HEXHUNTER

Hexworld 4

JORDAN L. HAWK

Hexhunter © 2019 Jordan L. Hawk
ISBN: 978-1-941230-35-0

Cover art © 2019 Jordan L. Hawk

Edited by Annetta Ribken Graney

CHAPTER 1

THE ORPHANAGE SEEMED a grim place for a nun to die. Bill Quigley only hoped she hadn't been murdered.

Four stories tall and wide enough to take up most of a city block, the Belfastian Catholic Orphanage presented a forbidding exterior to anyone passing by. It might have been a prison or an asylum of some kind; certainly nothing from the street indicated the presence of children. No toys, no colorful books, just unrelenting gray stone and barred windows on the lowest floor.

Bill's captain had called for him the moment he'd set foot in the precinct an hour earlier. The sun had barely risen above the roofline, and sweat already ran down Bill's forehead, gathering under his collar. Thanks to the heatwave, he'd spent the night trying to sleep on the tenement roof, surrounded by neighbors just as desperate for a breath of air.

"We've a dead nun at the orphanage on 50th," Captain Donohue had told him.

"God rest her soul," Bill said automatically. "Something unusual about the way she passed, then?"

There had to be; otherwise, Donohue would have given the case to one of the detectives not in a state of permanent disgrace. All the easy solves, or the prestigious ones, went to fellows the captain actually liked.

Bill had been one of them, once. Before his best friend Tom had joined the Metropolitan Witch Police, and Bill got tangled up in their affairs.

Before he'd met a dark-haired familiar, whose soulful eyes pierced Bill straight to the core. He'd volunteered to be the liaison between the regular police and the MWP, in hopes of seeing those eyes again.

Now, Donohue viewed him as the dumping ground for anything with a bit of strangeness or difficulty about it. The captain drew on his cigar, then expelled a lungful of smoke as he answered, "Aye, you could say that. She died from a snake bite sometime during the night."

A snake bite in the middle of New York City surely didn't sound natural. "You think she was murdered by a familiar?"

"I think it's your job to find out." Donohue made a shooing motion. "You've your assignment, Quigley. Get to it."

A priest waited for Bill just inside the orphanage, pacing back and forth along the short hall forming the entryway. At the sight of Bill's badge, he perked up visibly. "Thank you for coming, officer. I'm Father Patrick."

"Detective Bill Quigley," Bill said as they shook hands. "I'm sorry to hear about your troubles."

A stricken look crossed Father Patrick's face. "Sister Brigid's death has been a shock, no doubt about it. Of course, we're comforted by the thought she's with the Heavenly Father, but the manner of her departure from the earthly coil has frightened the other sisters."

"How are the children taking it?"

"We haven't told them yet. Sister Brigid was a favorite among them. She had a way of finding a home for the most unlikely among the orphans." Father Patrick shook his head. "It's a sad day for us all."

A clatter of hooves echoed from the street, and Bill spotted the coroner's wagon pulling up to the curb. If any of the children glanced out a window, they'd soon realize death had come for a visit. "I'd like to see the body before it's taken away."

"Of course. Come with me."

Bill followed the priest deeper into the building. The walls were painted a cheerless white, faded to a sort of dingy gray. Though the place had been wired for electricity, most of the lights were shut off, no doubt to save money. As a result, a gloomy air hung over the halls, one which only intensified when they passed a line of children dressed in identical, ill-fitting gray uniforms.

He might have ended up in such a place himself, if some tragedy had found his mother earlier than it did. When he was a boy, she'd done everything in her power to bring whatever small happiness into their lives she could, even on the nights when they'd gone to bed with empty

HEXHUNTER

Other books in print from Jordan L. Hawk:

Hainted

Whyborne & Griffin:
Widdershins
Threshold
Stormhaven
Necropolis
Bloodline
Hoarfrost
Maelstrom
Fallow
Undertow
Draakenwood
Deosil

Spirits:
Restless Spirits
Dangerous Spirits
Guardian Spirits

Hexworld
Hexbreaker
Hexmaker
Hexslayer

SPECTR
SPECTR: Volume 1
SPECTR: Volume 2
SPECTR Series 2: Volume 1
SPECTR Series 2: Volume 2

bellies.

The nuns' quarters were on the ground floor, away from the street. "Many of the sisters share rooms," Father Patrick explained as they walked. "But Sister Brigid had been here for many a year, and seniority earned her a bit of privacy." His look grew troubled. "If she hadn't been alone…"

"Aye," Bill said. Though if someone had it out for her enough to kill her, they would likely have found another way.

Father Patrick opened the last door on the hall. "There's a small garden on the other side of the wall," he said. "I suppose that's how the serpent got in."

The priest hovered just outside, clearly not wanting to enter the room. When Bill got a good look at what was inside, he didn't blame the fellow.

Only a small fireplace gave the tiny chamber any hint of luxury. A narrow bed took up much of the righthand wall, a crucifix above it the only decoration. A small window looked out onto the back garden, open to let a breath of air into the stuffy chamber.

Sister Brigid's mortal remains lay sprawled near the fireplace, one hand flung into the ashes. The stink of burned flesh filled the air. The dead woman had either been in bed already, or preparing to turn in. She wore a nightdress, and the bedclothes had been dragged half onto the floor, perhaps by convulsions.

"The other sisters rearranged her nightdress for modesty," Father Patrick said from the doorway. "But the bite was on her right leg."

Lifting a nun's nightdress—Bill was going to have quite the confession to make if he ever got around to attending mass again. Hoping the wound wasn't too high off her ankle, Bill crouched by the body and cautiously lifted the edge of the concealing cloth.

The whole leg was badly swollen, or at least the part of it he could see. Unmistakable puncture marks showed in the taut skin of her calf.

After putting her nightdress back in order, Bill rose to his feet and stepped carefully around the body to the fireplace. No one in their right mind would've had a fire going last night, not in this heat. Not unless they had a damn good reason.

Charred bits of paper still showed amongst the ashes. Someone—perhaps Sister Brigid, perhaps not—had lit a small fire to destroy…what? Letters seemed most likely, but pages from a diary could be another. Something the burner had wanted to keep anyone else from seeing.

The dead woman's hand had fallen into the fireplace while it was still warm enough to scorch her skin. No doubt she'd been in her last extremity; streaks of ash showed where her fingers had dragged out of the firebox and onto the hearth.

No, wait. The streaks were wild and messy, but they weren't random at all. Bill squatted down, peering at the messy letters they formed. It took a bit to decipher them, but once he did, their message was clear enough.

FIND THE CHILDREN.

Exhaustion slowed Isaac's steps as he approached the marble stairs leading into MWP Headquarters, more colloquially known as the Coven. He'd been up half the night, sitting with Freida, a familiar who was scheduled to testify soon against the gang who had kidnapped and force-bonded her to a witch.

It wasn't Isaac's case—that honor belonged to Cicero and Tom Halloran. But over the last year or so, he'd been unofficially working with the victims in the force-bonding cases they investigated. Making sure they got to court all right, that they had everything they needed once they arrived. Offering a comforting shoulder when possible.

Or, like last night, just listened while they talked. He'd sat in the stifling heat of Freida's apartment while she spoke of…everything, really. Her childhood, her hopes and dreams.

How she couldn't sleep for the nightmares. Flinched at every loud sound. How even the walls of the tiny tenement room she shared with the rest of her family seemed too confining.

"I don't know how I can get past this," she said in a small voice, long after everyone else was asleep.

"You're strong," he'd assured her. *"You can do it. Just try to stay busy."*

"Is that what you did?"

"Yes." Inactivity had been the worst thing about his stay in the hospital, after Cicero and the rest rescued him from the tunnels where he'd been caged and used for his magic. Nothing to do for long hours but lie in bed and remember, too afraid of the nightmares to sleep.

The normal crowd closed around Isaac as he started up the stairs to the Coven, and his skin twitched. Witches, in uniform and out, and familiars in both human and animal shape, made their way around the knot of reporters eternally stationed at the bottom of the steps. Too many people to keep track of at once, brushing up against him, moving behind his back where he couldn't see them.

Usually, Isaac ignored the newspaper men and women, other than to note their presence, their distance from him. But this morning, one of them shouted: "Isaac, isn't it? Isaac the familiar?"

Startled, he made the mistake of stopping. He took in the patched elbows of the reporter's suit coat, the battered hat, the worn shoes. A film of sweat stood out on the man's amber skin, which was almost the same shade as his tightly curled hair. "Eli Valentine with *The Daily Owl*," he said in a rush.

The three nearest familiars took on their animals shapes as they hurried past. It was a common trick, to escape talking to reporters. At one time, Isaac would have done it himself. Now the thought made his throat tighten and his hands go clammy.

"I'm investigating the possible existence of a ring of criminals shanghaiing familiars, breaking their spirits, and selling them to witches for bonding," Valentine went on. "You've been assisting Detective Halloran and his familiar, haven't you?"

"Talk to them," Isaac said, and started to turn away.

"I tried." Valentine's long fingers snagged Isaac's elbow.

Isaac spun. His hands curled into fists, the taste of metal filling his mouth.

The reporter hastily stepped back, holding up his hands. "Sorry—sorry—"

"Don't touch me again," Isaac snarled. Turning his back on Valentine, he stormed the rest of the way into the Coven.

By the time he reached the office he shared with another familiar, his hands had almost stopped shaking. He'd gone the long way around to reach the office, cutting through the detectives' area rather than taking the back stair.

Sometimes he could walk up that stairway without remembering the feel of hands shoving him from behind. The hard risers cracking into his jaw, his arm breaking under him. The heavy kick of a boot when he survived the fall.

But today his equanimity was already fractured, thanks to the blasted reporter. At least he had nothing to do but catch up on paperwork. The rote monotony suited him, gave him something to focus on.

His officemate, Sionn, wandered in a bit later. Sionn's hair was the same bright copper as his screech owl form. A galaxy of freckles spotted his face and hands, startling against his milky skin. They exchanged brief pleasantries, and Sionn launched into a long, meandering story about a party he'd gone to last night. They made good officemates, if only because Sionn enjoyed talking and Isaac could be counted on not to interrupt.

Sionn was halfway through explaining why taking a midnight splash in Bethesda Fountain had seemed like a good idea, when Cicero knocked on the open door. "Good morning, darlings."

Isaac's gut tightened. "Freida—has something happened? She was all right when I left her."

"No need to give yourself wrinkles." Cicero draped his arms around Isaac's shoulders from behind. The touch was worlds different from Valentine's unexpected grab, and after a moment of stiffness, Isaac relaxed into the embrace. "I have a job for you. Or rather, your nose."

No. Cicero couldn't be suggesting what Isaac thought he was. "My nose."

"Well it ain't mine," Sionn said from the other side of the room. "I can't sniff things out any better than an ordinary human. Owls ain't known for their sense of smell."

"We've a request for a dog familiar to do a bit of tracking, and Lavinia is having her lying in," Cicero said, naming the MWP's resident bloodhound. "You're one of our best trackers."

Isaac's heart beat so fast he felt light-headed. "Was."

"Then time to get back to it, don't you think?" Cicero asked. As if it were that easy. "The requesting officer is our very own William Quigley."

Sionn leaned over the desk, freckled face alight. "Oh, Quigley's the adorable liaison, isn't he?"

The walls of the tiny office felt as though they were closing in. Turning into a cage.

Isaac stood, shoving his chair back. "No." He brushed past Cicero, though he didn't have any destination in mind other than *out*. "Find someone else. I won't do it."

"Isaac!" Cicero called after him. "Wait!"

Isaac walked faster. He felt blindsided as anger seared through him, directed at Cicero. How *dare* he ask Isaac to do this?

But that wasn't fair. Cicero didn't know, couldn't understand.

A black streak dashed in front of Isaac, Cicero using his cat form to slip ahead. He shifted back into human and stood with his hands on his hips, blocking the way. "Why don't you want to do this? You aren't having some sort of quarrel with William, are you?"

Isaac's heart stuttered against his ribs. Bill.

He still remembered the warmth of Bill's strong arm around his shoulders the winter night he'd been rescued from the tunnels. Helping him to the nearest precinct, bundling him in blankets, fetching hot drinks for Isaac to cautiously sip. Visiting him at the hospital later, awkward and uncertain.

If only they could have met some other way. If only…

If only a lot of things, none of which mattered. If Cicero thought invoking Bill's name would convince Isaac to change his mind, he was wrong. Bill was the last person Isaac wanted to expose that part of himself to.

"No," Isaac said. "I just don't want to, all right? Find some other dog."

"You used to be one of our best trackers." Cicero watched him carefully. "But I can't remember the last time you volunteered to lend your nose."

Isaac could. It had been almost four years ago, when he'd been trying to impress the charming, charismatic man whom his magic had identified as his witch.

He flinched from the memory, refusing to allow himself to recall what it had felt like to be in mastiff form. He couldn't think about it, because thinking about it brought that part of him—the weak part, the tainted part—too close to the surface.

The memories were starting to disappear on their own, anyway. Not the ones he really wanted to get rid of, but surely those would follow.

"When did you last take on your other shape?" Cicero asked, his eyes narrowing.

"That's none of your business, cat."

Now worry showed clear in Cicero's kohl-lined eyes. "The other day, when Rook and I were talking about that trip we all took to Central Park right after I joined the MWP. When we were all in animal form. You said you didn't remember."

Fur and feathers. He was caught. Isaac tried for a casual shrug. "People forget things—"

"*Familiars* forget things when they stay in one shape for too long. The memories of their other form start to disappear."

"I don't care." The words were out before Isaac realized he was going to say them. The expression on his friend's face told him they'd been a mistake.

"Isaac…" Cicero for once seemed at a loss for words. "You can't do this to yourself. Staying in human shape is literally eating holes in your mind, and you say you don't care?"

It would all be worth it, if Isaac could just forget his witch, forget

Noah, forget the tunnels. But if he said that aloud, Cicero might go to Ferguson, tell the MWP chief that Isaac was refusing to shift, in the hopes of getting some sort of help for him.

Or he might not. The MWP didn't have any use for a familiar who didn't want to use magic. Ferguson had let Isaac return to the barracks, looked the other way in the years since, and made no mention of him finding a witch. But it couldn't last forever, and Cicero knew that. He wouldn't draw Ferguson's attention to Isaac unless he had no other choice.

Cicero wouldn't just let it go, though. He'd tell their friends. Isaac would end up with an entire circle of worried people badgering him day and night, instead of just one.

"Fine," he said. "I'll help Bill. Satisfied?"

A relieved smile bloomed on Cicero's face. "Yes."

CHAPTER 2

ISAAC FOLLOWED A nun down the hallway of the orphanage, his nerves thrumming. He felt acutely out of place, the sideways looks from the nun and the crosses on the walls alike making it clear he didn't belong here. And yet, his heart leapt at the thought of being in the same room, of smelling Bill's reassuring scent, even as his stomach cramped at the prospect of taking on his animal form again.

Easy for Cicero to say it was for Isaac's own good. Cicero's magic wasn't tainted, wasn't corrupted. His familiar nature had led him to a good man in the form of Tom Halloran.

Isaac's magic longed to bond with a man who seemed kind on the surface, but beneath was filled with hatred and violence. And after, when Isaac was forced into animal shape, muzzled and caged, deprived of water and food until he gave in to bonding, his magic had been used to fuel hexes drawn in blood. Hexes that caused madness and death.

His magic was twisted. Wrong. Surely it would be best for Isaac, best for the world, if he could forget it even existed.

Except here he was. Bullied into taking mastiff form, into starting over again. Cicero was his best friend, and Isaac was certain he truly believed he was acting in Isaac's best interests. Isaac didn't know how to explain to Cicero just how wrong he was.

Maybe if he could keep it short, he wouldn't set his progress back too far. Though it was hard to say just how much he'd made, since there was no way to know exactly what he'd forgotten unless someone drew attention to the blank spot in his brain, the way Rook and Cicero had the other day.

Bill waited in a room that reeked of death. He leaned against the wall by the fireplace. Isaac's first thought was that he looked almost as tired as Isaac felt. Fine lines sprang up around his hazel eyes, and his honey-brown mustache seemed to droop. He'd been promoted to detective after agreeing to liaise with the MWP, and wore a sack suit rather than a uniform. Even so, it was impossible to miss the breadth of his shoulders, or the curve of a thigh against the cloth.

"Here he is," the nun said unnecessarily, before departing back the way they'd come.

All traces of exhaustion dropped from Bill when he spotted Isaac. He straightened, shoulders back, a smile spreading over his face. "Isaac! Didn't realize the MWP would be sending you over."

"Lavinia is having her lying in," Isaac said, the words thick in his throat. "I'm afraid you're stuck with me."

"I'm glad," Bill said. "Give Lavinia my wishes for a healthy delivery." He paused uncertainly. "Should I be offering my congratulations to her witch…?"

"The father is another familiar." Sometimes familiars and their witches fell in love, and sometimes they were just friends. Or treated each other as business associates, if that was how things panned out.

Sometimes a witch turned out to be the worst thing that could happen to a familiar.

"Cicero said there'd been a murder," Isaac said, to stave off any dark thoughts.

Something flashed across Bill's face he couldn't quite interpret. But Bill only said, "Aye. Or most likely, that is. The coroner's man took away the body already, but Sister Brigid died from a snake bite."

"We aren't that far from Central Park," Isaac pointed out. "But I don't think there are any snakes native to the area whose bite is that venomous. I suppose it might have been the pet of some sailor and escaped?"

"I hadn't thought of that," Bill admitted. "But what's in the fireplace makes me think she didn't die by accident. Someone burned papers in it last night. Not to mention what she wrote in the ash before she died."

Isaac stepped closer. Bill had splashed bay rum cologne on this morning. So near the scent filled his senses, as though Bill had reached out and slipped a hand beneath Isaac's ribs, tugging on his heart. He wanted to lean in, to catch Bill's natural smell beneath the cologne.

Wanted to nuzzle closer, press his face against warm skin with nothing in between. See just how much hair pelted Bill's chest, let alone the rest of him hidden under clothing.

Isaac kicked himself mentally. Bill was a good man—far too good for him. He focused on the words scrawled in the ashes. They were difficult to puzzle out, but after a minute he read, *"Find the children.* What does that mean?"

"I don't know. Father Patrick might be able to shed some light on it, but I haven't asked him yet. I wanted to know for certain what we're dealing with first. I hoped we might track the serpent, at least far enough to guess whether it was a familiar or a natural snake somebody tossed through the window."

Isaac didn't want to do this. Fur and feathers, if only Lavinia were here instead.

He took a deep breath and shut his eyes. He could still feel his magic, the fading remnants of his mastiff form. All he had to do was reach for it.

Reach for something polluted, bad, wrong, and in front of Bill. Bill would see then. He'd remember just how worthless Isaac was, recall how Isaac's magic had fueled the blood hexes, and he'd turn away in disgust.

Isaac's eyes snapped open. His throat constricted so he could barely breathe, and his heart battered itself against his ribs. "I can't. I'm sorry, but—I can't do it."

A knot of worry pulled tight in Bill's chest. Isaac's olive skin had gone pale and a sheen of sweat sprung up across his forehead. The nostrils of his handsome nose flared, and his tawny eyes blinked rapidly.

Something was wrong—bad wrong. Bill ached to draw him close, stroke the dark brown hair Isaac wore long. But he'd seen Isaac flinch from being touched before, so he only said, "Is there anything I can do?"

Isaac shook his head. "No. No, I…I'm sorry. I'm useless. I'll go back and tell them to send someone else, I'll—"

"Here now." Bill pitched his voice to soothe. "You ain't useless. Tracking the snake any farther than the walls of the orphanage was a long shot anyway, given how many people walk up and down the street. As for figuring out if it was a familiar or a wild animal, there are other clues we can look for."

Isaac glanced at him uncertainly. "Yes, but that isn't what you wanted."

Bill shrugged. "So this way takes longer. What of it? I ain't got pressing business elsewhere, do you?"

The smile fluttering on Isaac's lips made Bill feel like a shaft of sunlight had fallen over him. "No. Have you searched the room?"

"Not thoroughly." He hadn't wanted to confuse the scent, but he didn't say that part, not wanting to make Isaac feel worse.

"Then you check her belongings, and I'll scour the rest of the room."

Bill shook his head. "Going through a nun's knicker drawer—I'll be reciting Hail Marys until Judgment Day."

Isaac snorted. As Bill went through the small chiffonier, he couldn't help but steal glances at the other man. Isaac seemed to have recovered, at least outwardly. He knelt near the hearth, his hair tucked behind his ears, his trousers pulling tight over his backside.

He was beautiful, though that wasn't a word Bill would've thought to use for another man up until the moment he'd met Isaac.

Bill shook his head, trying to clear away such thoughts. Some days, he wasn't even sure Isaac liked him. Half the time, Bill's attempts at small talk, like when he'd asked about the pregnant familiar, were cut off abruptly. True, they were here to work not socialize, but it reminded Bill all over again he was never quite certain where he stood with Isaac.

Which was a damn shame, because he'd spent the last two and a half years wondering what the skin of Isaac's throat would taste like against his lips. How that lithe body would fit with his.

Now he was going through a nun's knicker drawer with a half-hard prick.

The chiffonier had only three drawers, each of them inscribed on the inside with anti-moth hexes. All the clothes inside were disarranged, as though someone had hunted through them and not bothered—or had the time—to put things to rights. Whatever they'd been looking for—the burned papers? Something else?—they either didn't find or removed, because Bill discovered nothing unexpected.

"Did Sister Brigid have black hair?" Isaac asked.

"Nay. Blonde going to gray. Why?"

Rather than answer, Isaac held something up. Shutting the last drawer, Bill joined him. A short black hair lay across Isaac's palm. A man's, most likely, given the length. Still. "I suppose it might belong to a priest."

"Do priests often join nuns in their bedrooms?"

"Not usually. Well, they ain't supposed to, anyway." Bill took the hair and carefully placed it in an envelope.

They finished inspecting the room without finding anything further. "The open window seems the most likely path of entry," Isaac said. "It's too narrow for anyone in human form to fit through, but it looks out onto a small garden."

"Then let's see if we can find anything out there," Bill suggested.

A small door at the end of the hall let out into the garden, bounded on three sides by the orphanage. The fourth side, which faced the street, kept out the city by means of a high brick wall topped with iron spikes.

The area seemed to double as both a place of contemplation for the nuns and a patch to grow vegetables. Red tomatoes ripened on the vine, mint rioted wherever it could take hold, and plums bowed the branches of a small tree near the wall.

In the center of the garden, a statue of the Holy Familiar lay overturned onto its side. Raw earth showed where it had stood, dug up and tossed aside to form a small hole.

They exchanged a glance, and Bill nodded for Isaac to approach first. Isaac did so, peering at the statue and earth from all angles. "There's part of a shoe print," he said. "It looks as though whoever did this used their hands to dig. Whatever was under here wasn't buried very deep."

Bill joined him, lifting the statue and examining it carefully. Nothing seemed odd about the figure itself, other than depicting the Holy Familiar. Which, yes, this was a Belfastian institution, but he still would've expected Saint Jerome, patron of orphans.

Isaac went to Sister Brigid's window, inspecting the wall and ground below it. "Nothing." He glanced at the other windows looking out onto the garden, then crossed the heat-wilted grass to the wall bordering the street. "Snake skin."

Bill carefully set the statue upright beside the shallow hole, then hastened to Isaac's side. A patch of shed skin, perhaps five inches in length, clung to the rough brick. He plucked it off carefully and placed it in a separate envelope.

"Do you think Owen's hexes could tell if the skin and the hair come from the same familiar?" he asked.

"Yes. I'll take them to him, if you'd like."

Bill passed him the envelopes. "So this is what I think happened. The familiar crawled in over the wall, crossed the garden, and went in through Sister Brigid's window. He—or she—waited under the bed until Brigid came in and knelt for her prayers, then bit her. As she lay dying, he took on human form, searched her room for the papers, lit a fire, and burned them. Then he came back out, took whatever was buried under the statue, and left back over the wall. Does that sound about right?”

“We still have to confirm the hair and scales came from the same person,” Isaac said. “But no snake pushed over that statue and dug up what was underneath. So yes, I think you have it. This was no strange incident with an escaped pet or wild animal. Sister Brigid was murdered.”

The next morning, Isaac approached Chief Ferguson’s office with a sense of trepidation. It had been a long time since he’d been summoned by the chief himself. Probably because if they didn’t meet face to face, Ferguson wouldn’t have to think about Isaac. If he could plausibly say he’d semi-forgotten a familiar, he didn’t have to bring up the fact Isaac was still unbonded.

Ferguson had let him return—offered him a place, even, after the New Year’s Eve massacre. He didn’t have to; Isaac had walked away from the MWP of his own free will a year before. But Ferguson had given him shelter back behind the Coven’s walls, a place to stay while he healed. Something to do to fill the long hours.

It hadn’t been easy for Isaac to accept. He’d almost died here, when his witch turned on him, leaving him with broken bones and a broken heart. Coupled with the terrible knowledge some part of him must have wanted it, because why else would his magic have called out to his witch so?

Striking out on his own hadn’t gone well, to say the least. Isaac could have returned home—his parents would have gladly made room—but after the blood hexes, he couldn’t stand the thought of exposing them to the sickness inside him. So he’d come back to the barracks, even knowing he’d never take animal form again, let alone bond with any witch.

He’d stay long enough to forget why he was even here. Until he didn’t remember part of him was tainted; until the tunnels no longer invaded his dreams and he didn’t feel the need to keep track of everyone around him. Then he’d find another career, another life.

Maybe Ferguson suspected Isaac’s decision, or maybe he just wanted to give Isaac the time to heal, because the fact Isaac remained unbonded had never come up since. The MWP wasn’t a charity; familiars had only so long to make a choice, and Isaac was well past the usual deadline.

So Ferguson calling him here could mean time was up. Or Cicero had said something to the chief after all, thinking he was doing Isaac a favor.

Isaac had sneaked down to Owen’s lab with the hair and shed skin, careful to avoid being seen by Cicero. So when his friend cornered him later, Isaac said yes, he'd discovered they belonged to the same familiar.

It hadn't been a lie, though of course Cicero assumed Isaac had taken on dog form and sniffed it out. Isaac felt ashamed to mislead Cicero, but what choice did he have?

Bill hadn't pushed, when Isaac said he couldn't shift. Hadn't demanded an explanation. Just offered an alternative, something Isaac *could* do, something that wouldn't make him feel entirely useless.

Bill had been kind, just as he'd been last October, when they'd gone to the Menagerie together to question the warden about a prisoner who'd ended up murdered in Central Park. It hadn't been the easiest assignment, but Bill had spent the whole ferry ride back talking in low tones. His eyes stayed focused on the water, not asking anything from Isaac, but offering whatever distraction or comfort Isaac wanted from him.

Isaac hadn't fallen in love with Bill that day. Only realized he already was.

Fur and feathers, if only things had been different. If only Isaac had been born without this darkness in him, there might have been a chance for something more than friendship. If only…

"Isaac!" Sionn called. "Wait up."

Sionn made his way through the detectives' area. When he reached Isaac, he said, "Ferguson sent for you as well, did he?"

Some of the tension eased from Isaac's shoulders. If Ferguson wanted Sionn there, it wasn't to either order Isaac to find a witch or leave, or to pry into whether or not he took mastiff form. "Yes."

"Any idea what he wants?"

"Not a clue."

Sionn knocked on the door and received a gruff "Come in!" in response. As usual, the chief sat behind his desk. His familiar, Athene, perched in owl form. Her golden eyes fixed on Isaac, then on Sionn.

"Isaac," Ferguson said. "That murder scene you investigated yesterday, with the dead nun. There's some confusion as to whether the case falls under our authority, or that of the regular police."

"There was no hex magic involved," Isaac objected. The MWP had jurisdiction over crimes involving hexes. Yes, a familiar had killed Sister Brigid, but the only magic he'd used was his own natural ability to take on a different form. Under the law, that didn't put the case under the MWP's auspices.

Ferguson held up his hands. "I know. But Captain Donohue has a

history of fobbing off what he considers to be problem officers on us."
At Isaac's blank look he said, "He was Tom Halloran's captain, before he
joined the MWP. Halloran wasn't bringing in much revenue to the
precinct, so Donohue 'lent' him to us while Cicero investigated the blood
hexes."

Which Cicero had only done because he was searching for Isaac.
Isaac felt even worse about misleading him now.

"At the moment," Ferguson went on, "Donohue is claiming he's
unsure of jurisdiction, and offering Quigley to us to help investigate. I
want the two of you to lend him a hand."

Yearning gripped Isaac, unexpected in its strength. If nothing else, it
would be an excuse to see Bill for more than a few hours here and there.

But that was stupid. There was no point in tormenting himself with
a glimpse of what could never be. Bill deserved better. Deserved
someone who didn't flinch when touched unexpectedly. Who could take
on animal form without fear. Who didn't need to be coddled with kind
words all the time. Someone who could be Bill's equal, as opposed to a
burden.

So instead of jumping at the chance, he said, "I don't have the time.
I'm helping Cicero and Tom. I can't assist with two investigations at
once."

"I've plenty of time," Sionn said cheerfully. "Sounds like a treat."

Isaac ground his teeth.

Ferguson watched Isaac from across the desk, his gaze almost as
inscrutable as Athene's. "You're assisting Halloran and Cicero with the
key witness."

Isaac nodded. "Yes. Plus I've been checking in on some familiars
from previous cases, to establish whether or not there's a link between
them." Which wasn't exactly true. It was more that he felt a responsibility
to the victims. He knew what they'd been through, and how hard it could
be after. They needed someone who understood.

Inspiration struck, and he added, "Why not just send a detective pair
to help Bill? We have the manpower." After the disgrace of the Heirs of
Adam, the anti-vice mania had died an embarrassed death. It would
return eventually—it always did—but for now the MWP was free to
pursue more serious crimes.

"Because I don't think this is our case," Ferguson replied frankly. "I
think this is a simple instance of murder, and even the regular police
could solve it if they just did the work. So *if* this should catch the
attention of the Police Board for some unknowable reason, they won't be

able to claim I overstepped my bounds by assigning detectives to work it. I'm merely lending Captain Donohue a pair of unbonded familiars, as requested."

On her perch, Athene fluffed her feathers smugly. Sionn let out a hoot of laughter.

"I'm glad you're amused." Ferguson sat back and glanced at Isaac. "This won't take long. I'll tell Halloran and Cicero you'll be unavailable for a day or two. Any further questions?"

Isaac knew when he'd been given an order. "No questions, chief."

As they left Ferguson's office, Sionn grinned. "We get out of doing paperwork *and* get to work with the charming Detective Quigley. Lucky us, eh?"

"Yeah," Isaac said, stuffing his hands into his pockets. "Lucky."

Chapter 3

"So, you two are the ones Ferguson sent, then?" Bill asked, trying to sound casual. A moment later, he realized he only sounded like a fool.

"Apparently," Isaac said dryly, confirming the thought.

Since the first order of business was to question the priest, Bill had returned to the orphanage to wait for whatever help the MWP could spare. He'd half-hoped they'd send Isaac, even if he wasn't at all sure his heart could take it.

He'd let himself entertain thoughts about Isaac, even when he likely shouldn't have. Thoughts he'd never had about another man. Oh sure, he and Tom had tossed each other off on nights when they were both on reserve, bunking next to one another in the lightless attic of the precinct house. But that was just the sort of thing particular friends might do for one another, wasn't it? It didn't *mean* anything.

So he'd been shocked the night they rescued Cicero and Isaac, when Cicero had kissed Tom with obvious passion, and been kissed back.

Bill had thought Isaac was handsome even when he was in terrible shape from the treatment he'd received during his captivity. Brave, too—Isaac had risked death to have the bond broken so that bastard Noah couldn't use him anymore. Though not before he'd told them everything they needed to know to stop the theriarchist plot. Or Pemberton's plot, as it seemed given what they now knew.

Bill found himself thinking a lot about Isaac afterward. Of course he'd visited Isaac in the hospital; he would've done that for anyone. The more he saw of Isaac, though, the more he liked the man. And the more he thought about him, the more he wondered what it would be like to kiss those lips. Do other things.

So he'd hoped. And hoped. Now here they were, two and a half years on, and he still wasn't entirely sure if Isaac even liked spending time with him. Certainly the familiar had never sought him out.

"Hello, Bill," said the other familiar, who thrust out his hand. "I'm Sionn. We haven't been properly introduced."

"Bill Quigley," Bill said, shaking his hand.

Long, freckled fingers curled around his, and Sionn offered him a warm smile. "Such a pleasure to properly meet you."

Isaac cleared his throat. "We have work to do."

"All work and no play." Sionn shook his head. "Honestly, Isaac, I can't believe you're actually friends with Cicero."

"What sort of familiar are you?" Bill asked.

"Screech owl."

Bill glanced at the orphanage with all its open windows, struggling to let in a breeze. "Any chance you might fly up and take a look and listen at some of those windows? The children likely won't know much, but I'm sure the murder will be the only thing the sisters have on their minds."

Sionn's grin widened. "Oh, I like the way you think."

Isaac's brows drew down. "Spying? Do we really want to start off with spying?"

The note of censure in his voice made Bill wince. Still, he tried to keep his answer light. "My ma's probably turning in her grave, me spying on nuns. But the truth is, people see a badge and they don't talk as freely."

"Isaac told me something was buried under a statue in the garden," Sionn put in. "If anyone here knows or guesses what it was…well, a bit of gossip like that isn't something you're going to share with coppers, is it? Especially if it might make Sister Brigid or the orphanage look bad."

Isaac nodded reluctantly. "You have a good point."

"Of course I do." Sionn said. "I'll meet you back out here."

Sionn vanished in a flash, and a tiny owl glided on copper-colored wings up toward the orphanage windows. Bill glanced at Isaac, whose eyes were focused on the sidewalk, rather than following Sionn's flight. "Ready?"

Isaac glanced up, and for a moment his gaze held the haunted look Bill had seen in them far too often. Then he nodded. "Ready."

A hush hung over the orphanage halls. The eyes of the nun who ushered them into Father Patrick's office were red from weeping, and Bill wondered if Sister Brigid had been a favorite among those who served here, or if it was simply the shock and upset of murder in their midst that had so disturbed her. Father Patrick rose to his feet when they entered, extending his hand. "Detective Quigley, good to see you."

"You as well, Father. This is Isaac, a familiar with the MWP. We're here to ask you a few questions about Sister Brigid."

A shadow passed over Father Patrick's face. "Draw up some chairs and sit," he invited as he sank back into his own seat. "As much as I hope to see Sister Brigid's killer brought to justice, I can't imagine I have anything to contribute to your investigation."

Bill dragged two chairs from where they stood along the wall, and he and Isaac sat. The office was simply appointed and meticulously clean. Even the corners of the papers on the desk lined up neatly with each other.

"Why don't you begin by telling us about Sister Brigid," Bill prompted.

Father Patrick steepled his fingers. His pale hair had begun to recede, emphasizing his long face. "She was a good woman—that goes without saying, of course. Like many of the sisters, she felt called to help the unfortunate children of this great city. There are an endless multitude of hardships that can befall the innocent, especially those with no parents to guide them."

"We're quite aware," Isaac said. His stoic expression gave nothing of his thoughts away. "How long had she worked here?"

"About a dozen years, give or take. If it's important, I'm certain I can look into our records."

"I'd appreciate it," Bill replied. "I hate to ask such a thing, Father, but did Sister Brigid have any enemies? Anyone who'd want to do her harm?"

The priest drew himself up, chest puffing out in affront. "Certainly not! She was a nun, not a-a seamstress. She spent her days tending to the children and her nights in contemplation of the divine."

Bill doubted Brigid had been nearly as holy as the priest insisted. Saying so would only make Father Patrick even more defensive, though, so he kept the thought to himself.

"She had no outside interests?" Isaac asked. "Did she leave the premises often, or remain here for the most part?"

"The younger sisters go into the city regularly, to do shopping or run other errands. Sister Brigid had long ago handed off such tasks to others, preferring instead to concentrate on ministering to the unfortunates in our care." Father Patrick hesitated. "She did occasionally visit some of the children who had found permanent homes outside of our walls."

Bill exchanged a glance with Isaac. It could be nothing, but the detail had his copper's instincts tingling. "Were there any in particular she kept in touch with?"

"I wouldn't know." Father Patrick frowned a bit. "I can have a list drawn up of the children she worked with, if you like."

"That would be very helpful, Father." Bill shifted his weight, causing the chair to creak softly under him. "Her last message was a plea to *find the children*. Do you think she meant the ones she'd paid special attention to?"

"I wish I knew," Father Patrick said heavily. "I'm sorry not to be of more use to you, gentlemen. I spent all last night wracking my brain, trying to think of a reason anyone would have done this. But there's nothing. Sister Brigid stood out only in that she'd been here for some time. She lived a quiet life of devotion. I never heard of so much as a quarrel between her and any of the other sisters. I've prayed for guidance, of course, but at the moment I have only questions, and no answers."

It was obviously a dismissal. "One last thing before we go," Isaac said. "Do you have any guesses as to what might have been hidden beneath the statue in the garden?"

Father Patrick's expression grew rigid. "I'm certain I don't."

"I was a bit surprised to see a statue of the Magdalene here," Bill put in. "Her being the patron of familiars and all that. I would've imagined the sisters would have preferred the inspiration of Saint Jerome, as they worked with orphans."

"There was a statue of Saint Jerome at one time," Father Patrick replied. "But it was damaged about six months ago. Sister Brigid chose to replace it with the figure of the Holy Familiar, and as we follow the one true pope in Belfast, I allowed it to stay."

The explanation would have made sense, if not for the hiding place beneath. "Could Sister Brigid have been the one to damage the original statue?"

An expression of profound discomfort distorted the priest's features. "I…suppose. Saint Jerome's figure was larger and heavier."

"And the new one smaller and easier to move," Isaac murmured.

"Yes." Father Patrick licked his lips. "At the time, I thought nothing of it. Given the nature of Sister Brigid's work, her choice of the Holy Familiar made sense."

Bill frowned. "What do you mean?"

"She felt a special calling." Father Patrick slid his chair back from his desk. "Naturally, it's impossible to know who will be a familiar and who won't be, before the initial change. But the blood does run in families. If both parents are familiars, chances are quite high their children will be as well. It can be difficult to find anyone willing to adopt such children." He shot Isaac an apologetic look. "Not because they're any less children of God than the rest of us, but people generally assume a familiar will leave as soon as they find their witch. Most families prefer to adopt a child who can be counted on to remain and contribute to the household in the long term. Brigid thought it tragic—she said every child deserved a home. She took it upon herself to find placements for such potential familiars."

Beside him, Isaac stiffened. Bill swallowed against a knot of worry in his throat. "I see," he said. "Thank you, Father. You've been most helpful."

Isaac hunched his shoulders as they walked back out through the orphanage. A sick feeling had started growing in his stomach the moment the priest spoke of Sister Brigid's work with potential familiars. Children vulnerable to all the usual horrors, and more if the blood ran true.

"I don't like this," he said softly. "She wrote 'find the children' in the ashes even as she was dying. Now we learn she was working with potential familiars."

"She was murdered by a familiar." Bill's jaw was set, his eyes dark with worry. "I don't like it, either. My gut says this is bad. Real bad."

"The case I'm assisting Cicero and Tom with. I've been talking to one of the witnesses. She was kidnapped by a gang of men who were shanghaiing unbonded familiars and selling them to witches." He took a deep breath, or tried, his throat suddenly too tight. "It was organized. Underground tunnels and everything. There were arrests, and most of the gang is behind bars awaiting trial, but some might have slipped the net."

Bill frowned. "You think there might be a connection between that case and this one?"

"I don't know." A feeling of helplessness swept over Isaac. Too many familiars went missing every year, and it was impossible to say how many had been taken by the gang, or by would-be witches, or vanished due to some other misfortune.

"It doesn't make sense." Bill glanced around and lowered his voice as they passed a line of orphans in dull gray clothing. "The priest specified she worked with *potential* familiars. Would an organized gang really want to risk kidnapping kids, and then what…keeping them until they either shifted or didn't? That could take months, or even years. Not to mention they'd have no way of knowing how dangerous the familiar's form would be. Would they risk suddenly finding an angry young polar bear or moose on their hands?"

"You have a point. The gang only took easily managed familiars. Cats, lizards, smaller birds." Dogs, but the word stuck in his throat.

"We don't know for certain if these children are even missing," Bill said gently. "Possibly one or more of them saw something that might tell us who killed Brigid. They might all be in happy homes, and it's only we need to find them and ask a few questions."

It was possible. Not likely, but possible.

They emerged back into the sunlight and noise of the busy street. Isaac scanned their surroundings for any threat, a habit he couldn't bring himself to break. He spotted Sionn swooping down. The owl shifted just before he touched the ground so his boots hit the sidewalk with a soft thump. "Luck was surely with me today. Some of the younger sisters were tending to the foundlings and having a good chat. I hope gossip ain't a mortal sin."

Bill snorted. "It had better not be, or from what Tom tells me, most of you familiars at the MWP are in trouble."

"Aye, that's true enough," Sion agreed with a grin. Lowering his voice, he said, "One of the sisters swore up and down she saw Brigid tuck a stack of money into her prayer book. When she asked about it, Brigid said it was a charitable donation from one of the families who had adopted an orphan. It seemed a little odd, Brigid putting it in her book, but she didn't think on it again until now."

"I assume she believes Brigid hid the money under the statue," Isaac said.

"Aye."

"Could it have been a case of robbery?" Bill's brows creased in thought, a line springing up between them. Isaac had the sudden urge to kiss it away. "But then why kill Brigid? It would have been simple to sneak into the garden, dig up the money, then leave without raising an alarm. Brigid couldn't exactly have reported the theft without exposing herself."

"Don't forget the burned papers." Now it was Isaac's turn to frown in thought. "Brigid might have burned them, but my guess is her killer did. Why else would he take on human form in her room, rather than simply escape back out the window after biting her?"

"Too bad we don't know what the papers contained," Sionn said.

"Blackmail?" Bill suggested.

Isaac shrugged. "Maybe." It seemed as likely an explanation as anything at this point.

"So what next?" Sionn asked.

Bill took off his hat and wiped the sweat from his brow. "Isaac, if you'd look into any possible connections with Tom and Cicero's case, I'd appreciate it. I don't expect you to find anything, but we need to make sure. Other than that, I don't see there's much we can do until we get the list of the children Sister Brigid took a special interest in. She told us to find them, so that's what we'll do. Maybe if we can interview the families who adopted them, we'll learn something."

Hopefully not that she'd been blackmailing the families. Isaac's skin crawled to imagine some of the reasons a person might want to adopt a familiar child, reasons they wouldn't want anyone else to know about. Bile rose in the back of his throat, and chills ran over his skin despite the breathless heat of the day.

"Isaac? Are you all right?" Bill asked.

The worry in Bill's voice brought him back to his surroundings. "I'm fine," he lied. "If you don't need us, Sionn and I will go back to the MWP. Let us know when you have the list, and we'll help in whatever way we can."

"I will." Bill didn't look as though he quite believed Isaac's reassurance, but he let it go. "I'm sure I'll need all the help I can get."

Isaac told himself the only reason he looked back was to make certain no one in the crowd posed a danger. Not to get a last glimpse of Bill. "So," Sionn said, once they were well out of earshot, "is there anything between you and Detective Quigley?"

Isaac stopped. His lungs tightened and the muscles of his shoulders went tense. There was only one reason Sionn would ask such a question, and for a wild moment Isaac wanted to answer in the affirmative. To tell Sionn to back off. That Bill was *his*.

"No," he forced out between gritted teeth.

Sionn beamed. "Then you won't mind my asking him to dinner?"

"Of course not." The second lie in ten minutes, and it felt heavy on Isaac's tongue. "It's nothing to me."

"Excellent." Sionn's grin was as bright as his hair. "Listen, do you mind if I fly back to the Coven, instead of taking the El? It's so slow."

"Go right ahead," Isaac replied.

Sionn didn't waste any time taking on owl form and making for the sky. Isaac did his best to ignore the jealousy beginning to pool in his belly and continued on alone.

Chapter 4

Bill didn't particularly want to return to the precinct, but at the moment he had no real excuse to stay away. Not to mention it was where Father Patrick would send the list of children, and Bill wanted to be on hand to receive it the moment it came.

Isaac had looked shaken, there on the sidewalk. He'd gotten that blank expression Bill glimpsed on occasion, where he seemed to lose track of the world around him in favor of some inner vision. The first time, back when Isaac was still recovering in the hospital, Bill had made the mistake of touching him. Just a light hand to the shoulder, but Isaac recoiled as though Bill had struck him.

Bill made sure he kept his hands to himself after that. The last thing he wanted to do was make things worse. What Isaac had gone through would have broken most people, but he'd come out the other side. Not only that, but according to Tom, he'd thrown himself into helping other familiars who'd endured similar captivities, being there for them in the interview room, or in court, so they didn't have to face it alone. That was the sort of courage you didn't see every day.

No wonder Bill had fallen for him.

"Come back from visiting the fairies, have ye, Bill?" one of the other coppers called as he entered the main room. A burst of laughter accompanied the remark, which apparently passed as the height of wit.

Bill bit back a curse. He'd suspected what he was in for when he accepted the post of liaison between the regular Metropolitan Police and their counterparts in the MWP. The MWP viewed ordinary coppers as corrupt thugs, and the coppers considered everyone in the MWP to be mincing fairies at best. Still, he'd hoped the novelty would wear off for his fellow officers after a while, and he'd be able to do something to bridge the gap.

Unfortunately, all that happened was the other police looked at him as a source of humor, and Captain Donohue as somewhere to send the cases he didn't want to burden his favorites with.

The door opened behind Bill, admitting a dark skinned man clutching a newspaper. "Is Detective Quigley here?" he asked, waving the paper. "I have to talk to him right now."

Anything to get away from the smirking coppers. "I'm Quigley," he said. "What's the trouble?"

The man thrust the paper out in front of him. "This woman!" he said, tapping the small article. "Sister Brigid, the one who was murdered. She stole my little boy!"

"Back so soon?" Mal asked, when he spotted Isaac in the doorway to the forensic hex lab.

While he'd ridden the El back to the Coven, Isaac recalled hearing a rumor about the fox familiar's past. Mal had been a thief before he joined the MWP, working for one of the biggest fences in New York City. When he'd bonded with Dr. Owen Yates, the entire MWP had been abuzz over what seemed like the worst possible match between witch and familiar.

Isaac had tried to stay away from the gossip, but being best friends with Cicero meant he got an earful whether he wanted it or not. In the end, Mal and Owen had proved surprisingly suited to one another, and interest over Mal's criminal past waned.

Now, Mal was hard at work at one of the laboratory tables, grinding amethyst into powder to make one of the specialized inks used for hexes. Owen sat hunched over a different table, carefully drawing an elaborate hex with a brush that looked to be comprised of a single hair. Whatever the hex was for, it wasn't the sort of thing the hexmen downstairs would be tasked with duplicating en masse.

"I just can't stay away from your charm, Malachi," Isaac replied. "Or, possibly I have a question. Can you take a few minutes to talk?"

"Gladly," Mal replied, putting down the pestle and stripping off his gloves. The lab windows were flung open in hopes of catching a breeze, and sweat darkened Mal's brilliant red hair. "Owen's been working me to the bone."

"Honest work is good for you," Owen said without looking away from his task.

"Honest work is overrated," Mal shot back, but he grinned fondly when he said it.

The obvious affection between them sent a small pang of envy through Isaac's heart. He'd dreamed of having such a rapport with his witch.

The man had seemed so perfect, at the beginning. So handsome and charming. Isaac had been half in love with him from the start. Ready to bond, to pledge himself forever.

What a fool he'd been.

"I'm afraid your reprieve will be short," Isaac said, keeping his voice light as he could. "I just have a question about your upbringing."

Mal stilled. Now Owen did look up, a frown of concern on his face.

"What do you want to know?" Mal asked warily.

"I've been helping Bill—Detective Quigley, that is—look into the case of the murdered nun. She worked at the Belfastian Orphanage on 50th. You were in an orphanage yourself, weren't you?"

"Aye." Mal perched on the edge of a table. "Not that particular one, mind. There used to be a smaller Belfastian-run orphanage not far from the Bowery, but it was closed shortly after I left. A dozen years or so ago, I'd say."

It had been too much to hope for. "So you didn't know Sister Brigid."

Mal's eyes widened. "Sister Brigid? Fur and feathers, was she the one murdered?"

Owen sighed. "Honestly, Mal, we have a newspaper delivered every morning."

"Aye, but I only read it for the baseball scores."

"Obviously." Owen stood up and crossed to Mal. Resting his hand on Mal's shoulder, he said, "I'm sorry."

"Thanks, but I ain't seen her in years." Mal shrugged. "We weren't what I'd call close. Still, she's the one who saw I'd make a good thief and arranged for me to go to Madam Galpern."

Isaac's extremities went cold. "So she was sending children into lives of crime?"

Mal appeared as if he wanted to deny it, but couldn't. "Well, I suppose you could look at it that way."

"As opposed to some other way?" Owen asked. "She knowingly

gave you to a fence who trained you to be a second story man."

"Aye, but at the time, it seemed like she'd done me a favor. Otherwise, I would have spent those years in the orphanage, then been turned out on the street and left to fend for myself the second I was old enough. I figured being out in the world, learning a trade—so to speak— was the better deal."

Owen forewent any further comment, and instead turned to Isaac. "Perhaps Sister Brigid kept up her ties to the criminal element once she went to the orphanage on 50th. If she angered or threatened to expose the wrong person…"

"They might have sent an assassin after her." Isaac caught himself playing with the silver chain around his neck, and dropped his hand back to his side. "She left a message for us, before she died. 'Find the children.'"

Mal frowned uneasily. "Did she mean kids like me? Ones she'd sent along to people like Madam Galpern?"

"Possibly. When you knew her, did she work exclusively with familiar potentials?"

"Nay." Mal's expression grew puzzled. "Now, I did find out Madam Galpern wanted me because I was a familiar, but I'd already shifted by then. But Sister Brigid sent along plenty of children who weren't familiars. Ones who had quick hands, and were small enough to fit through transoms, that sort of thing. My friend Sophie was one of them, and she didn't have a drop of familiar blood in her."

Grief flashed across Mal's face at the mention of his friend. Owen gave Mal's shoulder a comforting squeeze, and Mal leaned into him.

Isaac looked away.

"Do you need our help?" Mal asked uncertainly. "I'm sure Owen could spare me."

"Ferguson doesn't want any of our detectives involved yet." Isaac rubbed at his eyes. "Besides, you have important work to do here. I'll let you know if we need anything."

Mal nodded. "All right. Good luck, Isaac. Sister Brigid may not exactly have been the most saintly nun, but a part of me still feels like she did me a good turn."

Would the children Brigid had asked them to find feel the same way? Or had they ended up in far darker situations than Mal? Sister Brigid had been involved with the criminal underworld. Had her ties included the sort of men who would kidnap and sell familiars?

Freida had enough problems of her own. Isaac was supposed to be helping her, not adding to her burdens. But if there was any possibility she knew whether the children might have been passed along to the gang who'd taken her, he had to find out.

Squaring his shoulders, Isaac headed back toward the Coven's main doors and into the blazing sunlight.

"Now then," Bill said. He closed the door to the interrogation room, while the man settled himself into a chair on one side of the table. Bill sat down across from him and took out a notepad and pencil. "What's your name?"

"Elwood. I'm ship's familiar aboard the *Sheltonia*." He leaned forward, hands clasped anxiously in front of him. "Sister Brigid stole my son. Can you get him back for me?"

This had to be related to her command to find the children. Bill's pulse quickened, but he maintained a stoic demeanor. "Slow down, sir. One thing at a time. Why do you say she stole your son?"

Elwood ran a nervous hand over his close-cropped hair. "As I said, I serve aboard the *Sheltonia*. I'm the ship's cat, in addition to working with the ship witch. The *Sheltonia* is a merchant vessel, and sometimes our voyages are long ones. When we put in last month, I hadn't seen my family in a year."

"That must be hard," Bill sympathized.

"Hard." Elwood let out a bitter laugh. "You could call it that. I came back to find my wife and her witch dead from influenza, and my boy gone. Neighbors said he'd been taken to the Belfastian Orphanage, so I went there to get him back. The orphanage claimed he'd been adopted, and one of the sisters gave me the address. I went to retrieve him, only the people living there hadn't ever heard of him!"

Bill's heart sank. "Are you sure the sister gave you the right place?"

"I copied down the address myself. I can write a little, enough for that much, and Teddy's name was beside it in the nun's book."

"And the folks who took him hadn't moved away in the meantime?" Bill asked, even though he already guessed the answer.

"No. The people I talked to said they'd been living there for the last five years or so." Helpless anger flashed in Elwood's eyes. "I went back to the orphanage. The first sister told me Brigid had been the one to find new parents for Teddy, so I tracked her down. Demanded she tell me where the hell my boy was!"

The poor man. Bill couldn't imagine how desperate he must have been. "I'm guessing she wasn't forthcoming."

"She called the coppers on me." Elwood's yellow eyes narrowed with remembered fury. "Once the coppers came, though, she said she didn't want this to go to court. She'd be happy if I just never came back. The coppers roughed me up, then told me if I showed my face at the orphanage again, they'd do worse." He bit his lip. "It won't help my boy if I end up dead or in the hospital, so I didn't go back. I've spent the last month looking everywhere for him, but he's just…disappeared."

Find the children. Christ, what had Sister Brigid been involved in?

"How old was your son?" Bill asked. "Was he a familiar, too?"

"He turned twelve while I was at sea." Elwood stared at his hands, mouth tight. Regretting he'd been forced to miss so much of his child's life, no doubt. "He hadn't shifted yet, but with two familiar parents, odds are he'll be one too." He looked up again, eyes pleading. "You have to help me. It ain't right, what happened. I don't know where Teddy is, if he's well or hurt or…"

The man clearly couldn't bring himself to say *dead,* and Bill didn't blame him. "I understand. I'll look into it, Mr. Elwood, you've got my word on that."

A tiny spark of hope showed in Elwood's eyes. "Thank you. I didn't think…the other coppers didn't give a damn."

"Be as that may, I do. Now, if you'd give me your address, or your witch's, so I've some way of contacting you."

"I don't see my witch off the ship," Elwood said. "We work together on board, that's all."

He gave Bill his address, along with a description of the boy and his full name. Bill escorted him out, then stood alone on the front steps of the precinct house, pondering.

Father Patrick had made no mention of the incident with Elwood. Possibly he'd not known, though if the police had been summoned, it would have been hard for Brigid to conceal. News of such a disruption would surely travel fast, unless Brigid had bribed the other sister involved to keep it quiet. Maybe the gossip about the hidden money Sionn had overheard was fueled by more than just a single incident.

What had she meant to do with the money? Being a nun wasn't the sort of job one usually retired from. Maybe she'd planned on leaving the church, leaving New York, even, and going somewhere that didn't burn in the summer and freeze in the winter.

Likely he'd never know what she'd intended.

With a shake of his head, he went back inside to wait impatiently for the orphanage to send the list, and prayed not all of the children on it would be as hard to find as Elwood's son.

Freida's apartment wasn't far from the Coven. Isaac walked the few blocks to First Street, struggling to ignore the scents wafting from the food carts as he dodged around wagons and pedestrians. It was Friday afternoon, and the pig market—which sold everything *except* pigs—on Hester Street would still be bustling by the time he finished with Freida. With any luck, he could find some peaches to take to his parents' apartment for Shabbat dinner.

At one time, he would have spent the night at their apartment, then gone to the synagogue the next morning. When he'd left the MWP to work at the Spitting Rooster, he'd stopped visiting at all for a time.

After he was rescued from Noah's clutches, his family had begged him to move back in. But at least in the barracks he didn't have to worry about the darkness inside him soiling his parents, his siblings. Friday dinner and important holidays were the most he could give them.

Freida's family lived on the second floor, too close to the ground to escape the stench of the heat-baked streets. Her mother answered Isaac's knock, expression going from suspicious to relieved in an instant. "Isaac! Come in, come in. We weren't expecting you today."

Isaac managed a smile. "I just had some questions to ask Frieda, if she's available."

Multiple German families shared the small, two room apartment. Most of the adults were at work this time of day, but a swarm of young children played on the floor. Freida herself sat near the window, mending a torn shirt with work-roughened fingers. When Isaac entered, she let it slip from her fingers. "Something's gone wrong," she said, despair in her voice. "They've been let out of jail, haven't they?"

Isaac shook his head quickly. "No. I had some questions to ask you, that's all. About another case that might be related to yours."

Her expression cleared. "Oh."

"Have a seat," her mother said. "I'm sorry none of the children are old enough to fetch a pail of beer. I could…?"

"No, no need." Isaac sat at the table, and Freida joined him. "This won't take long."

He explained his suspicions to Freida, leaving out the details of Sister Brigid's murder. A line slowly formed between Freida's brows as he spoke, and when he was done, she shook her head.

"The gang wouldn't take potential familiars," she said. Her fingers tightened in the skirt of her dress, then relaxed. "There's no knowing how long children would have to be held before they shifted…or didn't, and then what would you do with them? The longer you keep someone imprisoned, the more food they need, and the more likely they are to die and leave you with nothing. Or escape and bring the coppers." She closed her eyes, then opened them again. "The gang…they wanted to move familiars through as quickly as possible. Holding children indefinitely, just hoping they turn out to be useful, wouldn't be good business." Her mouth quirked sourly. "They considered themselves businessmen above all else."

The lack of inflection in her voice was a scab over a wound, hiding the pain beneath. Forced into animal shape, caged, starved, left in the dark until Isaac—Freida, that is—was willing to do anything just to make it end.

Bile coated the back of his throat, and his breath came fast and shallow. Isaac forced himself to inhale deeply, to still the trembling of his fingers. "Thank you, Freida. I'm sorry to have disturbed you, but this was important."

She nodded. "I can see that. You're always welcome here, Isaac." A watery smile touched her mouth. "I don't know what I would have done without you, these last few weeks."

"You would have done what you needed to," he said. "I'm just glad I could make things a little easier."

"You'll be at the trial?"

It wasn't the first time she'd asked. "I'll be right there by you, every step of the way," he confirmed. "I promise."

He took his leave after. But as he made for the door, Freida called after him, "Isaac? If something…bad…did happen to those children… you're going to find them, right?"

Isaac hesitated. This wasn't his case. It was almost certainly within the jurisdiction of the regular police. There was no evidence of hexes being involved.

But familiar children…magic had to come into it somewhere.

"I'll do my best," he said at last, and gently shut the door behind him.

CHAPTER 5

SUNDAY MORNING, ISAAC found Bill waiting inside the small office he shared with Sionn.

Isaac didn't sleep much anymore, and when he did, nightmares were a regular occurrence. But his dreams Friday night had been particularly disturbing. For the first time in months, Isaac had dreamed he was back in mastiff form. He'd been trying to find someone—Bill?—but his nose hadn't worked any better than in his human shape. He'd ended up lost in the dark, certain Bill was going to die, because of course Isaac's dog self had proved worthless yet again.

Sionn leaned half over the desk, chin propped on his hand, his yellow eyes fixed on Bill. Bill sat in Isaac's chair, canted forward, apparently listening to something Sionn had murmured.

Isaac felt a shiver across the back of his neck, as though hackles tried to rise, and a growl clawed at his throat. The reaction caught him off-guard. Fur and feathers, he'd almost succeeded in letting his dog form fade away, and now he was nearly *growling?*

It didn't mean anything. It couldn't. He wouldn't let it.

He just had to be patient. Eventually he would forget he'd ever been anything but human.

At the sight of Isaac, Bill scrambled out of the chair hastily, as though he'd been caught doing something wrong. Sionn sat back more slowly, not a trace of guilt on his features.

Why should there have been? Isaac had no claim to Bill. He ought to be surprised Bill hadn't found anyone sooner.

"Isaac," Bill said with a nervous smile. "The orphanage sent the list. I came by to see if you two were available to help."

Isaac went to his chair and sat down. The wooden seat was still warm from Bill's body. "I've learned some things since last we spoke."

"Is that why you have such a sour face?" Sionn asked.

He'd thought he'd kept his expression neutral. Apparently he wasn't as good at hiding his emotions as he'd hoped. "Yes," he lied.

Isaac related what he'd learned from Mal and Freida. When he was done, Bill told them about Elwood's visit to the precinct.

"Fur and feathers," Sionn said. "That ain't good, not a single bit of it. If the nun had ties with the criminal underworld, there's no telling what happened to the kids."

Bill leaned against the wall beside the door. "It sounds as though her interest in familiar potentials is new," he said slowly. "I'm guessing whatever she was involved in most recently, it began around the time the statue of Saint Jerome was broken."

"Because she needed somewhere to hide the money," Isaac supplied.

Bill nodded. "I'm thinking we should try to track down as many of the children as we can, starting a year ago."

Sionn cocked his head. "Why a year?"

"Because we'll know for sure if something *has* changed." Bill glanced at Isaac. "I'm guessing Sister Brigid wasn't sending too many orphans to people like Madam Galpern at once. It'd be noticed. But the fact she suddenly had enough cash to need a place to hide it…"

"That kind of money doesn't come from an occasional service," Isaac finished.

Their eyes met in a moment of understanding. Bill's hazel irises absorbed the colors around him, shifting their shade by mood and day. At the moment they tended toward green; not brash emerald but something softer. Warmer.

A man could get lost in eyes like that.

Isaac tore his gaze away, suddenly afraid Bill would look too deeply into *his* eyes in return. "So we start down the list. See how many of the children we can find."

"Aye." Bill hesitated. "If you've nothing else to be doing, of course. I don't want to interfere in your other work. I know you've been helping Tom and Cicero."

"I have the time," Isaac said with a shrug. "At least for now."

Sionn gave Bill a wicked smile. "I'm all yours."

Bill cleared his throat. "I've divided up the list. There are thirty-three names on it over the last year, but they're spread all up and down Manhattan. Sionn, if you don't mind taking these twelve, Isaac and I will see to the rest."

Isaac frowned. After his inability to take on dog shape the other day, did Bill think he wasn't capable of conducting a single interview on his own? "Why don't we each take eleven addresses?"

"Because some of these ain't in the sort of neighborhoods where people appreciate the coppers coming around asking questions," Bill replied. "I'm not looking to get taken by surprise from behind. But if you'd prefer, you can switch with Sionn."

That would give Sionn all day alone with Bill. "I didn't say that," Isaac said hastily. "I'm just surprised there are any names from those areas on the list. Why would anyone eking out a living in the poorest neighborhoods adopt another mouth to feed?"

"A good question," Bill said grimly. "I doubt we'll like the answers. Sionn?"

"Knock on doors in the swanky parts of town, where they usually wouldn't let the likes of me polish their boots?" Sionn grinned. "I can't wait to flash my badge at the swells and watch them squirm."

Bill laughed. "Aye, I thought that might be the case. Don't have too much fun, though; we don't want them complaining to the Police Board."

"Spoilsport," Sion replied, grinning back at Bill. As they gazed at one another, Isaac felt suddenly excluded. As though he could sink into the furniture and never be missed.

"We should get going," he said, more harshly than he intended. "There's no sense wasting any more time sitting around here."

Bill looked taken aback. Sionn frowned slightly, but only said, "That's our Isaac. Mind on business, and business only."

"True enough." Bill's smile curved beneath his mustache, but there was a wistfulness to it. Or maybe that was just Isaac's own wishful thinking. "All right, then. Let's go find these kids."

Their first address was on Hester Street, not far from the Coven. When Isaac saw the location, he frowned.

"That doesn't make sense." Fine lines showed around his eyes, crinkling in thought. "The area is mainly Jewish."

Bill had wondered about it as well. "For certain no Catholic orphanage is going to hand over children to anyone who doesn't follow whichever of the seven popes they do."

Isaac nodded. "Not to mention we have our own aid societies for orphaned children and destitute families. A Jewish family would turn to them."

"There are some Irish families mixed in the area, though, right?" Bill asked. "Maybe it was one of them. They'd likely be Belfastian, so the adoption would be approved."

"There are," Isaac said dubiously. "But that still raises the question as to why a poor Irish family would want another child to feed."

"Only one way to find out," Bill said. "Let's go talk to them ourselves."

They made their way toward Hester Street. Families bustled in and out of the restaurants or clustered around the food carts. The shops showed only closed signs, thanks to the Sunday laws. Children chased one another through the streets, while adults chatted on the stoops or along the sidewalk. Most of the signs were in Hebrew, sometimes with English written below and sometimes not.

"Did you grow up here?" Bill asked.

"Yes. On Allen Street. I visit every Friday, and on the major holidays like Passover."

"Saturday's the sabbath, right?"

"Not exactly. We mark the days starting at sundown, so it's really Friday evening to Saturday evening." Isaac glanced at Bill out of the side of his eye. "I take it you didn't go to mass this morning, as early as you arrived at the Coven."

Bill shrugged. "Aye, well, I ain't really the church going type. My ma dragged me to mass every week when I was a little one, but by the time she passed we only went on Christmas and Easter." What little faith she'd retained after Da left had been ground away bit by bit with every hard year after.

As they walked, a few people called out "Izak!" in recognition. He stopped in front of a bakery, chatting with the man sweeping the stoop in a language that sounded vaguely like Spanish to Bill's ear. The heavenly smell of the bread inside competed with the summer reek of the street: sweat, manure, and spoiling garbage.

The baker laughed at whatever Isaac said, then ducked into the shop. A moment later, he returned with something wrapped in a bit of paper, which he held out. "Kome kon gana."

When Isaac tried to pay him, he shook his head, holding up a hand and responding with another laugh.

As they left, Isaac said, "Mr. Bacellar is an old friend of my mother's. Their families lived next to each other in Constantinople, and they emigrated together. I introduced his daughter to her witch last year."

Bill nodded at the small package. "So what did he give you?"

Isaac's long fingers unwrapped a mouthwatering confection of pastry, honey, and nuts. "Baklava. Ever had it?"

Bill shook his head. "Nay, I can't say I have."

Isaac grinned. The expression transformed his face, erasing the fine lines around his mouth. Bill couldn't remember him ever looking just happy before, as though he had no cares in the world.

He wanted to see that look again. He wanted to be the one to put it on Isaac's face.

"You're in for a treat, then," Isaac said, and held the baklava up to Bill's lips.

Honey like liquid sunlight filled his mouth, flavored by the nuts and sheets of pastry. Bill let out an involuntary moan, and Isaac laughed.

"Like it?" he asked, a teasing note in his voice. He lifted the pastry to his own mouth and took a bite.

"Aye," Bill said. A fleck of pastry clung to Isaac's lower lip, drawing Bill's gaze.

He wanted to lean over and tongue it away. Isaac's mouth would taste like honey.

The elegant column of Isaac's throat worked as he swallowed. "One bite left," he said, and pressed it against Bill's lips.

Bill took it, mouth brushing Isaac's fingers. He wanted to lick the honey off—no, suck it off, each slender digit at a time. His prick hardened, and his skin ached with desire.

Isaac's lips parted, and his tawny eyes darkened. It felt as though they were suspended in the moment, neither of them able to move or look away.

Then Isaac snatched his fingers back, as though burned. Took a hasty step away as well, putting space between them.

Heat collected in Bill's face. Isaac had seen his desire, clear enough. Seen it, and wanted nothing to do with it. "Isaac, I…"

"We should get moving," Isaac interrupted, turning away from Bill. "We have a lot of ground to cover, after all."

Bill wanted to protest. But there was nothing he could say. If only he could turn back the clock just five minutes, take the moment back.

Live a little bit longer in ignorance.

"Aye," Bill said heavily. He followed Isaac down Hester Street, the sweetness of honey gone to ashes on his tongue.

"None of the adoptions from the last six months were real," Bill said that evening. They'd met back up with Sionn at the Coven, in the office he and Isaac shared. "We couldn't find a single person who had ever heard of the families listed, not even at the addresses they'd supposedly lived at as recently as two weeks ago."

The day had been long and frustrating. Isaac had worried when no one at the Hester Street tenement knew the family who'd supposedly adopted one of the orphans. But then the next address had proved to be real—they'd not only spoken to the man and woman on the list, but the girl they'd adopted. She seemed to be thriving in her new home, and some of the bands of fear had eased from Isaac's chest.

She'd been one of the few they'd found. Out of the twenty-one orphans on their part of the list, Bill and Isaac had located less than half. Three more had apparently lived at the addresses the orphanage had on record, but moved since. All of them had been adopted prior to six months ago.

As for the remaining nine, those who had passed through Sister Brigid's hands in the last six months, no one recognized the names of the supposed adoptive parents, let alone knew anything about potential familiar children. That number included Elwood's son, Teddy.

"Same." Sionn looked uncharacteristically glum. "Out of my twelve, eight were genuine, and all of them prior to February. The other four families didn't exist. I had a couple of servants threaten to call the coppers on me—they thought I was trying some sort of swindle."

"No wonder Elwood couldn't find his little boy." Bill sat back in the chair they'd dragged in for him. A weary look flashed over his face. "Saint Mary preserve us. That's thirteen familiar potentials—kids—gone missing since January."

Cold crept up Isaac's spine. Whatever had happened to the children, it couldn't be good. Where were they now? Afraid? In pain? Trapped in cages in the dark?

"We have to save them," he said past the bands of fear tightening his chest and cutting off his air.

"Aye." Bill's shoulders straightened. "That we do. Right now, our best clue is the viper who killed Sister Brigid. There can't be many snake familiars with venom that deadly."

"You're thinking we should check the rogue's gallery?" Isaac asked.

Bill nodded. "I'll take the one at regular police force. It includes the familiars listed as dangerous by O'Malley's old squad."

"I'll look through the one here," Isaac agreed. "First thing in the morning."

Sionn leaned back in his chair. "I don't know about you, but I'm famished." A coy smile touched his lips. "What do you say to getting a bite of dinner, Bill?"

Bill glanced briefly at Isaac—then away again, just as quickly.

They hadn't been easy with each other all afternoon, thanks to Isaac's stupid stunt with the baklava. The memory came back to him forcefully: the sticky heat of summer on his skin, the tips of his fingers just grazing Bill's lips.

He'd ached for Bill. Wanted nothing more than to taste the warmth of his mouth. To stand on tiptoe and kiss the tall Irishman. To press their bodies together and feel something even hotter than the sun beating down on them.

Bill had certainly read it in his eyes. Seen his secret longing, displayed naked on Isaac's face.

So Isaac had pulled away, before the inevitable rejection. Because he was spoiled, broken, unworthy. Bill surely knew it as well as Isaac did. Now he knew, too, that Isaac wanted him.

At least Bill was kind enough not to have betrayed any revulsion. Instead, they both pretended the moment had never happened.

Isaac focused his gaze on the desk in front of him. "Have fun," he said, and the words came out far colder than he intended, because a part of him was selfish enough to want to keep Bill to himself, despite everything.

"Aye," Bill said to Sionn. "Dinner sounds nice."

Sionn grinned and jumped up. "I know just the place," he said, steering Bill out the door. "Have fun with your paperwork, Isaac."

Chapter 6

Sionn led the way to a small Irish-run restaurant a short train ride from the Coven. It was a step up from most of the dives Bill found himself in, with good food served alongside the beer, and crisp linens on the tables. Fans overhead stirred the air, making the place less stifling than it would have been otherwise. Bill pitied the poor fellows in the kitchen, though.

For a foolish moment back at the Coven, Bill had half-hoped Isaac would say something. Offer to join them, or ask Bill to stay and help out. Of course he hadn't; he'd made his feelings toward Bill clear enough earlier.

Spending the rest of the day together, after the disaster with the baklava, had been its own kind of torture. Being so close to Isaac, knowing he didn't return Bill's feelings, hurt like a thousand rose thorns in his skin, snagging deeper every time he glimpsed Isaac's handsome profile, or heard his voice.

Which was why he'd agreed to Sionn's invitation. It was time to move on. Time to accept Isaac would never return his affection. Bill's own da hadn't wanted him; stupid to have imagined anyone else ever would.

"So, Bill," Sionn said, watching Bill over the lip of his glass, "tell me a bit about yourself, then."

It was a question Bill always dreaded. To buy time, he took a deep drink from the cool beer the waiter brought, the lager crisp enough to wash away a bit of the day's heat. "Not much to tell. I'm just a simple Irish lad from the East Side. What about you?"

"The same, or close enough." The waiter served their food, and they tucked in. "You work for the regular police, but you liaise with the MWP. Have you ever thought about bonding?"

Bill's stomach tightened around his brisket. He could still hear Da's words ringing in his ears: *You're no use to me. Your lying whore of a mother said her family was witch-blooded, but look at these scores. You're such a disappointment compared to Martin, I can't imagine why I kept coming here. I'm leaving.*

"Nay. Not since I was young." He took a deeper drink of his beer. "I've got some potential, but not much. Barely enough to register on the tests, to tell the truth. There's no familiar out there waiting for me."

"I see." Sionn tucked into the boiled cabbage. "Can I ask why you decided to liaise with the MWP, then?"

What was he to say? That he'd taken the job when it was offered because he'd hoped to see more of Isaac? It sounded pathetic—it *was* pathetic.

"Tom Halloran suggested it to me," he said, which wasn't quite a lie. "We knew each other back when we were both beat coppers at the same precinct. I'd been hoping for a promotion, but that fox Malachi put an end to my chances when he escaped custody on my watch." Not his finest moment on the force, that was for certain. "After, liaison seemed like the only way to make detective."

"Not interested in spending the rest of your life wearing out your shoes on the beat? I don't blame you. But you like the work?"

"Aye. There are days I wish I was assigned out of the MWP, rather than the precinct, but that's the way it is."

They finished their meal, then lingered over drinks. Sionn carried most of the conversation, chatting lightly about some of the other familiars. "I've had a good evening, Bill," he said when they finished their drinks. He stretched ostentatiously, and his ankle rubbed against Bill's. "It'd be a shame for it to have to end early."

Well, hell.

Bill wasn't a fool; he'd seen the looks Sionn had been giving him. Still, he wasn't exactly the type for casual encounters.

Back when they were both beat coppers, he and Tom had given each other a hand on the nights they spent on reserve, their cots only inches apart. He'd liked Tom, respected the man, but he'd never thought about taking things further.

After that, Bill had fallen for Isaac. He'd known Isaac needed space, needed time, so he'd waited almost three years with only his hand and a dildo for company. Hoping.

That was over with now. Isaac wasn't interested. It was time to move on.

Bill liked what he'd seen of Sionn. The fellow was handsome, with his coppery hair and freckles over every inch of his skin. But was Bill interested in going to bed with the fellow? This wouldn't be just a silent grope in the dark, never to be spoken of, like it had been with Tom.

Maybe it was what he needed. Something to clear the last thoughts of Isaac from his mind. Surely if he slept with Sionn, it would be easier to put Isaac behind him.

"I'm not saying no," Bill said carefully, because he didn't want Sionn to think it a rejection.

Sionn's smile wavered. "But you're not saying yes."

"Not tonight." Bill touched his fingertips to the back of Sionn's hand. "I've a lot of things tangled up in my head right now. I know most fellows would welcome a chance to stop thinking about them for a while, but I'm not like that."

Sionn's smile firmed back up. "A raincheck, then?"

He had to let go of his hopeless longing for Isaac. Had to. "Aye. A raincheck it is."

Isaac stared unseeing at the images in the MWP's rogues gallery, seething silently. Though whether he was angry at himself, or Bill, or Sionn, he didn't know.

Sionn had come back to the barracks late, after most everyone else was asleep and snoring. Isaac had been awake, of course. In addition to his usual insomnia, his treacherous imagination had supplied all the things Bill might be doing with Sionn. When Sionn finally returned, Isaac rolled over, face to the wall, and pretended to be asleep even as jealousy etched his veins with acid.

Over and over again, he'd told himself it was for the best. But the words didn't stop the ache in his chest, or the bile churning in his gut.

Then, to make things even worse, he'd dreamed himself in mastiff form again. For a second time, he'd been frantically searching for Bill, with only his nose to guide him. Just as before, he'd failed.

Now Isaac swore at himself and forced his attention back on the photos. Familiars were photographed in both human and animal form, which made his job a bit easier. All he had to do was look for the snakes. Non-venomous ones like black snakes he could discard immediately.

Though he doubted even the venomous native snakes like copperheads could kill an adult woman so quickly, if at all, he wrote their names down just in case.

At least this job didn't need two people working it, which meant he didn't have to put up with Sionn. If he'd had to see Sionn's satisfied grin, knowing he'd been with Bill, Isaac would have lost his mind.

There came a knock on the door, and Cicero let himself in. "There you are. Sionn said I'd find you here."

Isaac's heart picked up its pace. "Is there something wrong?" His mind went immediately to Freida. Had the gang sent someone to stop her from testifying? "Is Freida all right?"

"She's fine, darling, at least as far as I know." Cicero leaned against the wall beside the rogues gallery. "As for something being wrong, you tell me. Sionn says he had a very pleasant dinner with our William last night."

No. No, he was not talking about this with anyone, not even Cicero. "He's not 'our' Bill."

"Touchy." Cicero arched a brow. "I came to see how you were taking the news. Not well, I assume."

"Bill invited me to go with them. I chose not to."

Cicero's peridot eyes widened. "You did what? Have you gone utterly mad?"

Why couldn't Cicero leave well enough alone? First he had to badger Isaac about not taking his other shape, and now this. "I don't know what you're talking about."

Cicero crossed the room and shut the door, before turning to Isaac. "I'm talking about the fact that you're letting William slip through your fingers, and I don't understand why. Don't deny it—I've known you since I was practically a kitten. I can see how you look at him. You're halfway to being in love with him."

"You're wrong," Isaac said, and tried to put conviction behind the words. It wasn't even a lie. Cicero *was* wrong, because Isaac wasn't just halfway to being in love with Bill.

He was all the way there, and had been for a long time.

His face must have betrayed him, because Cicero's expression softened. "Oh darling. I'm sorry. But if you would just tell him, I'm sure you could work it out."

"What is there to work out?" Isaac demanded. "There's something wrong with me, Cicero. You said it yourself, when you found out I haven't been taking animal form."

"I said nothing of the sort!" Cicero reached for him, but for once Isaac avoided his touch. "There's nothing wrong with you, other than you aren't taking care of yourself."

"I don't want to talk about it. And I don't want to talk about Bill."

"Then stop talking *about* him, and start talking *to* him." Cicero flung up his hands. "If you just stand by while Sionn wines and dines him, you're going to lose him. Take my advice."

Something hardened deep inside Isaac. "Take your advice?" he asked, and felt a terrible satisfaction when Cicero cringed at his tone. "I took your advice and told Martin Granger he was my witch, and ended up in the hospital for my troubles. I took your advice and asked Noah for help finding a job, and was eventually force bonded and held captive." He took a step forward. "So do me a favor, and don't give me any more advice."

Cicero blanched. Then he bowed his head and turned toward the door. "Y-you're right," he said, voice muffled. "I'm sorry. I should mind my own business."

"Yes," Isaac said. "You should." He turned resolutely back to the rogues gallery, and pretended he didn't feel even the slightest twinge of guilt at the sound of the door shutting between them.

Bill stepped up to the bar beside Tom Halloran. "What do you know about poisonous snakes?"

"A good day to you, Bill," Tom said. "I'm doing well, thanks for asking."

They'd been meeting in the same saloon for years, even before Tom had gone to work for the MWP. Back when Bill had teased him about being "Saint Tom," and made him buy the drinks. It was a working-man's sort of place, a bit rough around the edges, but the owner was quick to toss troublemakers out on their ears. There were no chairs at the bar, which meant they stood elbow-to-elbow along the simple plank. The barkeep caught Bill's eye and slid him his customary whiskey.

"Sorry." Bill picked up his whiskey but didn't toss it back yet. "How are you, Tom? Cicero doing well?"

"Cicero and I are fine." Tom sipped from his pint. "What's this about snakes?"

Bill told Tom about his long day sorting through the extensive rogues gallery of the regular police force. From there, he moved on to the records confiscated from the defunct Dangerous Familiars Squad, which held photographs of all the poor bastards they'd sent to the

Menagerie. "All of the snakes I could find were ordinary species you'd see around here. I didn't think any of them were too poisonous, but I must be wrong, because Sister Brigid surely died quick."

"That, or the assassin ain't in the rogues gallery, and didn't run afoul of the Squad," Tom said.

"Aye." Bill drank some of his whiskey, enjoying the smooth burn against his tongue and throat. "But if we're to start looking for him, it would be a good sight easier if we knew what sort of snake to keep an eye out for."

Tom shrugged. "I don't know a thing about snakes. What do you mean to do?"

"I'm going to call at the Museum of Natural History over near Central Park tomorrow. Surely they have someone there who could help. I'll see if Sionn has time to go with me."

Ordinarily, he would have asked Isaac to help. But he could hardly move past the man if he sought him out at every turn, and Sionn would likely enjoy the excuse to stretch his wings.

Tom shifted his weight from foot to foot, eyes focused on the beer in front of him. "I hear you had dinner with Sionn last night."

Bill stiffened. "So what if I did?"

"No reason." Tom still didn't look at him. "I was just a little surprised, that's all."

"We've been working together a bit." Bill downed the rest of his whiskey and signaled for another. "I'm guessing Cicero was the one who told you about dinner."

Tom looked abashed. "Aye."

"Which means the entire Coven knows."

"Nay!" Tom finally turned his gaze to Bill. "That ain't the case. Cicero wouldn't spread this around. He only told me because he was worried."

Bill frowned. "Worried about what?"

"Isaac."

It was too much. "Why the devil would he be worried about Isaac?"

"Because they're best friends, and he—both of us—thought there might be something between the two of you."

Apparently Bill hadn't done as good of a job of hiding his interest as he'd thought. "Then you're both wrong." The lingering burn of the whiskey failed to wash away the bitterness of heartbreak. "Isaac's made it clear as day he ain't interested. So I'd thank you to let the matter drop, and let me get on with my life."

"I'm sorry, Bill." Tom held up both hands. "I'll tell Cicero to keep his nose in his own business from now on."

"See you do," Bill snapped. He stepped back from the bar. "I'm leaving. You can have the drink I ordered. Seems I ain't as thirsty as I thought."

Chapter 7

THE NEXT DAY, Isaac made his way to Freida's apartment once again. The court date was fast approaching, and he wanted to make certain she knew what would happen when she took the stand. He'd been to enough trials over the last few years that he wanted her as prepared as possible. Freida's testimony had the power to sway the jury one way or the other. To put away the gang who had kidnapped her and too many others.

Even on the walk to her apartment, though, he acknowledged the visit was an excuse. He could go any time before the trial; there was no great urgency to the task.

No, he'd left the Coven because Bill sent around asking Sionn to join him at the museum.

After Cicero had departed, Isaac felt increasingly guilty throughout the day and night. He'd treated his best friend badly, made Cicero feel as though Isaac blamed him for everything that had happened with his witch, with Noah, with the blood hexes. He'd vowed to keep a tighter control on his emotions from now on.

Sionn's brilliant grin at the prospect of spending more time with Bill had sorely tested that vow.

The heat in the tenement's stairwell was stifling, adding to Isaac's foul mood. As he neared Freida's door, it swung open, causing Isaac to startle. "Thank you for your time, Miss Freida," a man said as he stepped out.

It took Isaac a moment to place the figure, and when he did, his fists clenched. Eli Valentine—the reporter who'd been after him on the steps of the Coven the other day.

Now he was here, badgering Freida.

Isaac's lip curled, a protective snarl thrumming in his chest.

Fur and feathers, those stupid dreams were dragging old instincts back into his waking life now. He swallowed the snarl and strode toward the reporter. "Mr. Valentine," he said coldly.

Valentine's light brown eyes widened in alarm. "Well, it's good to see you again, Mr. Isaac. I don't suppose you have anything to say to the press?"

Isaac's teeth ached from clenching his jaw. "What are you doing here? Freida's been through enough—leave her alone."

"Isaac, it's all right." She stepped out after Valentine.

"It isn't." He didn't take his glare off the reporter. "If you print something that causes us to lose this case, if they walk free because of you…"

"That's not my intent!" Valentine held up both hands. "Let me explain. I'm not just looking for something to fill column space. I want to help."

Isaac folded his arms over his chest. "Explain, then."

Valentine lowered his hands cautiously. "I became a reporter because I wanted to make things better, not worse. Expose corruption, shine the light of truth into the dark places. Help the honest people of this city who just want to live in peace." His generous mouth tightened. "I'm still new to the newspaper business, so my editor has me writing all the silly stories no one else wants to take. Maids who claim to be lost princesses, drunken fishermen who see monsters on islands in the East River, that sort of thing. I wasted three inches of column space on a dancing cat last week."

Isaac felt a headache coming on. "So you think writing about the trial will advance your own career?"

"When you put it like that, it doesn't sound so good," Valentine muttered. "It's what I want to write about. I want an exposé, run during the trial, detailing all the ways familiars are mistreated. By the time I'm finished, I want everyone in New York demanding to know why nothing's being done, why the penalties for mistreatment and force bonding aren't harsher. I want to make so much noise the politicians can't afford to ignore the issue."

Isaac frowned. "You aren't a familiar, though."

"No. I'm a witch. Unbonded." He shrugged. "But I don't have to be a woman to think they deserve the right to vote, do I? Or a factory worker to think the man who's doing the labor with his own hands ought to get more benefit from it than the man who owns the mill."

"An idealist," Isaac said. "I used to be one myself."

"The world's a dark place, Mr. Isaac. If it's in my power to bring a little light into it, shouldn't I?"

"You sound like my rabbi." And himself, once upon a time. He'd gone into police work believing he was going to stop bad people, help innocents. Fix the world.

"Then he's a smart man," Valentine said.

Isaac sighed. He couldn't forbid Freida from talking to the journalist, and at least Valentine's heart seemed in the right place. "All right. Work on your exposé, but don't do anything to jeopardize the trial."

Valentine grinned. "I won't. I don't suppose you'd be available for an interview…?"

"No," Isaac replied flatly. "I wouldn't."

Valentine shrugged. "Can't blame a man for trying. Let me know if you change your mind."

With a tip of his hat, Valentine trotted away. Isaac suppressed a sigh and turned to Freida. She wore an anxious expression, her hands twisted in front of her. "I'm sorry. I thought he could help."

"It's fine," Isaac said, though he wasn't at all sure about that. What was done was done, and there was no sense making Freida feel bad about it. "But let's go inside, just in case the good Mr. Valentine is tempted to eavesdrop from the stairwell."

Bill and Sionn took the Ninth Avenue El to the American Museum of Natural History. The owl was good company, Bill had to admit. Clever and funny, always ready with an anecdote or bit of news any time conversation lagged. Bill liked him, liked spending time with him.

Whether he wanted it to be more than that, he wasn't sure yet. Sionn flirted, but he didn't press, which was nice.

It was a short walk to the enormous sprawl of the museum. The place wasn't terribly crowded on a Monday, and Bill flashed his badge at the ticket taker and explained what they needed. In short order, they were escorted through the public galleries and back through a series of long corridors lined with specimen cabinets. A witch and familiar pair worked their way down one hall, carefully recharging the hexes on the cabinets to help preserve the contents.

Their guide left them in a cluttered office. "Wait here a moment, and

I'll fetch Dr. Berry."

Sionn began to inspect the office as soon as they were alone. "Would you look at this!" he said, pointing to an enormous snake skeleton mounted on a wooden plaque on the wall. "I'd hate to have met that fellow when he was still alive."

"Aye." A window let in a beam of sunlight, and dust motes danced in it. Shed snake skins, notes, and papers cluttered the desk. Preserved snakes curled in jars on the shelves, and the sight of their coils gave Bill a little shiver. Maybe because they were dead; he'd never been afraid of live serpents before.

He turned away from the creatures and stared out the window. "Can I ask you a question about familiars?"

Sionn paused in his investigation of the office. "Aye. What do you want to know?"

Bill hesitated. He shouldn't ask. Isaac wouldn't thank him, if he found out. "I've heard it ain't good for familiars to spend too much time in one shape or another. Why is it bad?"

Sionn was uncharacteristically silent for a few moments. "It's hard to explain," he said at last. "Denying a part of yourself is never a good thing. Familiars who stay too long in animal shape start to forget they were ever human, and those who stay human forget they were ever an animal. They lose half of themselves either way."

Bill frowned. "You mean literally forget?"

"Aye. If I stayed in owl shape for too long, someday I wouldn't remember we'd ever had this conversation. I might recall flying around outside the orphanage, but not what I was looking for. My entire childhood would just be…gone."

Could this be happening to Isaac? Except he'd be forgetting memories made as a dog. "Oh. That ain't good."

"Having your mind turned into cheesecloth usually isn't," Sionn agreed. "I'm no alienist, but a familiar I knew as a boy ended up in the lunatic asylum on Blackwell's Island, after she refused to take animal shape for years. Thought it was sinful or something." Sionn paused. "By the end, she was just…lost. Couldn't function, because she wasn't a whole person anymore."

"Did they help her? The doctors at the asylum, that is."

Sionn snorted. "Nay. They locked the patients in at night, you see. One of the other women took the bucket they used for a chamber pot and beat her head in."

Bill wished he hadn't asked. Before he could say anything else, footsteps approached, and a spry older man dressed in a sober suit walked in.

"Dr. Frederick Berry, at your service," he said, shaking their hands. His palms were soft, and a heavy silver ring set with a large emerald encircled one finger. Either the museum paid very well indeed, or Dr. Berry came from money. "I must say, this is a bit exciting for me. It isn't every day the police seek out the opinion of a herpetologist."

He listened attentively while Bill explained the particulars surrounding Sister Brigid's death, and produced the scrap of snake skin and the coroner's report. When Bill was done, he read over the report carefully, then took the shed skin to his desk and examined it closely with a magnifying glass. Bill exchanged a glance with Sionn while Berry worked, but neither of them wanted to disturb the man's concentration by speaking.

Finally, Dr. Berry sat back in his chair. "Ordinarily it's difficult to identify snake species based on nothing more than a bit of shed skin, even for the expert."

Bill's spirits plummeted. "So you can't help us?"

"I didn't say that, my good man." Berry favored him with a smile. "This patch of skin was shed from the side and back of the head. Do you see this pair of large scales here, behind the nine-plate arrangement?"

"I think so?" Bill said doubtfully. It all looked pretty much the same to him, but the man obviously knew what he was talking about.

"Those scales are called occipitals, and occur in only a single species. *Ophiophagus hannah*, the king cobra."

Sionn let out a low whistle. "Well, ain't that a spot of luck."

"Likely I would have been able to identify the species based on the coroner's report, even if we didn't have such concrete proof," Berry said. "Fortunately for humankind, there are few vipers on earth which can cause such a rapid death in adults as was visited on your victim. The king cobra is one of those few."

None of the familiars in the rogues gallery had been king cobras. Or at least not listed as such. "Could they be easily mistaken as something else? A rat snake, say, or a copperhead?"

"I wouldn't think so. If nothing else, they have the hood associated with other cobras, though theirs is narrower than some. I'm certain we have a specimen or two here, if you'd care to have a look."

"Could you write up a short description?" Bill asked.

"Of course."

They departed a short time after, Bill carrying the description in his pocket. "What next?" Sionn asked as they made their way back toward the El.

"This king cobra familiar might not be known to the police," Bill said, "but someone out there might recognize him. I figure we'll make use of the reporters hanging about the Coven, have them run the description in their papers and send word to me at the precinct if anyone recognizes his serpent form."

"Good idea." Sionn glanced up at him, then away. "Fancy a beer after? There's a saloon I'm partial to not far from the Coven. I think you'd like it."

Bill hesitated. But what was his alternative? Go back to his apartment after work and stew there alone, wishing for something he could never have?

"Aye," he said. "I think I would."

A rap on the door woke Bill from a sound sleep.

The apartment was breathlessly hot once again, but the beers he'd knocked back with Sionn had let him collapse into unconsciousness the moment he reached the bed. Only the faintest breeze leaked through the open window. The gray light of dawn crept in with it, and he cursed whoever had waked him so early.

The knocking came again. "Hold on!" he called and found his trousers and shirt abandoned on the floor beside the bed. He struggled into them, then stumbled to the door with an aching head.

A familiar stood there, her bright red eyes startling against her brown skin. "Isaac sent me," she said in a clipped voice. A bird familiar of some sort, then, as they most often acted as couriers. "There's been a body found in the East River, at the floating baths south of the Brooklyn Bridge. He thinks it might be related to your case."

"Christ." Bill scrubbed at his face. "Did he say why?"

"No. Just to meet him there." Her job done, she hurried out, no doubt eager to be back on the wing.

Bill splashed water on his face, skipped his morning shave, and finished dressing as quickly as possible. It was a long way from 47th Street to southern Manhattan, and every clank and jerk of the El aggravated his headache.

Still, he felt more awake by the time he reached the pier and its floating bath. The floating baths were popular every summer, especially during hot spells like the one currently gripping the city. A group mainly composed of men crowded near the pier this one was anchored to; no doubt they'd hoped for a cool dip before whatever work awaited them. The bath bobbed in the river past them, its huge pontoons blocking any outside view of the central wells where bathers would cool and clean themselves.

Isaac stood on the pier, near the police wagon that had come for the body. Bill didn't recognize the young witch driving it. The task had once belonged to Jamie MacDougal, who'd not only bonded but left police work altogether.

The early morning wind blew over the East River, bringing some relief to the close air and stirring Isaac's dark hair. The dawn light gilded his profile, and Bill's breath caught in his lungs at the sight. A pensive expression pinched Isaac's eyes and mouth, but he was still so beautiful it made Bill's chest ache.

If only it had been Isaac with him at dinner last night. Isaac drinking beer and swapping stories until after midnight.

But that wasn't fair to Sionn. Bill let out a sigh. He needed to keep his mind on business from now on, whenever he was near Isaac. Had to let this longing go.

At the sound of his boots on the pier, Isaac turned sharply. Momentary alarm replaced his pensive expression, easing when he saw it was only Bill. "Bill. Take a look at this."

The body lay sprawled in a pool of water, bronze eyes open. The flesh was in fairly good condition, which meant he couldn't have been in the water for more than a few hours. His black hair was shaved short, his brown skin tinged gray with death. The shabby clothes hanging on his frame looked to have been made for a larger man.

"Who is he?" Bill asked.

Isaac crouched by the body, and Bill followed suit. "He was in the MWP rogues gallery. Alfonso, a rat snake. He was arrested for peddling fake hexes during the anti-vice campaign last year."

"So what does he have to do with Sister Brigid's murder? She was killed by a king cobra."

Instead of answering the question, Isaac said, "An attendant came to get the baths ready for the day. The body had fetched up against one of the pontoons, caught on one of the anchoring lines. The attendant summoned the beat copper, who pulled Alfonso out of the river. Then the copper saw this, and decided it was ours to deal with."

Isaac took a pencil from his pocket and used it to ease the dead man's mouth open. Jammed in amidst the ordinary human teeth were two needle-like fangs. His soft palate bulged behind them, as if distended by a pair of sacs.

Bill stared at the impossibility. "They couldn't...I mean, familiars don't shift just parts of their bodies, do they?"

"I've never known anyone who could," Isaac said.

"Then what the devil are those doing there?"

"I don't know." Isaac pulled the pencil back and wiped it off absently with a handkerchief. "I suppose it might not have anything to do with missing potential familiars and a dead nun. But rat snakes don't have fangs like these, or venom sacs."

"And the good sister died from the bite of a venomous snake that ought not to be in this city," Bill agreed. "I think your instincts are right, and we've just found our murderer."

Chapter 8

"Quigley," Nick said by way of greeting when he arrived at the morgue a few hours later, his witch Jamie in tow. "What's this about a man with snake teeth? Rook's yammering didn't make much sense, not that it ever does."

Isaac had gone back to the Coven, while Bill accompanied Alfonso's body to the morgue. Once there, he'd had Rook fly a message to Nick at his saloon. Nick might not have gone to medical college, but he'd studied for it, and he likely knew as much about familiar anatomy as anyone.

Nick was a big man, brown skinned and possessed of a glorious mane of wavy hair, and Bill had to crane his neck to look him in the eye. "To be honest, the situation doesn't make much sense."

Jamie gave Bill an easy grin and held out his hand. "Good to see you, Bill," he said. "It's been too long. How are you?"

Bill shook his hand warmly. He'd always liked Jamie, back when he drove the police wagon for the MWP. "Doing well. You? How's business?"

Nick stamped a foot impatiently. "We're here to see the body. Catch up over a beer when we don't have to breathe in this air."

"You've a point," Jamie allowed. "It ain't pleasant."

Jamie wasn't wrong. The area around Bellevue Hospital and the City Morgue never smelled exactly good, but in the heat the stench of sickness and decayed flesh was more pervasive than usual.

"The coroner already started," Bill said. "He said we could join him once you arrived."

Jamie wavered, just slightly. Nick put a hand to his witch's shoulder. "The last time you were here was with Wyatt, wasn't it?"

"Inside the actual autopsy room, aye." Jamie swallowed thickly. "But I'm fine. Don't you worry about me, horse."

"Someone has to."

The undisguised affection in Nick's voice conjured up a wave of loneliness in Bill. Everyone had been shocked when Nick agreed to temporarily bond with Jamie, and even more so when they made it permanent. But theirs had been a love match, astonishing as it seemed.

Maybe things with Sionn would work out. They were to have dinner again tonight. Bill honestly liked Sionn.

But Sionn didn't send his heart to racing the way Isaac did.

"Come on, then," he said, a bit roughly. He turned his back on Nick and Jamie and started toward the viewing room and the hall beyond. It took a few moments to realize they weren't close behind him.

Saint Mary curse him, he'd forgotten about Jamie's leg. Jamie limped along at his own pace, and Nick ambled beside him, seeming in no hurry at all.

"Sorry," Bill said, feeling the heat rise to his face. "I forgot."

"I'm usually faster," Jamie said with a shrug, "but I overdid things a bit yesterday. We went picnicking at Coney Island to escape the heat, and sand ain't the easiest thing to walk on with a wooden leg."

They continued at a more sedate pace, passing through the viewing room where unidentified bodies were displayed in the hopes a friend or family member would recognize them. The autopsy room was set deep in the building, and a gust of cool air came out when Bill opened the door. Hexes kept the air chilled—and the stench down—and hexlights illuminated the bodies in clear, steady light.

The coroner glanced up from his gruesome work. "The victim drowned," he said without preamble, "but there was foul play involved."

Somehow, Bill wasn't surprised to hear it. "What happened?"

"He received a blow to the back of the head. It wasn't enough to kill him, but he would likely have been either unconscious or nearly so when he went into the water."

"The fangs?" Nick asked. "Were they real, or put in by dental work?"

The possibility hadn't even occurred to Bill. The coroner glanced at Nick. "You aren't a doctor?"

Nick's nostrils flared. Jamie put a hand to his arm, and they exchanged a look. "No," Nick said, surprisingly subdued. "But I know my anatomy, and I've been around familiars all my life. I've never known a one to keep their teeth or claws when they turned human. Or any human characteristics when they turned animal. Unless you count our eyes changing color, when we first shift. Though mine were always this dark, so it's not necessarily noticeable even then."

"They aren't dental work." The coroner opened the body's mouth, and Nick stepped close to take a look. Bill stayed well back, along with Jamie. "Not only are they growing from the gums, but I believe they're connected to venom sacks. I'll need to do a more thorough dissection to be certain."

"What about the rest of him?" Nick cocked his head. "Are his internal organs completely human, or…?"

The coroner paled. Once again, Nick had considered something the rest of them hadn't. "I looked at the lungs first, to determine cause of death, but I haven't explored further."

Nick folded his arms. "Then let's get to it."

Jamie nodded to the pile of clothing laid out on the nearby table. "Bill, it might be best if we look through his clothes, just in case there's some clue, while they worry about the blood and guts end of things."

"Aye," Bill said, grateful for something to focus on other than what was happening on the table. The clothing was still damp after immersion in the river. One shoe was missing, along with the sock, though both garters were there. Probably tugged off by the currents once the shoe was lost, but Bill made a note of it anyway.

He and Jamie went through the small pile, checking pockets as they went. Bill's fingers encountered something in an inner suit coat pocket, and he pulled it out carefully. It proved to be a square of newsprint, folded into quarters and utterly waterlogged.

"That ain't going to be easy to unfold without tearing," Jamie said with a grimace. "Might be best to let it dry a bit."

"Dear heavens!" the coroner exclaimed from behind them.

Bill set the paper aside and turned to the table. "What is it?"

"His heart only has three chambers," Nick said. "Like a snake's."

"It…it is a condition known in humans," the coroner said uncertainly. "But those so afflicted usually die quite young."

"So what does any of this mean?" Jamie asked.

Bill didn't like the picture starting to form in his head. "There was no mention of fangs in the rogues gallery. It's possible someone forgot to write them down, but it seems to me something like that would stand out more than a tattoo or birthmark."

"To say the least," Nick said.

Bill met the familiar's black eyes. "He was an ordinary rat snake familiar who suddenly has fangs and venom. His heart isn't some sort of defect he's been living with his whole life. This—all of this—was something done to him."

Nick's nostrils flared. "Rook said this case has something to do with missing familiar children?"

"Potential familiars, yes." Bill felt suddenly sick. "Saint Mary, Holy Familiar of Christ. You don't think whoever has them is doing this, whatever this is, to them too?"

Nick and Jamie exchanged a look. "I think you'd better do whatever it takes to find those children, copper," Nick said. "I'll put the word out among the ferals. Maybe I can find out who the dead man's friends were, or where he lived."

"Anything will help," Bill said fervently. "Thank you."

Nick only nodded shortly and turned to go. Jamie stayed long enough to shake Bill's hand. "Good luck, Bill. Saint Mary look over us all."

Isaac stared at the commendation hanging on the wall of the office.

He'd been trying to concentrate on his paperwork, while he waited for Bill to return from the morgue, but Sionn tapping his pencil against the edge of his desk made it nearly impossible. He'd looked up to chastise Sionn, but found his attention caught by the medal hanging on the wall next to him. A commendation for service, and Isaac was certain it was his. He remembered being proud of it.

He just had no idea what it was for.

Service. Maybe he'd tracked down a criminal as a mastiff? Followed the trail of a missing child? Detected some other danger in dog form?

The memory was simply…gone.

The tapping of Sionn's pencil intensified. "Could you stop?" Isaac snapped.

"Sorry." Sionn sat back. His expression grew pensive, and he glanced down, then back up at Isaac. "I'm having an attack of nerves."

Chances were, this was nothing he wanted to hear. But he still asked, "Nervous? Why?"

Sionn let out a long breath. "I'm going to ask Bill Quigley to bond with me."

Isaac felt as though the Coven floor had collapsed beneath him, dropping him into an abyss with no stable footing left.

"He seems a good man," Sionn went on. "I could wait for my witch to show up, but why take the gamble when there's a decent man right here in front of me? Not to mention my time's running out. I need to bond or leave the MWP. With Bill, I get to stay. Our hexes won't be much to speak of, but so what? Magic ain't everything."

A hand seemed to grip Isaac's throat, cutting off his breath. This shouldn't have taken him by surprise. Sionn was right—Bill was a good man. Any familiar would be lucky to have him.

But Isaac wanted him.

Longing rose in him, pressing against the bands around his throat and chest. Bill could have his pick of men, of familiars. He deserved someone like Sionn, who would be a help to him, not a burden. Whose magic wasn't hopelessly tainted.

Telling himself that didn't help. Just as telling himself to let go of his infatuation for Bill hadn't helped.

"Good for you," he said, and tried to keep the bitterness from his voice. Judging by Sionn's frown, he hadn't succeeded.

"You ain't angry, are you?" Sionn asked uncertainly. "You said you were fine with—"

"I *am*," Isaac snapped. "Bill can do what he wants, and so can you."

A tap on the door interrupted them. "Sionn, we need a winged familiar to take some letters to City Hall," said the young witch who'd recently been working as Ferguson's secretary.

"But I'm an owl," Sionn protested.

"Yet here you are awake in the middle of the day."

"Not by choice," Sionn muttered. "All right, all right. This had best not take too long, though. I've got something important to do later."

Sionn left. No sooner had Isaac turned his attention back to his desk, than there was another knock. Malachi stuck his red head inside. "There you are," he said. "Bill's back, and he's waiting downstairs in the lab."

Isaac rose to his feet. "In the lab? Why?"

Mal shook his head. "Better to tell you once we get there." He glanced down the hall. "Away from any chance of prying ears."

When they reached the laboratory, Isaac found Dominic and Rook there as well as Bill. Dominic sat by Owen at one of the desks, both wearing slight frowns.

"What did you find?" Isaac asked. He stopped near the door, closest to Bill. Mal perched on one of the desks beside Rook.

"Few answers, and too many questions," Bill replied wryly. They all listened intently as he explained what the autopsy had revealed—and what he and Nick surmised.

"He used to be a rat snake," Bill finished, "but now he's got the fangs of something more venomous, and his insides are wrong. There has to be magic involved."

"There's no hex that could do that," Owen said.

Dominic looked less certain. "We would have said the same about the blood hexes. Or the hexes of bone that gave the Wraith his power. Let alone the one that would have turned the reservoir in Central Park to poison."

Bill's mouth thinned. "If it is hexes…the jurisdiction is clear. This is an MWP matter. I should report back to Captain Donohue and let you lot investigate."

Unless Bill agreed to bond with Sionn. Not that Bill knew what Sionn intended.

He would soon enough, though. Then he and Sionn would bond. Sionn would have to be brought into their inner circle, the only ones who knew what had truly been going on over the last few years. Isaac would see them together anytime they had a meeting such as this, smiling affectionately at one another while he remained alone.

Owen paced across the room, then back, deep in thought. "Don't go to your captain just yet, Quigley. Dominic, do you really think this could be another old hex, similar to those we've seen before?"

"I don't see why not."

"Then Senator Pemberton might be involved, as he was before."

The thought chilled Isaac to the bone. If Owen was right and Pemberton was involved, they were likely crossing some very powerful men. Ones who would do anything, kill anyone, to have their way.

"Saint Mary, I hope not," Bill said. "But it's possible."

Owen stopped his pacing. "Then we must tread very cautiously. Pemberton's lackeys already tried to take over the MWP once. Likely they have spies among our ranks." Owen clasped his hands behind him. "I doubt the Police Board would let Ferguson assign the case to Dominic and Rook, given their link with Nick. Tom and Cicero already have work. I'm not inclined to trust anyone else with the full story, given we have no way of knowing who might be reporting back to Pemberton."

"So what are you saying?" Bill asked.

"I'm saying we keep things as they are currently." Owen gave Bill a pointed look.

Bill paled. "The only way to do that would be to lie on my reports to my captain."

Owen made no reply. Isaac fixed his gaze on Bill's face, and the struggle written there. Bill was a good man, and lying didn't come naturally to him.

Bonding with Sionn would solve the problem; Ferguson might not tell the Police Board he had his new detectives working the case, just as he hadn't when Nick had briefly joined the MWP. Isaac knew he should say something, even though it would spoil Sionn's moment. But he couldn't bring himself to do so.

Bill's shoulders straightened. "There are kids out there, having God alone knows what done to them at this very minute. I'd lie to the Pope's face if it would help get them back."

The children. What would a hex like this do to someone who hadn't yet taken on their familiar form? Or to someone destined to be an ordinary human, for that matter?

"I'll help too," Isaac said. Starting tomorrow, Bill would have Sionn's aid on a permanent basis. Even though it would hurt to see them together, Isaac couldn't keep away from the investigation, not with children in danger.

A faint smile lightened Bill's expression. "Thank you."

"So what do we think happened?" Rook asked. "We're assuming Alfonso killed Brigid, and someone then killed him to cover it up? If so, how does it relate to the missing children? Are they having this hex cast on them, or something else?"

Mal cocked his head. "What if Alfonso took this hex to change himself from one type of snake to a more dangerous one, because he wanted to get into the assassination business? He was hired to murder Sister Brigid, then killed to keep him quiet, but the hex is unconnected with the missing kids."

"Which just means something else bad is happening to them," Bill said. "Nick's trying to find anyone among the ferals who knew Alfonso, but in the meantime, maybe this will help."

He pulled a folded scrap of paper from his pocket. "This was found in his clothes. I haven't tried to open it yet—I was too worried about tearing it."

"Let me see." Owen held out his hand, and Bill passed it over. Owen put it on the desk, then took out a pair of fine-tipped forceps and began to tease the folds apart. The rest of them crowded around.

"You're blocking the light," Owen said in annoyance. "It looks to be a scrap torn from a newspaper. These are advertisements for rooms to let."

"Alfonso was looking for somewhere to stay?" Rook peered over Owen's shoulder. "I don't think any of these are feral colonies, but Nick would likely know for sure."

Owen took a small hexlight from a drawer. "Illuminate," he murmured, and cold white light poured from the crystal set into the silver base. He lowered it to the table, so the light hit the paper from the side. "Look. There are faint impressions in the paper. The ink must have washed off in the river, but one of them was circled."

Rook read the ad aloud. "Beekman Place—clean, well-ventilated rooms. Low rents. See Mrs. Zabaldo."

"I'll go straight away," Bill said. "Isaac? Do you want to come with me?"

This was probably Isaac's last chance to work with the man he'd fallen in love with. Isaac's throat tightened, and he nodded. "Of course. Anything you wish."

Chapter 9

Something troubled Isaac; that was plain to see. Bill waited for the other man to speak up, but they settled onto the Third Avenue El without exchanging a word on the whole walk.

The heat had grown more and more oppressive as the day went on. The muggy air dampened clothes, kept sweat from drying, and put more of a curl into Isaac's hair than usual. The atmosphere felt close and ominous; surely a storm was building. Bill hoped so; any break in the heat would come as a relief.

"Is something bothering you?" he asked at last.

Isaac stared doggedly out the train window. "Why would anything be bothering me?" Before Bill could answer, he said, "You'll miss dinner. I hope you left Sionn a note."

The change in subject caught Bill off guard. "I did."

"Good. Good." Isaac sighed deeply. "The two of you seem to be getting along well."

"He seems nice," Bill agreed cautiously. "Good company. Why?"

Isaac shrugged. "No reason."

Well that was a lie, and no mistaking it. Maybe Bill had misjudged Sionn in some fashion, and Isaac was trying to warn him. "Is there something I ought to know? Some reason I shouldn't be going to dinner with him?"

"No!" Isaac said, far more vehemently than the simple question called for. "That is—Sionn is a fine familiar."

"You don't say that like you mean it."

"The station at 52nd is coming up," Isaac said quickly. "We need to disembark."

Bill wavered between confusion and annoyance as they descended to the street and turned their steps back toward 51st. If there was some quarrel between Isaac and Sionn, he ought to just tell Bill outright. Bill would cut things off with Sionn right away.

The thought took him aback. So much for putting Isaac behind him, if he was willing to break off the prospect of a relationship with Sionn at a word from Isaac.

Which wasn't at all fair to Sionn. The realization made Bill hot with shame. Sionn deserved to have someone who wanted to be with him for his own merits. Not as a way of getting over another man.

Bill would apologize to Sionn tomorrow. Hopefully they could stay friends, so long as Sionn understood it couldn't be anything more.

As for Isaac, was he simply in a bad mood? Did he have a quarrel with Sionn? Or could he be feeling the effects of staying in human form for too long?

He'd not been able to take on mastiff shape at the orphanage. Which didn't mean he wasn't doing so in the safety of the barracks, but what if he wasn't? Could it be affecting his mind, his mood?

Bill wasn't sure how to ask. It was the sort of question Isaac was likely to take offense at. Even if it wasn't, he might not be comfortable with Bill asking something so personal.

By the time they reached the boarding house near the waterfront, lightning danced on the horizon, and a line of dark clouds bloomed to the west. Beekman Place had been well-off thirty years ago. But in the intervening time, the slums had swept north, and most of the current inhabitants worked the coal yards along the East River. Anyone with enough money to get out had done so.

An older woman in matronly garb answered their knock. "No rooms," she said in a heavy Italian accent.

Bill opened his coat to show his badge. "We're here to ask a few questions about an ad you put in the paper."

Fear flickered over her face. "Good house. No trouble."

"You're not being accused of anything," Isaac said, and offered her a smile. "Are you Mrs. Zabaldo?"

"Sì," she answered warily.

"I'm Isaac, and this is Detective Bill Quigley."

Bill gave her a nod and a smile of his own. "Did you run this ad?" he asked, holding out the scrap of paper, much worse the wear for its dip in the river.

She examined it carefully, then nodded. "Sì. Last week. A man answered it. Is he in trouble?"

"Not as such," Bill said. "Alfonso? Dark hair, gold-brown eyes?"

Mrs. Zabaldo nodded warily. "Sì."

"Did you ever notice anything…strange about Mr. Alfonso's appearance?" Isaac asked.

She shook her head. "No, no. But he does not speak, you understand?" She gestured to her mouth. "Only write."

Probably to conceal the fangs. Or the bulge of the venom sacs might have kept him from being able to talk.

"I'm sorry to tell you he's no longer among the living." Bill pitched his voice as calmly as he could, but she still blanched at his words. "We were hoping to see his rooms."

She whispered something that might have been a prayer. "Come with me."

"Did he have any family that you know of?" Isaac asked as she led the way up the stairs. The house was shabby, but better kept than some of the places Bill had laid his head. The once-fine domicile had been broken up into a series of smaller rooms, but traces of its former grandeur remained in the worn bannister and large entryway.

"No." Mrs. Zabaldo stopped at the uppermost floor and took out her keys. "But he did not speak, as I said." She unlocked the door and stepped back. "I go?"

Bill nodded. "Thank you. Grazie."

She bustled away. Bill opened the door and led the way inside.

The tiny room was roasting from the trapped heat. Alfonso had left the lone window closed. Bill crossed the room and shoved it open. A noticeably cooler breeze blew in; the storm was on its way.

Isaac stood in the center of the room, gaze roving over its contents. There wasn't a great deal to see. The narrow bed was jammed against the sloping roof that formed one wall. A desk stood under the window, along with a rickety chair. An open trunk spilled clothes out at the foot of a washstand and basin. There didn't seem to be much in the way of personal artifacts: no books, no photographs, none of the knickknacks people inevitably accumulated.

A newspaper lay on the desk. *"The Daily Owl,"* Bill read. "Woman Lassoes Bear. Three Dead in Boiler Explosion. Palace of King Minos Uncovered in Crete."

"I met a reporter who works at that paper," Isaac said absently. He'd pulled back the blankets on the bed and lifted the mattress. "He probably wrote the article about the bear lassoing. Anything else in the desk? Any letters?"

Bill pulled open the only drawer. A pencil stub lay inside, along with a knife and small collection of clipped bits of paper. "Here now, what's this?" he murmured.

Isaac joined him at the desk. The rapidly freshening breeze stirred his long hair as he bent to look at what Bill held. "It looks like they were cut from the personals."

PATIENT, A WOMAN OF GOOD HABIT IS WANTED. BCO 50-4. -DR G

PATIENT, GENESIS 3:1. WINDOW 1. MARY STANDS UPON IT. -DR G

PATIENT, NO LETTERS. -DR G

PATIENT, THE TIME IS NOW. -DR G

"It's some kind of code," Bill said.

Isaac leaned close enough for Bill to smell the faint musk of his skin. He didn't wear cologne, so far as Bill could tell, and the scent of him made the blood rush to Bill's groin. "It's instructions to Alfonso. Sister Brigid—a nun—is the woman of good habit. BCO 50-4 is the Belfastian Catholic Orphanage at 50th Street and Fourth Avenue." Isaac paused. "Genesis 3:1 refers to the serpent in the Garden of Eden—instructions for the snake familiar to go in through the garden. The first window belonged to Sister Brigid, and the statue of Mary Magdalene hid the money. No letters is an order to destroy any incriminating writings Sister Brigid may have kept."

Bill shook his head in admiration. Maybe he'd been worried for nothing; Isaac's mind was clearly sharper than his own. "You're brilliant, to figure that out."

Isaac's cheeks flushed slightly. "Not really. The last one is self-explanatory. Let's take a look in the paper—perhaps something's there he didn't have time to cut out."

Bill opened the intact paper and turned to the personal column. "Here," he said, then read. "PATIENT, RETURN FOR TREATMENT.

-DR G.”

"Probably a signal to return to a prearranged meeting place." Isaac frowned. "What do you think all this 'patient' and 'Dr. G' business means? They're code names, clearly, but I'd bet there's some deeper reason behind them."

"I don't know, but if we find out who placed the ads, we find out who this Dr. G is who ordered Sister Brigid's murder. I'd bet Dr. G has the kids, too, or at least knows where to find them." Bill carefully gathered the clippings and tucked them into an envelope, which he then placed in an inner pocket of his coat along with the whole paper. "Do you think your reporter friend would help?"

"He isn't my friend," Isaac said. He hesitated, then his shoulders slumped fractionally. "But I might have something to offer him in exchange for his help."

Isaac's obvious reluctance worried Bill. "What?"

"It doesn't matter now." There came a distant boom of thunder, and Isaac reached past Bill to shut the window. A moment later, rain pelted against the glass. "If we hurry, we might catch him before he leaves for the day."

There came the soft scuff of a shoe from the hall outside.

Bill and Isaac exchanged a glance—then Bill strode to the door and flung it open, just in time to see a figure hastening down the stairs.

"You there—stop!" he called.

An innocent boarder would have paused, or at least looked back in response to Bill's shout. Instead, the figure broke into a run.

Bill raced after him, down the stairs, with Isaac on his heels. As they rounded the final landing, their quarry came to an abrupt halt. Bill caught the flash of light on a gun barrel as the man turned toward them.

"Look out!" Bill flung out an arm to keep Isaac from rushing past him. He got a clear look at the fugitive's face—a light-skinned man with a hat pulled down low enough to conceal his hair. Recognition shocked through him. He'd seen the fellow before, hauled into the precinct by one of the other coppers not long ago.

The pistol cracked, and the bullet lodged in the wall above them, sending a puff of plaster dust into the air. The man swore, yanked open the front door, and rushed out into the storm.

Bill plunged out the door in pursuit, leaving Isaac no choice but to follow.

Isaac hadn't noticed the man in the hallway until he stepped wrong.

Hadn't realized someone was sneaking up behind their backs. Like a fool, he'd let his guard down because he felt safe in Bill's presence.

The storm exploded around Isaac the moment he hit the sidewalk. Rain poured down in sheets, soaking through his outer layer of clothes. Clouds blocked the light, transforming the day to near-darkness, lit only by incessant flashes of lightning. The wind screamed between buildings, wrenching off Bill's hat and sending it scudding away. Puddles splashed around Isaac's feet, flooding his shoes before they'd gone half a block.

"Stop!" Bill shouted. "Police!"

If the fugitive even heard him over the storm, he didn't slow. Rather, he put on another burst of speed, darting onto a cross street that led down toward the waterfront. Rain gushed from downspouts, loosening the filth of the roadway and turning it into a slippery morass. Most of the pushcart vendors had cleared away at the first sign of stormy weather, but a few had tried to wrestle their carts underneath awnings, blocking the sidewalk and forcing the chase into the thoroughfare.

A cart barreled past, the driver urging the horse to greater speed, no doubt hoping to get out of the weather. The fugitive dashed just in front of the horse's enormous hooves. Bill jumped back, barely avoiding getting run over, and a wave of water cast up by the wheels struck him and Isaac both. Bill swore and dodged around the back of the wagon, getting another soaking. Isaac chased after him.

The fugitive made for the waterfront. If they could just keep up, he'd find himself trapped between them and the currents of the East River.

Isaac's foot slipped on something slick. He went down, skinning one palm as he caught himself on the ground. He scrambled back up, but the few seconds had cost him. Bill and the fugitive both had longer legs, and were already pulling away. He had no hope of catching up.

Unless he took mastiff form.

He shoved the thought aside. The magic inside of him didn't help; it only corrupted. Even if it didn't, it had been too long since he'd changed. It would be too late by the time the shock had passed.

Gritting his teeth, he continued on two legs, running as fast as he could. His heart slammed into his ribs, his lungs ached, and a stitch burned in his side, but he forced himself onward.

There—he spotted them even through the rain and darkness. The street ended at the East River. Lightning forked over the water, revealing a steam launch bobbing just off shore. Their fugitive hadn't been running into a dead end—he'd been making for escape the whole time.

The man slowed slightly as he approached the water's edge. Bill took advantage, catching him in a flying tackle. They both went down, struggling against one another, and Isaac couldn't tell what had become of the gun.

But he did see the second man step out behind Bill. Lightning flashed again, revealing the blade of a knife poised to strike.

He was going to murder Bill, stab him in the back, right there in front of Isaac.

No.

Protective fury exploded in Isaac's veins, so strong the instinct swamped every other thought. Distantly, he heard himself snarling like an animal, barely aware the sound was coming from his own throat. Without hesitation, he flung himself bodily on the man with the knife.

They went down in a heap. Isaac grappled with the man's wrist, holding the blade away from his own flesh, growling the entire time.

Bill shouted. Then he was there, wrestling alongside Isaac to wrench the knife back. Over his shoulder, Isaac glimpsed the first man leaping into the water. Bill had abandoned the fight in favor of helping Isaac.

The man with the knife kicked Bill hard in the ankle. It must have loosened his grip, because the man tore free and sprinted for the end of the street. Without pausing, he leapt into the water and began to swim for the launch. The first fugitive was already aboard.

"Isaac!" Bill exclaimed. "Saint Mary, are you all right? Did he hurt you?"

Isaac blinked, his hands shaking as reaction set in. His throat was sore, and his very bones ached with the need to shift.

Bill pulled him to his feet. "Did he stab you?" Bill's hands, warm through Isaac's sodden clothing, gripped his shoulders. Then his eyes widened, realizing he'd touched Isaac without asking. He started to let go and step back.

It was all too much. Isaac was sick of grief, sick of loneliness and need. It was wrong, Bill was meant for Sionn, but at the moment Isaac didn't care. He grabbed Bill's hands, his arms, feeling the taut muscles beneath the waterlogged coat and shirt.

"Don't," he said, gripping tight. "Please don't let go."

They stared at one another. Bill's hazel eyes looked black in the dim light. He trembled beneath Isaac's fingers, and surely it was just from the cold rain. His lips parted, and Isaac's name on them sounded like a question or a prayer.

"Yes," Isaac whispered, and kissed him.

Chapter 10

THIS COULDN'T BE real. Bill had been stabbed, or shot, and this was just the last delusion of a dying brain. It couldn't possibly be happening.

But it was. Cold rain ran under his collar, his wet shoes chafed his feet, and Isaac was actually kissing him.

He'd dreamed about this a hundred times over the last few years, but none of his imaginings approached the reality. Isaac's lips were hungry, desperate, his fingers clutching Bill's forearms tight enough to bruise. He tasted of warmth and need, and Bill kissed him back, hoping against hope he was doing the right thing with his mouth, his tongue.

Their lips parted. Isaac pulled back, just a little. His grip loosened, but rather than draw away, he slid his arms all the way around Bill's waist.

A wave of something too keen to be described as relief swept over Bill, months and years of waiting suddenly at an end. He wound his arms around Isaac's slender body, felt his heat through their wet clothing. They pressed together from mouth to knee, and Bill's skin ached for more. His prick swelled in reaction, and he felt an answering hardness in Isaac's trousers.

Lightning cracked the sky, the titanic bolt nearly overhead, its simultaneous roar of thunder deafening. They both jumped in reaction.

"We should get under cover," Isaac said, his breath rough with desire. "Before we get struck by lightning like a pair of fools who don't know to get out of the rain."

Saint Mary, to think *he* was the one to make Isaac's voice tremble with need. "My apartment is only a few blocks from here," he said, then realized how it must sound.

But Isaac nodded. "All right."

Bill would have thought the walk through the cold rain would calm his racing pulse, but the closer they drew to home, the faster his heart seemed to beat. They hurried through puddles and across flooded intersections, and every brush of their arms together sent a jolt of heat through him. He led the way into the tenement where he lived, then up to his apartment. "No roommates," he said, just so Isaac knew.

He unlocked the door and gestured for Isaac to go inside first. Isaac did so, then stood with his arms wrapped around himself, surveying the room. The apartment consisted of a living and cooking area, and a bedroom, both tiny but Bill's alone. He wished he'd bothered to pick up a bit: clothes scattered across the bed, newspapers covered much of the table, and cobwebs clung to the corners near the ceiling.

Bill shut the door and took a hesitant step forward. Now that they were here, he wasn't quite sure what to do. What Isaac wanted him to do.

"May I kiss you?" he asked.

Isaac's throat worked as he swallowed. "I…I don't think that's a good idea."

Bill's heart plunged. He'd thought everything he wanted was in his grasp, but here was Isaac, pushing him away again. "Did I do something wrong?"

"No!" Isaac cast him a startled look. "No. Never. But…there's Sionn to consider."

"Sionn?" Bill said.

Isaac turned to face him. "I probably should let him tell you himself, but Sionn wants to bond with you. He's a good man. A good match for you." He took a deep breath. "Yet I can't stand the thought of you together."

Bill didn't know which part left him the most flabbergasted. "Why would Sionn want to bond with me?" he settled on. "I've barely any potential."

Isaac looked away. "Magic isn't everything," he said softly. "I know you've…been intimate."

"Who's been spreading rumors?" Bill asked. "Cicero? Tom swore he wasn't, but—"

"I live in the barracks," Isaac said, holding up a hand. "I know Sionn's been coming in late."

"That doesn't mean I've slept with the man." Bill carefully laid a hand on Isaac's arm, and was glad when he didn't pull away. "I ain't been with Sionn like that. I ain't been with anyone, not in the way you mean, at least."

Isaac's lips parted in shock. "I…oh."

"I like Sionn," Bill pressed on. "But I don't feel about him the way I feel about you. Only, I can't figure out how you feel about me. Some days it seems as though there might be something between us. Others you're as remote as the moon. Out of my reach." He swallowed, mouth suddenly dry. "Now you say you can't stand the thought of me with someone else. Can't you just…just tell me what it is you want from me?"

Desire darkened Isaac's brown irises, and a flush tinged his cheeks. Then he closed his eyes and took a deep breath, as though steadying himself. "I'm not what you want. I can't *be* what you want."

The raw pain in his voice caught Bill off guard. "What is it you think I want?"

"Someone who doesn't flinch when he's touched unexpectedly. Someone who can sleep at night. There are times when I can't think for the memories bleeding into the present."

"Is that why you don't take mastiff form anymore?" Bill asked, as gently as he could. "To forget?"

Isaac's eyes widened. Then he looked away. "It isn't the only reason."

Bill ached for him. "Is there anything I can do to help?"

Isaac glanced back, then let out a little laugh. "Of course that's the first thing you ask. But don't you see? You need someone who can be your equal. Not…not a burden, who has to be coddled."

"You ain't a burden," Bill said. "And it hurts my heart, to know you think so little of yourself." He ran his fingers along Isaac's jaw. "It's up to me to decide what I need, not for you to tell me."

Isaac trembled beneath his fingertips. Bill longed to slide his hand back through Isaac's hair, to pull him close. But what happened next was up to Isaac.

"You know what sort of work I did at the Rooster," Isaac said. As if he thought making his way in the world as best he could would change Bill's mind.

He was in for a surprise if he did. "Aye. My own sainted mother did a bit of honest whoring now and then, when she couldn't make the rent. Maybe it makes me a bad copper, but ain't nothing wrong with it so long as no one gets hurt."

A helpless little laugh escaped Isaac. "Why do you have to be so perfect?"

"I surely ain't that." Bill hesitated, but if ever there was a time to be honest, it was now. "I've been in love with you almost as long as I've known you. But my heart can't take any more of this uncertainty." He forced himself to let his hand fall, to take a step back. "I'm yours if you want me. But you have to decide, one way or the other."

For a long moment, they stared at one another in silence. Bill's pulse thudded in his ears, and his stomach twisted into a knot. Isaac was going to say no. He was going to turn away, and that would be the end of it, and—

Isaac stepped forward, grasped Bill's face between his hands, and kissed him.

"Yes," Isaac whispered, then kissed him again. "Yes, I want you, if you'll have me."

Bill buried his fingers in Isaac's hair. Isaac tipped back his head, exposing his throat, so Bill put his lips there. Isaac's skin tasted of salt and rain, and the little moan of pleasure he let out went straight to Bill's cock.

"We're soaked," Isaac murmured, throat working under Bill's hungry mouth. "We should get rid of these wet clothes, don't you think?"

"Aye," Bill managed past the desire thickening his throat. He caught Isaac's hand, drawing him to the bedroom, a grin of sheer delight shaping his mouth.

A return grin transformed Isaac's features, wiping away the lines of care. "Tell me what you want, mi corazón."

"To make you feel good," Bill said honestly. "Can I undress you?"

"Fur and feathers, please do."

His fingers shook on the buttons of Isaac's vest, his bracers, his shirt. Bill took his time, slowly unveiling Isaac's upper body. The silver charm he wore on a necklace, of a hand set with an eye, gleamed against his olive skin.

Isaac's breath quickened, and his skin pebbled under Bill's pale fingers. He was slender and beautiful, and Bill wanted to touch every inch of him.

He restrained himself, gently running his hands down Isaac's arms. "Is there anywhere you don't want me touching? Or anything you don't like?"

"If you don't touch me more, I think I'll go mad," Isaac panted. "I want your hands everywhere, your mouth. Just...I don't care to be restrained. And I'm not comfortable with anyone behind me."

Bill nodded. He let his hands explore, gliding over Isaac's flanks, up his chest, to the darker nubs of his nipples. Isaac gasped and leaned forward when Bill took one between his fingertips. "Harder. Please."

Bill did as requested, then, feeling daring, dipped his head and put his lips to it. Isaac's hand gripped the back of his head, urging him forward.

Bill trailed kisses over skin warm and smooth beneath his lips. From one side of Isaac's chest to the other, then down, across his belly. Isaac gasped when he found a sensitive spot, and his hips jerked forward involuntarily.

Bill paused at the buttons to Isaac's trousers. He could make out the rigid form of Isaac's prick, and the sight made his own even harder. "I ain't never…that is…" Heat collected in his cheeks.

"Never done it French, as Cicero would say?" Isaac asked. "You don't have to."

"No, I want to, if you like it." Bill tore his gaze from Isaac's tented trousers, forcing himself to look up into the other man's eyes. "I just wanted you to know it might take a bit of practice. I'm good with my hands, though."

Isaac's fingers grazed his face. "What have you done?"

"Another fellow and I tossed each other off now and again." No sense making things awkward by bringing up Tom's name at the moment. "That's it. Other than my own hand, of course. And, er, a, uh, 'ladies companion,' as they call them."

He didn't know why he felt nervous at admitting he'd used a dildo on himself, not in front of Isaac at any rate, who had likely seen it all. A startled grin crossed over Isaac's face, and he chuckled, though not unkindly. "Just when I think I know you, I find out there's more to learn," he murmured, his fingers gliding to Bill's lips.

Bill caught a fingertip into his mouth and sucked on it. Isaac's throaty gasp was like a hand to his cock. Bill would be lucky if he didn't come in his drawers, the rate things were going.

Isaac tugged him to his feet, then kissed him swiftly. "If you don't like something, just say so. There's no shame in it, and I won't be disappointed. I promise." He reached for the buttons on Bill's vest. "Now let's get you out of some of this damp clothing before you catch a chill."

Bill felt a flash of disappointment, that he wouldn't be touching Isaac's prick yet—but there would be plenty of time. No need to rush.

Then coherent thought disappeared altogether. Isaac attacked Bill's body like a starving man set before a four course meal. He kissed and bit Bill's throat as he undid the buttons of his collar, ran his hands over every inch of exposed skin, and sucked each nipple until Bill was afraid he would come just from the sensation. When Isaac's fingers plucked at the buttons of his trousers, he took a step back with a groan.

"Best not, unless you want me to spill right now."

"That would be a shame." Isaac's tawny gaze roved over Bill's exposed body, ravenous. "You should take them off yourself, then. Shall I do the same?"

Bill nodded, not trusting himself to speak. He stripped hastily, but Isaac took his time. Popping open one button, then another, exposing the bulge beneath. Sliding his trousers down over narrow hips, then off long legs. The cotton drawers were damp from the rain and clung to the outline of his erect prick. Isaac turned his back on Bill and bent over to remove his socks, the drawers shaping his arse.

"You're beautiful," Bill said, then felt like a fool. He tried to think of something Isaac hadn't likely heard from other men, the ones who had paid for his company, but his mind remained stubbornly blank as a sheet of paper.

The smile Isaac gave him was oddly shy. "I'm glad you think so. I want you to like what you see."

Bill glanced at his own erect cock. "I'd say there's little doubt of that."

Isaac licked his lips. "Indeed." He stripped off his drawers, and stood exposed to Bill's gaze.

Bill went to his knees and reached for Isaac's prick. "Can I taste you?"

"Please."

He took Isaac's prick in his hand, slowly palming its length before leaning in. No foreskin, of course, so a little different than Tom's or his own, but as beautiful as the rest of the man. His tongue darted out in an exploratory lick, touching the moisture gathering in the slit.

Isaac gasped, and his hand tangled in Bill's hair. The taste of bitter salt was on Bill's tongue, and he went back for more, circling the head until finally slipping his lips around it.

His free hand rested on Isaac's thigh, and he felt the muscles trembling beneath his fingers. He took in a bit more, even as he stroked the rest with his hand. Isaac's little moans and twitches goaded him on, and the feel and weight of Isaac's cock in his mouth had his own practically dripping with need.

Isaac's fingers clenched in his hair. "St-stop!"

Bill sat back quickly. Isaac panted, his chest and face flushed. "You're not the only one who's been wanting this for too long."

It seemed impossible. "Have you? Really?"

"Fur and feathers, yes." A sly smile touched Isaac's kiss-reddened lips. "I imagined you, so many nights, while I lay alone in my bunk. I had to be quiet, there in the barracks. Had to bite my lip to keep from shouting your name when I came."

Heat coursed through Bill's entire body. "What did you think about?"

"The feel of your skin." Isaac licked his lips. "How you'd taste in my mouth. Rubbing against you while we lay together in bed, until we came on each other's bellies."

"I want all of that," Bill said. "Do you think you'd like to bugger me?"

Surprise flickered over Isaac's face, there and gone. "Now?"

"Only if you like. *Is* that something you'd want?"

Isaac's long throat worked as he swallowed. "On the bed, on your back. I want to see your face when I fuck you."

Bill scrambled to comply, hastily snatching the clothes off his bed and tossing them to the side. "The oil is in that box on the shelf."

Isaac opened the box, then raised a brow. "Along with your 'companion' I see." He glanced at Bill. "Did you ever think of me, when you used it?"

"Every time."

The mattress dipped under Isaac's weight. Bill hooked his hands behind his knees, pulling his legs up. A moment later, he felt the cool drip of oil over him, followed by Isaac's probing finger.

It was different, having someone else touch him there. Different, but good, and soon he was writhing under Isaac's practiced hands.

"Are you enjoying this?" Isaac murmured. "Do you still want me to bugger you?"

"Aye," Bill panted. "Please, love, I need you."

Isaac took up position between Bill's legs. His lips parted—then he gripped his cock by the base and squeezed his eyes shut. "I'm *not* going to spend too soon," he growled. "When I do come, it's going to be deep inside, with you shouting my name."

Bill felt as though he'd spend with the slightest friction against his aching cock. "Christ, yes."

He kept his gaze fixed on Isaac's face, even as he felt the press of Isaac's prick against him, probing for entrance. A firm push, and then, God, yes, Isaac was in him, going deeper with every thrust. His back arched involuntarily, and a wanton groan escaped him that drew a hungry smile to Isaac's mouth. "You love this, don't you?"

A laugh of sheer joy escaped Bill. "Yes, yes, if you couldn't tell. Do you?"

Isaac swore softly in that language he sometimes spoke, that sounded a bit like Spanish but wasn't. He gave a harder thrust, hips angling in a way that nearly brought Bill off the bed and spangled his vision with stars of pleasure. Bill's cock leaked clear fluid onto his belly, and he was as hard as he'd ever been in his life.

"Touch me," Isaac whispered, and Bill did, running his hands over his lover's arms, across his chest, pinching one nipple. "I can't last much longer."

"Then do it," Bill urged. "Come in me, please."

A shudder went through Isaac—then he bore down hard, hips jerking in a fast rhythm for a few strokes before he stiffened. Bill grabbed his own prick, tugging twice before spunk striped his belly.

The sound of their breathing filled the room, along with the soft drip of rain from the eaves outside. Bill's head spun, and, after so many years of wanting, a part of him still couldn't believe this was real. That it was Isaac's weight on him, Isaac's softening prick in his arse, and not some dream or fantasy he'd wake from. The silver charm swung from Isaac's neck, flashing in the air between them.

Isaac gently slipped free, then bent to kiss Bill. "Mi corazón," he murmured.

"I love you." Bill threaded one hand through Isaac's hair. "Are you all right? Glad we did this?"

"More than I can say." Isaac stretched out beside him. Bill grabbed one of his damp socks from the floor and wiped his stomach, before rolling to face Isaac.

Isaac's hand lay palm-up between them, so Bill took it in his own. The storm outside had rolled past, and golden light drifted through the window, dusting Isaac's skin. The smile on his face sent a surge of uncomplicated joy through Bill.

"I've been in love with you for years," Isaac confessed.

Bill ran his thumb along the back of Isaac's hand. "Why didn't you say anything?"

Isaac glanced down, his long lashes hiding his eyes from Bill's gaze.

"I was afraid you wouldn't want me. I thought...if I told you, and you rejected me, then I'd know for certain you didn't. That I was too ruined."

The words threatened to break Bill's heart. "May I hold you?" When Isaac nodded, he let go of Isaac's hand and slid his arms around him. Isaac cuddled close, resting his head against Bill's shoulder, his own arms twining around Bill's waist.

"You could have said something, you know," Isaac murmured.

"Maybe," Bill allowed. "But at first I figured you needed a friend more than a lover. And after, I suppose I thought you weren't interested."

Isaac ran his hand lightly over Bill's chest. "Worth the wait?"

"Aye." Bill kissed Isaac's hair. "Worth everything."

Chapter 11

Isaac hadn't been at all certain he'd be able to sleep in another man's arms, given he could barely sleep when alone. So he was surprised to open his eyes and realize the light in the room had shifted from that of a long summer afternoon to twilight. Bill's scent enveloped him, comforting, and the feel of his skin brought a new stirring to Isaac's cock.

He'd fantasized about sex between them, but he'd always known reality would be different. It had been, but in a good way. A wonderful way. Bill's straightforward delight, his respect for Isaac's needs, were nothing Isaac had let himself dream of.

Though he probably should have. Bill always had a way of making him feel cared for; of course he'd do the same in the bedroom.

Isaac sat up and peered out the window, into the deepening dark. The electric streetlights gleamed, while the softer glow of gas came from the tenements across the way. The storm had left everything washed clean, and for a moment the city almost seemed new again.

The mattress dipped as Bill shifted. "Isaac?"

Isaac cast a glance over his shoulder and smiled. "You have a nice view."

"Aye. It's one of the best things about this place, to tell the truth." Bill's hand came to rest lightly on his spine. Isaac leaned into the touch, and Bill stroked his back slowly. Not sensually, but just for the feel of skin against skin. "Though I'll admit, even without the view, it's a sight better than most of the places I've lived."

"Were you born in the city?" Isaac knew all of the important things about Bill—his kindness, his loyalty—but none of the details.

"Aye. Not far off the Bowery, in a place even smaller than this one."

Isaac lay down beside him, and they linked fingers. "Any brothers or sisters?"

To his surprise, Bill hesitated. "My mother bore four others, but none of them survived past a few months, if that long," he said at last.

Isaac winced. "I'm sorry. That was a stupid question, given what you said."

"Nay, they weren't…this was before, when my da was still helping with the rent." A shadow crossed over Bill's face.

"I don't mean to pry," Isaac said gently. "I only wanted to learn more about you."

"You might as well hear it." Bill sighed. "When I was little, I thought my da had hung the sun and the moon. I thought him a bigger hero than Cú Chulainn, Fionn mac Cumhail, and all the others combined. Aye, he was gone a lot—long stretches of time—but it was because he had to leave the city to find work, you see. At least, that's what he told us."

It had been clear from the start there was no happy end to this story. Isaac drew their clasped hands to his heart. "I take it he was lying."

"One day, my ma had to run an errand farther north than usual. Up Third Avenue. There she sees him, walking arm and arm with another woman."

"Fur and feathers," Isaac said. "Did she kick him in the balls?"

He'd meant the words lightly, but Bill didn't laugh. "Nay. Maybe if he'd been with another poor Irishwoman, she would have. But he was dressed much finer than she'd ever seen him before, and so was the woman he was with. Not like the Astors or anything, but of better quality than anyone on our block could have dreamed of. She didn't know what to do, so she followed them to a nice house farther up the avenue. Da went in and the door shut."

Bill's mouth tightened. "She waited until he came back. Let him say how glad he was to see us, how much he'd missed us while he was away. Then she told him. It turned out he had a whole other family. Another wife, another son."

Isaac swore. "It wasn't your fault, Bill."

"Maybe not, but what happened next was." He shut his eyes, as if he couldn't bear to look at Isaac. "He wanted me to get tested for witch ability. Ma's people, the Quigleys, were supposed to be witch-blooded, you see. So I did."

Isaac's heart drummed against his chest. "You said…when Nick asked you in October, you said you had some ability, but not much."

"Barely any," Bill agreed. "As it turned out, his son by the other wife had it to spare. So Da left us and stayed with them."

Isaac parsed the words, then parsed them again. "Wait. He chose his other family because your half brother had stronger witch potential than you?"

"Some men want their sons to succeed in business. Some want them to become railroad engineers, or lawyers, or whatever thwarted dream they had for themselves." Bill turned his head away. "I wasn't enough to make him stay. So everything that came after was my fault. Without him paying the rent, Ma had to find other work. I did what I could, and when I joined the police, I thought I could finally support us both. But the pox took her just a few months later."

"It wasn't your fault," Isaac repeated. When Bill didn't look at him, he moved to straddle the other man. Startled, Bill turned his head, and Isaac caught his face between his hands. "Your father was a raging pustule of a man, but you aren't."

Bill gave him a weak smile. "I'm glad to hear you think that. Would you like to find some dinner? I need to hang up our clothes to dry, but you can borrow something of mine, if you want. Or I can go out and bring food back, if you tell me what's all right to get."

It was an obvious attempt to change the subject. Isaac let the matter drop. Bill had never pressed him when he didn't want to talk; he could at least return the favor.

"Maybe later," he said, bending low to kiss Bill. Their bodies slid together, and Bill's prick stirred against his. "For the moment, I'm hungry for something other than food."

The next morning, Bill opened his eyes to the sight of Isaac lying in his bed.

His heart leapt, and his mouth stretched in a smile. The sun hadn't quite risen. Grayish light filtered in through the half-drawn curtains. Isaac had rolled so his back was to Bill, his mussed hair spread over the pillow. Bill started to reach out a hand to stroke the curve of scapula, but caught himself.

"Isaac, love," he said softly.

Isaac stirred and made a small sound of acknowledgment. Bill did touch him now, and Isaac scooted back, until he was pressed against

Bill's chest. His morning stand took on new urgency with warm, firm flesh against him. Bill slid an arm around Isaac's waist and kissed the side of his neck. "Good morning."

Isaac wriggled his arse against Bill's erection. "Good morning to you, too."

Bill groaned. "You're tempting me, love, but we've got work that needs doing."

"I suppose you're right." Isaac shifted to face him, his own cock prodding Bill's stomach. "But I'd rather stay in bed and put this to good use."

"Later?" Bill asked. "You can spend the night again, if you'd like."

They hadn't spoken of where to take things from here. Unbonded MWP familiars lived in the barracks at the Coven, so he wouldn't be able to spend too many nights in a row with Bill, assuming he even wanted to. And if Isaac did eventually choose to bond, there would be his witch to take into account.

The thought made Bill ache. He wasn't so selfish he wanted to keep Isaac all to himself, but the thought of him losing him to another man, one who had more witch potential, stung.

He hadn't been entirely open with Isaac the night before, when they talked about his family. The sad truth was, Bill had gone into police work because he'd heard his brother had been hired by the MWP. It was a stupid motive, competing with a man he'd never met and likely never would. When he left the force for some reason Bill had never learned, for the first time he had felt as though he'd won out. Proved himself better than his brother.

Isaac smiled. "I'd love to, if you'll have me."

"Any time." Bill kissed him softly. "Now we'd best get up, or else we'll be in bed for another hour."

The air blowing through the window was already warm; the thunderstorm of the day before seemed to have offered only a temporary respite to the heat. Bill lent Isaac his shaving kit. Their clothing had dried overnight, and as they dressed, Bill said, "I'll go to the precinct and find out what I can about our friend from last night."

"Good idea." Isaac buttoned his trousers much more efficiently than he'd unbuttoned them the night before. "While you do that, I'll return to the Coven—the reporter, Valentine, seems to be there more days than not. With any luck he can help us find out who's behind the ads."

Fortunately, the slips of paper had survived the downpour last night, tucked as they were inside Bill's coat. He'd taken them out of the envelope and let the last of the dampness evaporate overnight.

Bill nodded. "It ain't the fellow we chased, that's for certain. I don't recall what charge he was brought in on, but he's no criminal mastermind. Certainly he ain't hexing anyone."

Isaac's hands slowed. "The hex Alfonso was under, turning him from one type of snake to another…we've seen what a hex like that does to an adult. But what about a child too young to have shifted?"

"I don't know." Bill shook his head. "What happened to Alfonso was bad enough. But to try it on a bunch of innocent kids…"

Isaac wrapped his arms around himself. Bill had only put on one shoe, but he left the other off and went to Isaac. "Whatever this is, we're going to put an end to it," he said, placing his hands gently on Isaac's shoulders. "I ain't going to stop until the children are safe, and these bastards are behind bars."

Isaac took a deep breath and nodded. "I know." He rested his hand lightly on Bill's chest, over his heart. "Send word when you find anything about the man from last night. I don't want you chasing after him without someone to watch your back."

His eyes darkened, and Bill guessed he was thinking about the close call they'd had. He caught Isaac's hand and raised it to his lips. "I will," he promised.

Isaac's expression eased, and they shared a kiss, before parting reluctantly. Once out on the street, they headed in different directions: Bill to the precinct, and Isaac to the El. Though early, the sidewalks were already crowded with men and women off to their jobs in sweatshops and factories. Pushcart vendors added to the growing traffic, battling for space on the sidewalks. Newsboys shouted the headlines from their corners, and wagons packed with barrels and produce rattled past.

Despite everything, Bill's heart felt lighter than it had in a dog's age. After all this time, he'd finally held Isaac, kissed him, told him he loved him. It barely seemed possible.

Bill hummed to himself as he entered the precinct. Luck was in his corner, and he spotted the officer he wanted immediately. "Liotta!" he called. "I've a question to ask about one of your arrests last month, if you've a moment."

Liotta gave him a guarded look. "Which one?"

Bill described the man he'd chased the night before, and Liotta nodded. "Oh, I remember him, all right. Lucius Young. He's been in and out of trouble most of his life. Did a stint in Sing Sing for beating a man half to death. Swears he's reformed, even has a job at Fulton's Fish

Market. He wasn't looking very reformed when I saw him pounding another man's head into a wall, though. They got into an argument while drinking swipes in a dive bar." Liotta paused, then glanced around, as if checking to make sure they weren't overheard. "So how do you figure a man like that ends up with a fancy lawyer?"

"Fancy lawyer?" Bill asked with a frown.

Liotta nodded. "The lawyer made sure the charges didn't stick. Acted like I was the one who'd done something wrong, arresting his *client*." A snort escaped him. "I figure Young's got someone by the short hairs, probably some rich swell he's blackmailing."

Or Young knew enough that those who hired him didn't want him talking to the coppers. He was lucky not to have ended up in the river alongside Alfonso. "You said he works at the fish market?"

"Yes." Liotta cocked his head. "What's your interest in him?"

There was no sense in not telling part of the truth. "He shot at me yesterday, and one of his friends almost knifed me in the back."

Liotta's eyes widened in outrage. Bill might not be the most popular man in the precinct, but coppers didn't take threats to their own lightly. "The devil! Need any help rounding him up?"

Bill shook his head. "Nay. I appreciate the offer, though."

"Quigley!" Captain Donohue called from his office door.

Liotta melted away, obviously not interested in attracting Donohue's attention. Bill suppressed a sigh and hastened to the captain's office. "Aye, sir?"

"You didn't report in yesterday." Donohue sat back in his chair.

"Nay, sir. I was a bit busy following leads before the trail got too cold."

Donohue eyed him closely. "You've been on this case for a few days now. Long enough to know if there's magic involved or not."

A few years back, Donohue had lent Tom Halloran to the MWP to help solve a series of murders. But that had been before the relationship between the regular and witch police went from semi-friendly rivalry to outright animosity.

Since then, an MWP familiar had masterminded an attack against the city's most powerful citizens. Then Jamie MacDougal helped expose the head of the Dangerous Familiars Squad. O'Malley had been popular amongst the rank and file, and a lot of people felt Jamie had broken the code of silence. Police officers protected one another against the rest of the world, and that was true even if O'Malley had been an accessory to murder and conspiracy. The fact O'Malley had been Jamie's uncle made things even worse; it proved the MWP detectives wouldn't even stand up for their own family, let alone the rest of the force.

Donohue was unhappy enough that one of his men liaised with the MWP. He'd deliberately kept Bill from assisting with the Wraith murders. If Bill told him the truth, that they thought hexes were involved, he'd pull Bill off the case instantly.

There was nothing for it but to do as Owen had suggested. Lie to Donohue's face and keep the coroner's report on Alfonso out of anyone else's hands.

Bill had never considered himself a saint, but he wasn't a liar, either. But as he'd said before, he'd do whatever it took to get the kids back. "Aye, I've been looking into it. It seems like Sister Brigid was killed to cover up some sort of criminal activity. Nothing about hexes so far, though."

Donohue didn't look pleased, but he nodded. "All right, then. Write up a report and have it on my desk in an hour."

Bill might have joined the police force for the wrong reasons, but the work had suited him. Now he'd just put his career on the line. If Donohue found out…

He wouldn't. They'd keep things quiet, and Donohue had no reason to look any closer into Bill's activities. "Aye, sir." He hoped the queasy feeling in his stomach didn't show on his face as he left Donohue's office.

Only to find himself face-to-face with Elwood, the familiar whose boy was among the missing.

"Have you found Teddy?" Elwood demanded. Bags showed under his eyes, and his fingernails were bitten to the quick.

Bill's heart plummeted. "Not yet. But I swear to you, I'm doing everything in my power to find him and the rest of the missing kids."

"The rest?" Horror crossed Elwood's face. "What do you mean? There are others?"

Bill winced. The commotion had attracted the attention of the other officers, which was the last thing he needed. "We're having trouble accounting for some of the orphans," he settled on. "But we're going to find them all. You have my word."

Elwood's eyes narrowed. "Your word. Tell me what you're doing to find them."

Hell. "Let's step into the interrogation room, where we can talk privately," Bill suggested.

"Just answer me. Are you any closer to finding my boy?"

"I'm trying—"

"You're not trying hard enough," Elwood shouted. "Do you have any idea what it's like? Not knowing where he is? Who has him? You don't care, do you?"

"That ain't true," Bill protested.

As Elwood grew more agitated, some of the other officers started to drift over, hands hovering near the nightsticks on their belts. Elwood saw them and took a step back.

"I've already been beaten by your lot for trying to find Teddy." The look he shot Bill burned with suppressed rage. "I should've known then you coppers would be useless. None of you give a damn about familiars."

"I do," Bill protested. But Elwood had already turned and started out the precinct doors.

"You shouldn't let civilians yell at you like that," Liotta said, taking his hand off his nightstick. "It undermines all our authority."

"Aye," Bill said, even though he didn't give a damn. As Liotta and the others drifted away, he sat down at his desk, trying very hard to focus on the lies he needed to put in his report, and not on Elwood's pain and fury.

Saint Mary, they had to find the kids. Had to.

CHAPTER 12

ISAAC SPENT THE ride on the El staring out the window. He'd found a seat in the back, where he didn't have to worry about anyone sitting behind him. Even though he knew his mind should be on the case, he found himself daydreaming about the night with Bill instead. It seemed impossible that just twenty-four hours ago, he'd been convinced Bill couldn't want him. That he'd had have to watch Sionn have the life Isaac longed for.

He could still smell Bill on his skin. The scent was both comforting and arousing, bringing back memories of Bill under him, gasping and eager.

Bill knew his history, knew what his magic had been used for, and still didn't think he was too tainted to love. He thought Isaac was worth spending time with.

Maybe after a while he'd get tired of Isaac, prefer a lover who didn't need such careful handling, but Isaac was determined to enjoy the moment while it lasted. At least, when things came to an end, he'd have the memories to help warm him during the lonely nights.

When he arrived at the steps leading up to the Coven's brass doors, Isaac was relieved to spot Valentine amidst the journalists. Catching the man's eye, he nodded to the side, away from the scrum.

Valentine joined him at the spot he'd indicated with alacrity. "Changed your mind about that interview?"

Isaac's mouth tightened. "In a way. I need your help with something.

In exchange, I'll let you interview me."

It wouldn't be easy, answering Valentine's questions. Reliving the worst time in his life. But there were children depending on him, and if it meant flaying his heart raw for the press, then he'd do it.

Isaac took out the clipped ads and passed them to Valentine. "We think these came from *The Daily Owl*," he said. "I need to know who placed them."

"That's our typeface, all right," Valentine murmured, examining them. "Do you need to know the dates they ran?"

"Whatever information you can get, I'll take."

"All right, then." Valentine carefully recorded the wording of the clippings in his notebook, before handing them back to Isaac. "I'll go back to the *Owl* and see what I can find. I'll send word to you here as soon as I have the information you need."

Isaac watched Valentine hurry off. His shoulders felt tight, and he did his best to shove aside anticipation of the interview to come. One thing at a time.

He restored his mood with thoughts of Bill. They'd spend the night together again, and even though they'd just parted, Isaac couldn't wait. The knowledge buoyed him up the steps, into the Coven, and up the stairs.

"There you are!" Cicero exclaimed, looming up in Isaac's peripheral sight. Isaac flinched, but for once Cicero didn't seem to notice. "Fur and feathers, we thought something terrible had happened to you."

Isaac stared at him blankly. "Why?"

Sionn hurried down the hall to join them. "Because it ain't Friday, and you didn't come back to the barracks last night."

"That predictable, am I?" Isaac asked lightly. But Sionn was right. Isaac's life for the last few years had fallen into a routine. At first, that had been a comfort, but maybe he'd let the habit linger past the time he needed it.

Sionn's freckled face was uncharacteristically somber. "Bill's note said you two were tracking down a lead. When you didn't come back last night, I started to worry. I waited for Cicero this morning, hoping he would know where you were. When he didn't, we thought something must have gone wrong."

Sionn's concerned expression sent a spike of guilt through Isaac. "We did have an encounter," he admitted. "A man with a gun came to the boarding house, likely to destroy evidence. Fortunately, we got there first."

"A gun?" Cicero gasped. He flung his arms around Isaac. "Thank heavens you're not injured."

"What about Bill?" Sionn asked. "Is he all right?"

Cicero took a deep breath. Then another. "Oh. My. God."

Isaac froze. "Cicero," he said warningly.

"What is it?" Sionn asked.

"I'd say William is right as rain," Cicero said. He didn't let go of Isaac, but leaned far enough back to grin at him.

Heat suffused Isaac's face. "Cicero, don't."

Sionn's freckles stood out against his suddenly pale skin. "You spent the night with Bill, didn't you?"

Cicero stepped back, looking abashed. "Oh dear. I probably shouldn't have said that."

Fur and feathers, this wasn't how he'd wanted to broach the subject. "Sionn, I—"

"I *asked* you if there was anything between you, and you said no!" Sionn's coppery brows dove into a glare. "I told you I wanted to bond with him, and you pretended to be supportive, and the whole time you meant to fuck him?"

"Sionn—"

"I was *worried* about you, damn it! Afraid something had happened, and instead you were off with Bill, stealing him out from under me."

"That isn't true!" Isaac exclaimed. "I wasn't trying to mislead you, Sionn, I swear. I didn't think he was interested."

Cicero rolled his eyes. "Really, darling, you'd have to be blind to miss it."

Isaac loved Cicero, but at the moment he was ready to strangle the cat. "Be quiet. You've done enough already."

Sionn folded his arms over his chest. "I suppose you're going to bond now. Or have you already?"

The words came like a blow to Isaac's gut. He opened his mouth, then shut it again. Maybe it was stupid, but he hadn't even thought of bonding last night. He and Bill hadn't been together as a witch and a familiar—they'd been together as two men who cared about each other.

Could he bond with Bill? He wasn't certain. Just the thought of bonding with anyone else made Isaac feel faintly ill. Bill, though…it might be different. The warm place behind his heart would surely feel welcome, not a violation, if it connected him with someone he loved.

But no. Bonding meant taking on mastiff form. It meant he'd never get rid of the memories. True, he wouldn't forget any more of the good things, but he'd be haunted by what happened to him in the tunnels for the rest of his life.

Cicero shot Sionn an angry glare. "Don't ask him something like that."

Isaac dropped his arms again. "I can stand up for myself, Cicero. Sionn, we honestly didn't talk about it. For what it's worth, I'm sorry. I know how this must look."

"It looks like you were playing me for a fool." Sionn snapped his teeth together, like an angry owl clacking its beak. "To hell with you. I'm moving to a different office, no matter who I have to suck to switch with me."

Sionn turned his back on them and stalked away, head held high. Cicero turned his back on Sionn dismissively. "So, tell me all about it. I want details, darling."

"You aren't getting any." Isaac leveled a glare at him. "That wasn't necessary. You don't have to blurt out every thought that crosses your mind. You had to have known how Sionn would react."

Cicero's shoulders slumped. "I *am* sorry. I didn't think."

"Do you ever?"

"Not when I can help it. Leads to wrinkles, don't you know." Cicero bit his lip. "I was just, well, relieved. The last time you went missing…"

The worst had happened.

Isaac wanted to tell Cicero he'd been wrong to fear. He was a grown man; he could surely be gone without explanation for one night, without everyone panicking for his safety.

But when he'd been held captive, Cicero had been the only one looking for him. The only one who refused to give up searching, no matter what.

He sighed and opened his arms. Cicero slipped into them, resting his head on Isaac's shoulder. "It wasn't fair to Sionn, to hear it like that," Isaac said.

"I know."

Isaac hugged him tighter. "I'm sorry about what I said the other day, when you tried to give me advice. It sounded like I blamed you for everything, and I don't. Fur and feathers, you're the one who did everything to save me."

"Of course I did. You're my best friend, and I love you."

"I love you, too."

Cicero grinned. "So…details?"

"No!" Isaac shoved him away, laughing.

"Now that's a sound I've missed." Cicero's wicked grin softened. "I can't remember the last time you laughed."

"Maybe you just aren't that funny."

"I'm wounded, darling." Cicero clutched at his chest melodramatically. "Utterly slain. Now come along. As I've cost you access to your office, at least until Sionn gathers his things, I'll sacrifice part of my desk. I'm sure William will be able to find you there."

"And give you a chance to demand details from him?" Isaac guessed.

"That, too," Cicero said with a wink.

Bill told Isaac what he'd learned about Young as they made their way to Fulton's Fish Market in the late afternoon. The market was held inside a large, shed-like building that backed directly onto the waterfront, in the shadow of the Brooklyn Bridge. Ships jostled for position at the back, loading their catch either directly into the hands of the fishmongers, or into the fish cages in the river. Wagons rumbled past, gulls screamed, and sailors shouted and swore.

The smell of the fish permeated the air a block away, and Bill wrinkled his nose as they approached. "It's quite the reek, eh? I can't see how the fishmongers stand it day after day."

"They're probably used to it." Isaac made a face of his own. "It's just…overwhelming, more than anything."

Bill wondered if the stench would be worse or better if Isaac had taken dog form recently. He hadn't forgotten what Sionn had said, about staying in one shape too long being bad for familiars. He wasn't sure if he should broach the subject with Isaac yet, or if he ought to give it some time and see if Isaac decided to shift on his own.

Isaac nodded in the direction of the river. "Alfonso was found just a little way downstream. Do you think he was killed near here?"

"Might've been," Bill said. "Young is obviously involved in something big. No other reason an expensive lawyer would come to get him out of jail and away from the coppers."

"So we wait and watch?" Isaac asked. "And hope he doesn't spot us first?"

"That's the plan." Bill tugged his hat lower, hoping it concealed his face. Isaac had tucked his long hair up under a cap, and both of them had dressed in shabbier clothing than usual. With any luck, they'd look like dockhands from a distance. "If Young does recognize us, we'll arrest him on the spot. I don't want him getting away a second time."

Inside the market, the reek of fish was so strong it seemed to thicken the very air. Shoppers perused the various tables, workers heaved baskets of fish onto tables, and filleting knives flashed like quicksilver. Blood and scales stuck unpleasantly to the floor. A uniformed copper roamed the building, keeping an eye out for trouble, and Bill felt a flash of sympathy for the fellow. He'd walked some unpleasant beats, but none that smelled quite like this.

"Should we split up?" Isaac asked in a low voice.

Bill shook his head. "Nay. I don't think Young would be so desperate as to try and kill us in the middle of the market...but I've been wrong before, and it ain't worth the risk." He glanced down at Isaac and grinned. "You might have to rush to my rescue again."

Isaac bumped his hip lightly with his own. "I'd do it. Now let's pretend to be deeply interested in fish."

They made their way around the market, stopping from time to time so as not to arouse suspicion. It wasn't long before Isaac nudged him in the ribs. "There he is. To the left, one row back."

Bill chanced lifting his head just high enough to spot Young from under the brim of his hat. Young stood behind a table, wielding his filleting knife expertly. A few feet away, the man who had nearly stabbed Bill gutted fish before tossing them onto the table in front of Young.

"I see him. And his friend."

"What now?"

"We wait and watch. Likely neither of them will be leaving anytime soon, not if they want to keep their jobs. We go outside and find some excuse to loiter until the market closes and the customers are gone. Then we move in closer and keep a sharp eye out for either Young or the other one. When they leave, we follow, and see who they meet up with."

Isaac nodded. They finished their circuit of the market, avoiding Young's table, and left. Bill took deep breaths of the fresher air as soon as they were outside. "We've a few hours to pass before the market closes," Bill said. "A shame there's no convenient saloon across the street."

"Drinking on the job, detective?" Isaac asked, a teasing note in his voice.

"When you're a beat copper, you take the chance to wash the dust from your throat when you can, and hope the roundsman doesn't catch you."

"Did the roundsman ever catch you?" Isaac asked.

"Oh, aye." Bill grinned. "Fortunately, his mistress lived on my beat, and she threatened to complain to his wife if he caused me any trouble."

Isaac laughed. "Did you enjoy it? Walking a beat, I mean."

Bill tipped his head back. The iron skeleton of the Brooklyn Bridge loomed against the sky, and the masts of the ships turned the waterfront into a forest. "Sometimes. When I wasn't getting rained on, or freezing my balls off, or sweating half to death in the uniform."

"I can see that might not be pleasant," Isaac agreed. "So what did you like about it?"

"Getting to know the people on my beat. Feeling like maybe I was making some of their lives easier." Bill shrugged awkwardly. "I met some good men on the force. Friends."

"Tom Halloran."

"Aye. Saint Tom, we used to call him." Bill shook his head. "When I found out he used to be part of a tunnel gang, I could hardly believe it."

"But you came to help him. You didn't abandon him."

"Didn't seem right for him to be judged solely for something he'd done when he wasn't even old enough to be called a man. Something he'd been born into, not chosen for himself." Bill shrugged again. "It seemed to me any judge looking to condemn him ought to know all the years he'd spent doing good as a copper."

Neither of them spoke for a few minutes. Then Isaac said, "A few weeks after I was rescued, Cicero told me you'd stood by Tom, even when no one else had. Even when Cicero himself hadn't. I think…I think that was when I started to fall in love with you."

Bill ducked his head, heat gathering in his face. "Anyone would have done it," he protested.

Isaac looked up at him, brown eyes warm. "No, Bill. They wouldn't have. But you did."

They kept a casual eye on the fish market from across the street. Even though Bill had wanted Isaac almost as long as he'd known the man, now that he knew what it was like to go to bed with him…well, his presence at Bill's elbow was twice as distracting as it had been before.

It seemed forever rather than just a few hours before the market closed for the day. Before long the various workers would be leaving. Including Young and his compatriot.

Likely the men would go to a saloon. If so, Bill and Isaac would have to wait outside, lest either man recognize them. If Young went back to wherever he called home afterward, how long would they spend surveying the place, instead of getting back to their own bed?

A damn shame they couldn't trust the other MWP officers enough to bring someone else in to help. But there had been too much betrayal already on that front to risk it. As for the regular police, given the Dangerous Familiars Squad's activities, Bill had the sinking feeling their chief was in Pemberton's pocket outright.

A crowd of workers exited the market, laughing and talking amongst themselves. In their midst were Young and his friend. But while the other men turned toward the city and away from the waterfront in a group, the two hung back until they were left behind. Walking shoulder-to-shoulder, they continued on along South Street, paralleling the wharf.

Finally.

"Come on," Isaac murmured.

Bill and Isaac followed at as slow a pace as possible, while still keeping the two in sight. The docks never truly slept, and there was still enough activity to prevent Bill and Isaac from standing out, should the men happen to look back. The sun crept down toward the horizon as the heat gripping the city began to ease.

The crowd thinned out as they began to approach one of the sanitation department's dumping wharves. The area along the wharf was largely empty, to allow carts filled with debris to back up to the river's edge. The contents would be dumped onto a waiting barge, then taken away to be used as infill or disposed of in the ocean. By this time of day, though, all of the city workers who drove the carts had gone home, and no barge bobbed in the river alongside.

While Young and his compatriot walked out onto the empty wharf, Isaac darted behind an empty guard shack. Moving as silently as he could, Bill joined him. He pressed his back flat against the weathered boards, then risked a peek around the corner.

The two men had come to a halt at the water's edge. In the relative quiet of the deserted wharf, their voices carried.

"This is your fault," said the one. "If you hadn't gotten caught—"

"How was I to know the coppers had beaten us there?" Young shot back.

"If you hadn't insisted on stopping for a pint on the way to the boat, you might have gotten there before them. Then we wouldn't be in this mess." He glared at Young. "I'd better get my damn money, or I'll take it out of your hide."

Young returned his glare. "I told you, my mate will smooth things over. Just like when that fucking copper arrested me. Now shut up—I think I see them."

Bill exchanged a glance with Isaac. Moving slowly so as to keep any noise to a minimum, he drew his gun.

Isaac leaned close, his breath stirring the hairs around Bill's ear. "Are we going to try and arrest whoever shows up?"

"It depends on how many of them there are," Bill whispered back. "I ain't looking to get killed, but if we can put an end to this tonight…"

Their eyes met in understanding. Stopping whatever was happening, finding the missing kids, was worth more than a little risk.

He and Isaac both leaned around the corner again. A small tugboat swung into position on the wharf, and Young and the other man moved to secure the lines. There were three men visible on the boat: the captain at the wheel and two hands working to bring it in.

The odds weren't good. But if Bill could get the drop on them before they had a chance to draw any weapons, it would help. With any luck, the tug would prove to be hired, and its captain and hands would stand down in a confrontation.

"Where's Granger?" Young called. "He said to meet him here."

Another man stepped out from behind the tug's small stack. He was fair haired and tall, with a square jaw and handsome face. A face that seemed damnably familiar, though for a moment Bill couldn't place it.

Isaac let out a horrified moan and pressed back into Bill. "No. No. Not him. Not Martin."

Recognition snapped into place like a blow to the gut. Bill hadn't seen him in over a decade, but he recognized Da's features in the strong jaw, the shape of his eyes. A younger version of this face had stared at him between the parted curtains, the day Da threw Bill into the street for daring to come to his other house.

Martin Granger. Son of Donald Granger.

Bill's half brother.

"It's him." Isaac's entire body shook against Bill's. "My witch."

CHAPTER 13

ISAAC'S HEART THUNDERED in his chest, and he couldn't look away from the man on the boat. The man his magic yearned for even now, filling Isaac's bones with the certainty they would be uniquely powerful together. That some part of them *matched*.

Unclean. Tainted.

He wanted to throw up. He wanted to run away, tail tucked between his legs.

"Martin?" Bill whispered, sounding stunned. "Your witch?"

Isaac nodded dumbly, too shaken to say anything else.

"Granger!" Young called. "There you are. Listen, I'm sorry about the coppers. But we got away, and no harm done, right?"

Isaac didn't want to see Martin's face, but his eyes seemed drawn to his witch's handsome features. His easy smile. Charm exuded from him, just as it had when they'd first met, four years ago.

Right up until the moment it hadn't.

"Come aboard, Luce," Martin said affably.

"You've got the money?" Young asked. "Because it wasn't our fault the coppers got there ahead of us. We deserve to be paid for our effort."

"Of course you do." Martin's white teeth flashed as he smiled. "Just come aboard and we'll see to it."

Isaac couldn't believe anyone would be stupid enough to get onto a tug with Martin. But Young climbed aboard without hesitation. Martin clapped him on the shoulder, as though greeting a friend.

Young's companion wasn't quite as dazzled. He remained on the dock. "I don't know. Something about this don't feel right."

Isaac bit back a hysterical bark of laughter. The man wasn't wrong: nothing about this was right. His witch—*his witch*—was involved in this horror of missing children and distorted familiars. Bad enough to know the person his magic connected with most strongly was filled with hate and violence, hidden beneath a friendly mask. But this was so much worse.

Young turned back to the man on the wharf. "Come on, Jake. What's gotten into you?"

Jake stepped back, frowning. "Just toss the money to me, and I'll be on my way. No need to drag things out."

Martin slugged Young in the back of the head, the blow so unexpected both Isaac and Jake cried out. Young slumped to the ground, and Martin drew a gun. "Get on the boat, Jake. No reason to make this any more unpleasant than it has to be."

Bill tensed, as though he meant to spring forward. No, he couldn't go out there. Not where Martin—not where Isaac's witch—could hurt him.

Jake's hands shook as he moved cautiously toward the tug, his gaze riveted on the gun. "What do you mean to do with us? Throw us in the river like that snake-guy?"

Martin's smile brought bile to Isaac's throat. "Oh no. It's the labyrinth for you."

Bill surged upright. Before Isaac could stop him, he stepped out from behind the shack, gun leveled at Martin. "Police! Drop your weapon!"

Martin swore and fired. The bullet took Jake in the head, dropping him instantly.

The sound shocked Isaac from his paralysis. He tackled Bill to the ground, just as Martin took aim and fired a second time. This shot struck the side of the shack, sending splinters into the air.

"You," Martin snarled. "I should've known."

The tug's engine roared as it pulled away from the dock. Bill shoved himself to his elbows, but didn't bother to lift his gun as the distance between them rapidly increased.

Martin moved to the stern, staring back at them. Far enough away Isaac's magic settled itself, but that didn't stop the bile from coming up his throat. He staggered to the side of the shack, belly heaving again and again. But he couldn't rid himself of the wrongness settled into his soul.

"Are you all right?" Bill asked softly. He hovered, as if uncertain whether or not to touch Isaac.

Maybe he didn't want to touch Isaac again, now that he'd seen— now that he truly understood—the sort of murdering bastard Isaac's magic craved.

"No," he said miserably, the taste of bile in his mouth. "I don't think I am."

Isaac sat with his back against a nearby building, while Bill instructed the beat copper to call the coroner, then inspected and searched the body. His head pounded and his mouth tasted utterly foul. He could sense Bill casting glances at him while other coppers came and went, but kept his attention fixed on the scene as a whole, rather than meeting Bill's gaze.

Bill hadn't touched him. He must be horrified. Disgusted.

At last the police wagon rolled away, taking the bodies with it. Bill approached cautiously, then crouched next to Isaac. "The river police will be on the lookout for the tug," Bill said. "Assuming no one's bribing them to look the other way."

Isaac's hands twisted together on his knees. "Good."

Silence. He could feel the weight of Bill's gaze on him, but he focused on his fingers. At last, Bill said, "What can I do? Do you need to go back to the barracks?"

Revulsion cramped Isaac's stomach, but there was nothing left to bring up. If he returned to the Coven right now, Martin was all he'd be able to think about. It was where they'd first met. Where Isaac had been swept off his feet by someone who seemed so dashing, so friendly. He'd been unable to believe his good fortune, that such a man could be his witch.

Why couldn't he have forgotten Martin, instead of the commendation, or the day in the park? Because too many memories were tied up with Isaac's human form as well as his dog form? Fur and feathers, he'd been clinging to the hope of erasing the memories, but it hadn't worked fast enough to spare him this. What if it never did? What if he lost everything that had been good about his life as a familiar, and kept only this darkness?

"Do you want Cicero?" Bill asked. "I'll walk you to his and Tom's apartment."

Isaac nodded. "That would be good."

They walked side-by-side to the El. Bill kept shooting him glances, as if worried Isaac wasn't steady on his feet. It made him feel even more unworthy. Useless.

When Cicero opened the door and saw them standing there, his yellow-green eyes widened. "Something's gone wrong, hasn't it?" He ushered them inside. "Thomas!"

"I'm right here, cat." Tom emerged from their bedroom, his face drawn with concern. "What's happened?"

The apartment was small but neat. The neatness was no doubt Tom's influence, as Cicero's discarded clothes, half-read books, and sticks of kohl had always ended up scattered over the space he and Isaac once shared in the barracks. Cicero's touch showed elsewhere, though: thick pillows strewn about, books of poetry, a painting that bordered on scandalous.

Cicero drew Isaac to the divan and sat down with him. "Talk to me," he ordered.

Isaac dragged in a breath. "Martin Granger is working with whoever is using hexes to turn familiars into monsters."

Cicero's accent came from the London gutters where he'd spent his childhood, but he'd been born in Italy and preferred his native language for cursing. Which he did now, at length and presumably with great inventiveness.

"Who?" Tom asked in confusion.

"My witch," Isaac said.

"Oh," Tom said softly. "The one who…"

"Who was thrown out of the MWP after he pushed me down a flight of stairs, and when that didn't work, tried to kill me more directly." The words were simple, but they were a skin of ice above a lake of pain. "The reason I initially left the MWP."

Only to eventually be forced bonded to Noah instead, and stripped to fuel the terrible blood hexes. As though his magic was drawn to corruption.

Cicero took Isaac's hands in his own. "I'm sorry, darling. I suppose it would have been too much to hope he'd been knifed in the kidney by now."

Tom looked to Bill. "Tell us everything that happened."

Bill did, from their trip to the fish market to Jake's murder right in front of them. When he was done, Cicero looked horrified and Tom thoughtful.

"He recognized you," Tom said.

"Yes," Isaac said, at the same time Bill said, "Aye." He'd hung back since they'd arrived, standing near the door seeming uncertain.

Maybe he wasn't certain. He probably wanted to leave, now that he understood about the darkness inside Isaac, only he was too good a man to simply turn his back altogether.

"Thomas, William, will you step out onto the fire escape and let the two of us have a little talk?" Cicero asked. "Familiar to familiar."

"Aye," Tom said. "Come on, Bill. I'll bring the whiskey and glasses." The fire escape was off the bedroom, and Tom quietly shut the door behind them, leaving Cicero and Isaac alone.

Isaac regarded Cicero warily. "What do you want to talk about?"

Cicero's eyes were steady, his expression uncharacteristically sober. "Martin. Even after everything that's happened, he's still your witch, isn't he? You still feel that pull toward him."

Shame heated Isaac's face, and he looked away. "Yes."

"That must be…fur and feathers, I can't imagine."

The sympathy in Cicero's voice made Isaac's eyes sting. He blinked rapidly, refusing to break down. "I hate Martin. He could have said no and walked away. I would've been heartbroken, but so what? He didn't have to…to…" Isaac swallowed thickly. "Now this."

"It's not fair." Cicero pressed his forehead against Isaac's. "And it isn't your fault."

Isaac couldn't bring himself to believe that. Everyone said magic didn't take into account whether a familiar and witch were anything alike in temperament. Certainly he'd seen witches and familiars whose magic was strong, but who loathed one another. The best among them spent as little time together as possible. The worst…

Cicero rubbed his hands gently. "Tell me what I can do."

"Nothing." Isaac sighed. "I have to see this through, even if it means being exposed to him again."

"I'll be right there with you, darling. Every step of the way."

"I know." Isaac breathed in Cicero's scent, held it in his lungs. "Thank you."

"A sorry business all around," Tom said with a shake of his head. He measured out some whiskey and passed it to Bill. "How are you holding up?"

"Fine," Bill lied.

In truth, his head spun. His half brother, the one their father had chosen, the son with the potential…was Isaac's witch.

Worse—he was the witch who'd hurt Isaac bad enough to put him in the hospital. Who'd made Isaac feel so unsafe at the MWP he left and ended up in Noah's hands.

"You're a lot of things, Bill Quigley," Tom said, "but a good liar ain't one of them."

Bill let out a long breath. "No one ever said the name of Isaac's witch in my hearing, so I didn't know. Not until today."

"Didn't know what?"

"Who the bastard was." Bill tossed back his shot. "Oh, nay, wait, that's not right—*I'm* the bastard, you see. My Da had a whole different family, a wife he was married to legally. Martin Granger…he's my half brother, Tom."

Tom's mouth gaped, as though he wanted to make some response, but couldn't think what to say. "I…oh," he managed at last. He drained his own shot, then poured them both a second. "Damn, Bill. That's a kick in the balls for sure. But it don't make any difference to me. You didn't judge me for my family, and I ain't going to judge you for yours."

"Thank you."

"Did you tell Isaac yet?"

Bill shook his head. "I didn't know how. He's going to hate me when he finds out."

"Maybe. But you still have to tell him."

"I know." Things had been going so well between them. Just this morning, Bill had been dizzy with happiness.

Isaac had looked so sick after seeing Martin, Bill had been afraid to touch him. Saint Mary, he was so scared of making things worse by doing or saying the wrong thing.

Cicero would know what to do. The cat wasn't perfect, but he and Isaac went back years. He'd be able to help in ways Bill just couldn't.

Bill took a sip of whiskey, rather than gulping the second shot. "What do you think they're talking about inside?"

Tom leaned against the rail of the fire escape. The night was still too young for the city to have settled. Hansom cabs clattered along the streets, and the El rattled past a block over. The saloons and gambling houses seemed to be doing a brisk business. Neighbors called greetings to each other from stoops and fire escapes, where they sat to escape the heat.

"There are some things we'll never completely understand, not being familiars ourselves," Tom said. "We can try, of course, and we should. But this business with Isaac's witch…Cicero told me how, when he first laid eyes on me, his magic 'knew' me somehow. But that don't mean I can really get, deep down, what it must feel like."

"Makes sense," Bill said. "I'm glad Cicero is here for him."

"Aye." Tom clapped Bill lightly on the shoulder. "So what do you mean to do next?"

Did their father still live on the same street? He would know where to find Martin. What he was up to.

Assuming he'd even agree to speak to Bill this time, instead of slamming the door in his face.

"I'll follow up on Martin," Bill said. "See if I can find an address for him, if nothing else. Isaac's been in contact with some reporter. Assuming Martin was the one running the ads in the paper, maybe they have some way of finding him."

"We'll help you, as much as we can with the trial coming up," Tom assured him. "Was there anything else you can think of? Any clue? Did the tug have a name, or did Granger say anything to Young and Jake that might give you a lead to follow?"

Bill started to shake his head, then stopped. "Aye, now that you mention it, he did say something strange. When Jake wanted to know if Martin meant to kill them, he said it was the labyrinth for them."

"The labyrinth?" Tom's brows drew down in a frown. "That's like a maze, right?"

"I think so?" Bill could read and do his numbers, but he wasn't what most would consider an educated man. Tom never had any formal schooling to speak of, what with growing up running with his family's tunnel gang. "Owen would know."

"I'll let him know when I go to the Coven tomorrow morning," Tom decided. "You see if you can't track down Granger, and Isaac can talk to his newspaper friend. We'll all meet up over lunch in Owen's lab."

"All right." Bill finished his whiskey in a gulp. "Do you think they're done in there?"

"I'll knock and see." Tom paused. "I hope Isaac's all right."

"Isaac's the strongest person I know," Bill said.

"That don't mean he won't be needing our help."

"Aye. Never meant to suggest otherwise." Bill stared down at the empty glass. "Sometimes strength means asking for help when you need it."

"True enough." Tom knocked on the bedroom door, then opened it when Cicero answered.

Cicero and Isaac still sat on the divan, hands interlinked. The cat tended to be flighty, but his kohl-lined eyes were solemn tonight. Isaac wore a neutral expression, as though he didn't want anyone else privy to his thoughts.

"Should I get out the blankets and make up a bed on the divan?" Tom offered Isaac. "Or do you and Cicero want to curl up in animal shape for a while?"

Isaac's eyes flicked to Bill.

Bill wasn't certain if he should offer. But he wanted to talk to Isaac in private, away from their friends. That way Isaac could shout at him, or throw things, or...

Forgive him. If Bill was lucky.

"You can come with me," he said. "Whatever you like."

The relief in Isaac's face caught Bill off guard. "If you don't mind."

"Of course I don't." Bill held out his hand, and Isaac rose to take it. "Tom and I have made a plan, but that can wait until tomorrow."

Isaac nodded. His fingers tightened on Bill's, not letting go. "All right." He glanced over his shoulder. "Thank you, Cicero."

Cicero's peridot eyes were sad. "Any time, darling. Any time."

CHAPTER 14

"WE NEED TO talk," Bill said, locking the apartment door behind them.

Isaac resisted the urge to wrap his arms around himself. He'd been so startled, so grateful, when Bill invited him back. When he touched Isaac's hand, like he still wanted him.

But maybe he'd made a mistake. Seeing Martin today had brought back so much. Reminded him of the darkest parts of himself. "Maybe... maybe I should go."

A worried expression grew on Bill's face. "If you want to, of course. But where do you mean to go?"

"Anywhere." Isaac shook his head. "Away from decent people. Away from you, before I contaminate you."

His breath hitched, and he found himself fighting back tears. He scrubbed at his face roughly, angry at himself. Bill must surely think him the weakest man in New York.

"Does this have anything to do with what you said last night?" Bill asked quietly. "Why you're so down on yourself?"

"You saw the kind of man my magic wants!" Isaac's voice rose and cracked. He turned his back on Bill, walked to the open window and stared out blindly.

"I don't know a lot about magic, but I've been around long enough to know that ain't how it works." Bill crossed to stand just behind him. Not touching, but Isaac was aware of his exact position, as if he could feel the beat of Bill's heart and the heat of his body through the air separating them. "You ain't responsible for Martin."

Isaac shook his head, not disagreeing exactly, but rejecting the proffered comfort. "He was so damned charming. Until I told him he was my witch. The things he said when he hit me." Isaac shuddered. "He was so full of hate, of rage, but my magic still wanted to make that connection. It still saw something of me in him."

"No," Bill objected. Isaac held up a hand, and he fell silent.

"So I left," Isaac said, his voice low. "Cicero thinks it was because I didn't feel safe in the MWP anymore, and that's true. I didn't. But it was more than that. I went to the Rooster. I danced and fucked men for money. Then there was Noah, and my magic, the same magic that wanted to bond with Martin, was used to fuel the blood hexes." He licked his lips and tasted salt. "I'm contaminated, Bill. My magic is spoiled. It's wrong; it only—only does bad things, and I've been so selfish coming between you and Sionn, and—"

"Shh." Bill put a hand lightly to his shoulder, and Isaac turned to him. Bill gathered him in his arms, rocking back and forth. "That ain't true, Isaac. That woman you've been talking to, Freida. Is her magic spoiled because she was force bonded?"

"No, but my witch—"

"So you've never known some miserable bastard who ended up bonded to someone who deserved better?"

Isaac swallowed. "You don't know what it's like," he said into Bill's shirt. "That sense of connection."

Bill had never thought witches were lucky for not recognizing their familiars the way familiars recognized them. If anything, he would have figured the opposite. If Tom had known Cicero was his familiar from the first moment, it might have made things a good deal easier for them both. But not everyone was as fortunate as Tom and Cicero.

"You're right. I don't." Bill let out a heavy sigh. "There's something I have to tell you, love. But I'm afraid, because you might not ever want to see me again once I do."

A new sort of worry threaded through the misery shrouding Isaac. He pulled back, and Bill released him. The look on Bill's face was utterly wretched, and for a moment Isaac was tempted to tell him not to speak. That he didn't want to know. "What?"

Bill bit his lip. "Let me say first, I'll go and sleep on the roof if you want me to. Give you the key to the apartment so you can lock the door behind me, and I can't come back in without you unlocking it."

Now Isaac did wrap his arms around himself. "What's wrong? Fur and feathers, just tell me, Bill!"

"I didn't know the name of your witch, not until today. I swear to God." Bill swallowed visibly. "You remember what I told you last night? How Da picked his other son over me?"

Bill couldn't be saying what Isaac thought he was. "No. That is, yes, I remember, but…you can't mean…"

"I can. I do. I never met the man, only saw him once through a window, but I knew his name. Martin Granger is my half brother."

Isaac put his hands to his mouth and stepped back. This couldn't be happening. It felt like some cruel trick, as though fate had gone horribly awry and given him the wrong man to be his witch.

"He's my brother," Bill said. "My flesh and blood, and he hurt you. He's killed people, and abused them, and Christ only knows what else." His shoulders slumped. "He's a hateful, evil son of a bitch, and Da still chose him. So what does that make me?"

Fur and feathers, Isaac could see the resemblance between them, now that he knew to look. They had the same shade of honey blond hair, the same hazel eyes.

Maybe that would have mattered a few days ago. Left him wary, afraid he'd see Martin's face instead of Bill's if they slept together. But he knew Bill's touch now, had felt his tenderness, and that was as different from Martin as it was possible to get.

"It makes you a good man," Isaac said. "You aren't responsible for Martin."

Bill shook his head. "That ain't the worst of it. I was so damned jealous. I heard Martin joined the MWP, so I joined the regular police, because…I don't know, I thought I might show him up somehow. Make Da regret picking him instead. I never heard why he left the MWP, you have to believe me, but when he did…I was glad. I felt like I'd won, for the first time. I stuck with the work when he couldn't make it." Bill closed his eyes. "Now I find out why he left, and know that feeling came at your expense, and I…I'm just so damn sorry. I won't blame you if you never want to speak to me again."

"You didn't know!" Isaac grabbed Bill's hands in his own. "Your father was a fool, and you aren't responsible for what Martin did. Or what he's doing now. It isn't your fault."

"Then it ain't yours, either." Bill opened his eyes and met Isaac's gaze earnestly. "Martin, Noah—they're the corrupted ones. None of what they did, *none* of what happened to you, is your fault."

Isaac's throat closed and his eyes burned. "I…"

"It ain't your fault." Bill brought Isaac's hands to his chest, above his heart. "You didn't do anything wrong. You ain't tainted. You survived everything they could throw at you, and you're the most wonderful person I've ever met, and…and I love you more than I can say."

Isaac couldn't see through his tears. He flung his arms around Bill, and they clung to each other. "I love you, too," he said hoarsely. "So much."

He lifted his face and kissed Bill, tasting both their tears. Bill's mouth was warm, and his body strong, and he smelled so good. Isaac's heart thrummed in his chest, his desire spiking in desperation.

Bill didn't think there was anything wrong with him.

Isaac couldn't bring himself to completely believe it, not yet, but maybe that was all right for now. Bill believed enough for the both of them.

Their lips parted, and Isaac leaned against Bill. "Will you make love with me?"

Bill's arms tightened around him. "Of course."

Bill led Isaac into the bedroom, then turned and kissed him gently. "If you change your mind, or just don't feel like continuing, say the word," he whispered.

His sweet consideration brought an ache to Isaac's chest. It seemed impossible Bill could be related to Martin. How could the same man have fathered two sons so utterly unlike?

Martin had seemed open, friendly, but it had all been an act. The mask of a man who used others to get what he wanted. But Bill…

Bill was simply good, all the way to the bone.

Isaac kissed him, wanting Bill's skin against his. Wanting to feel, viscerally, what Bill had said, that he didn't see any corruption in Isaac. "Undress me," he whispered.

Bill swallowed thickly. "Aye."

He peeled off Isaac's clothing one layer at a time, pausing to caress each inch of skin as it was revealed. His fingers encountered Isaac's necklace, and he slid them down to touch the silver charm. "What does it mean?"

"The hamsa? It's a symbol of protection. My mother gave it to me when I joined the MWP." Isaac smiled at the memory. "It's meant to keep away the evil eye, and to give a long and healthy life. I think…I wonder, sometimes, if it's why I survived the fall down the stairs, instead of breaking my neck." He shook his head. "But I don't want to think about that. I don't want to think at all."

"Got it," Bill said, and proceeded to kiss his way down Isaac's belly. He slid Isaac's trousers off, followed by his drawers. Isaac closed his eyes and gasped softly at the bristly brush of Bill's mustache against the inside of his thighs. "Want to lie on the bed?"

Isaac nodded. He sprawled on the bed, the sheets still thick with their mingled scent from the night before. Bill stripped quickly, then slid in beside him. He slipped a hand between Isaac's thighs, and Isaac let his legs fall apart with a groan as Bill fondled his sack.

"What do you want?" Bill asked. "Should I tug you off like this?"

The thought was tempting, but Isaac wanted more. "I want to feel you on top of me," he said. He hated feeling restrained, but he could probably do this much. At least with Bill.

"Aye." Bill rolled onto him, though he took most of his weight on his elbows. Isaac's breath hitched, then evened out. There was something about having his lover's body pressing him into the mattress, the feel of Bill's legs tangled with his, that stiffened his prick. It reminded him of all the good times he'd had, before being locked in a cage.

He writhed under Bill, rutting his cock against Bill's belly, his nails digging into Bill's back. The breeze blew in through the window, stinking of coal smoke and the muck of the streets, but free for all that.

He pressed a kiss into Bill's shoulder, breathed in the scent of his skin. Bill's cock brushed his own, and they both groaned. And with that, Isaac didn't want tender and slow anymore.

"Let me on top," he ordered, and Bill rolled off of him immediately. Isaac straddled his hips. "Hold our cocks together while I fuck you."

Bill grinned with wanton delight. "I love it when you talk filthy."

His big hands encircled them both. Isaac braced himself against Bill's broad shoulders and began to thrust. Silky skin glided against skin, and Bill's hand formed a tight tunnel. Isaac kept his gaze fixed on Bill's face, watched his eyes go dark with lust and pleasure. "Aye, please, faster," Bill begged, and now it was Isaac's turn to grin. Bill's thighs had gone taut under his, hips rocking up, adding to the pressure. "I ain't going to last."

"Then come for me," Isaac gasped.

The cords in Bill's neck stood out and his back arched, spunk spilling over his belly. Then he let go of himself and wrapped his strong fingers around Isaac's prick, even as his other hand gripped Isaac's ass. Isaac gave himself over, thrusting frantically into Bill's hand, until the rising tension within him shattered and he spent on Bill's chest.

Isaac's arms felt limp as wet string, but he didn't let himself fall forward. "We've made quite the mess of you."

Bill smiled up at him, an uncomplicated look of pure happiness. "Aye, that we did."

Isaac climbed off of him, fetched a cloth from the washstand, and gently wiped Bill's chest and belly clean. When he was done, he snuggled beneath the sheets, his head resting on Bill's shoulder.

"I might have dreams," he said quietly. "I don't know that I will, but…seeing Martin again could bring things back."

Bill's arms tightened around him. "Anything I need to know? Should I try to hold you, or…?"

"You can hold me. Talk to me." Isaac kissed the nearest available patch of skin. "Thank you. For…well. Everything. Taking care of me."

"We take care of each other," Bill said. "That's what friends—lovers —do."

The words brought a smile to Isaac's lips. "Yes. We do."

The next morning, Bill found himself standing in front of a door he'd never thought to lay eyes on again.

His gut churned at remembered shame and anger. Even at the time, he hadn't known exactly what he expected to achieve by coming here. Maybe deep in his soul he'd thought Da would change his mind, would leave this house where only one family lived, a place with servants and a dozen rooms, and come back to the cramped apartment Bill shared with Ma. Or maybe Bill had just wanted to lay eyes on Da's other family. On the boy he'd chosen over Bill.

It hadn't ended well, unsurprisingly. A servant had answered the door and told Bill to be off. Bill tried to force his way in, and the scuffle brought Da charging out like an enraged bull. Between the two of them, they'd thrown Bill off the stoop and into the street.

"Stay away from my family," Da had warned, before slamming the door and locking it after.

Bill could still recall the sting of shame, lying there in the gutter and trying not to cry. He'd just been a kid, no more than fifteen, but he'd thought himself a man. As he collected himself, he'd seen a face peering out at him from one of the second story windows. Another boy, about the same age as him, who he knew in his gut must have been his half brother Martin. The witch. The one Da had picked instead of him.

The neighborhood was shabbier now, the sidewalks dirtier. The brownstone had seen better days, its windows cloudy with accumulated soot, the curtains threadbare. A sign in the window indicated there were rooms to let. Likely Da didn't even live here still, might not have for years.

Bill tugged back his coat so his badge was visible. He'd worn his best suit today, and his best hat. Made sure to stop and get his shoes shined a block away. Even as he'd dressed, even as he'd let the shoeshine boy work his magic, Bill had called himself a fool. What did he think would happen, that Da would take one look and at him and beg forgiveness? Say he'd made the wrong decision all those years ago?

Taking a deep breath, Bill climbed the stairs and knocked on the door. A curtain in what he assumed was the parlor twitched, and he heard slow footsteps on the other side. His gut twisted itself into knots of anticipation. Da couldn't still be living here, now that it had turned into a boarding house, and he didn't know if he'd be relieved or disappointed when some stranger answered.

Then the door swung open, and even with half his life between their last meeting and this one, he recognized his father in an instant.

The years hadn't been kind to Donald Granger. His wrinkled skin hung loosely on his frame, and he leaned heavily on a cane. Brown hair had gone mostly gray, with only a few streaks of color still remaining. His worn suit looked to be second hand, matching the furniture Bill glimpsed through the open door.

Da squinted at Bill's badge. "What do you want, copper? I run a clean house. No disorderly conduct here."

Bill swallowed heavily. "You don't know who I am, do you?"

A frown creased Da's mouth as he studied Bill's face. Then his eyes widened. "Billy?"

No one had called him that in years. "Aye. It's me."

"What do you want? If you're looking for some kind of inheritance, I don't have anything for you."

It had been too much to imagine Da would be glad to see him. Bill found he'd hoped for it anyway.

"I ain't here for a reunion," Bill said, even though what he really wanted was to walk away, for good this time. "I need to find Martin. Police business."

Da scowled, but he stepped back from the door. "You'd better come inside, then."

CHAPTER 15

INSTEAD OF GOING to the Coven, Isaac took the El all the way to Park Row—or Newspaper Row, as it was often called.

A part of him had hoped he might sleep as deeply as he had the first night he'd spent with Bill. Instead, it had taken him hours to fall asleep. When he did, he'd dreamed of going into his office at the Coven and finding Martin waiting for him. He'd tried to ask everyone around him for help, but they'd only pointed out Martin was his witch, as though his presence were expected. As though he'd never left. Isaac was trapped with him.

He'd waked in a cold sweat, only to slip into another nightmare, featuring Martin in the tunnels with him in Noah's place. The dream morphed, and suddenly he was once again searching the tunnels frantically for Bill, while unseen dangers stalked them through the dark.

Isaac shook his head and let the bright sunlight banish thoughts of the night. Rather than turn his steps toward the architectural masterpieces dedicated to the publishing of *The New York World* or *The Tribune*, he aimed for a more modest establishment closer to the waterfront.

The Daily Owl was housed in a slightly shabby building, only two stories tall. Hundreds of statues of owls dotted alcoves in the exterior, hexlights in their eyes glowing an angry red even in the daylight. Clearly, either the architect or the building's owner were a bit eccentric. As Isaac approached, a hawk familiar swooped from the sky and through an open window on the second floor. A reporter, or simply the companion of the witch who kept the printers running smoothly?

The noise inside was deafening. The rumble of the presses in the basement echoing up through the floor competed with the ring of telephones, the clack of typewriters, and the shouts of editors. Resisting the urge to cover his ears, Isaac went to the first desk he saw. "I'm looking for Eli Valentine."

The harried woman pointed toward the back of the room. Isaac threaded his way through the maze of desks, and spotted Valentine in a dim, dingy corner. A man smoking a cigar stood over him, hands on his hips.

"The piece on the Fifth Avenue ghost was due yesterday!" the man said, bellowing to be heard over the cacophony.

Valentine chewed unhappily on a pencil stub held between his lips. "It turned out to be nothing but a maid frightened by a bit of laundry and a drunken swell. There wasn't a story, chief."

"Then make it into a humorous anecdote," the other man said, poking Valentine in his chest. "I'm paying you to fill column inches with stories of interest to the reading public, so have the piece on my desk in an hour, or I'll feed your liver to the owl."

He stomped off. Isaac took his place. "Who was that, and what owl is he going to feed your liver to?"

"My chief editor," Valentine said glumly. "The owl is a poorly taxidermied monstrosity the publisher keeps on his desk. We're certain the thing is cursed."

Isaac decided it was probably best not to inquire further about the owl. "I hate to interrupt your important work, but I don't suppose you have an address for the man who placed the ads?"

"No," Valentine said, even more glumly than before. He sorted through the papers on his desk and pulled out a pad with notes written on it. "He paid in cash and didn't give a name, unless he really is 'T. Roosevelt.'"

"It seems unlikely," Isaac agreed.

"I can give you the dates the ads ran on." Valentine tore a page from his notebook that already had them written down and handed it to Isaac.

Isaac scanned them. They'd run over a week and a half, which didn't tell him anything more than he already knew.

"We had a deal, and I didn't deliver on my end of it," Valentine said. "You don't owe me an interview."

"Thank you." Isaac had expected Valentine to argue the point. Even so, he couldn't feel relief. They could use all the information they could get, especially if Bill and Martin's father had moved from the last address Bill had for him.

Fur and feathers, Isaac still couldn't believe they were half brothers. He'd wondered before what sort of man would turn his back on Bill. Now he knew: the sort who could raise someone like Martin. Bill must have taken after his mother in every way that counted.

"I did get a description, for what good it's likely to do," Valentine added.

Isaac's fingers went cold. "He wasn't disguised?"

"That, I couldn't say."

Isaac swallowed. "Did he have dark blond hair and hazel eyes? Tall? Square jaw?"

"Indeed," Valentine said, surprised. "It sounds as though you already have your man."

Martin. They'd assumed he'd taken out the ad, but this confirmed it. He'd been the one to orchestrate the murder of Sister Brigid.

Isaac reminded himself what Bill had said. Nothing Martin did was Isaac's fault. It didn't reflect on him, or his magic. When Bill had held Isaac's hands, looked into his eyes, it was clear he believed that with his whole being.

Isaac might not trust his own judgment, but he did trust Bill's. He clung to that trust now.

"I wish we didn't," Isaac said. At Valentine's surprised look, he shook his head. "Never mind. I need to go."

He exchanged the noise and bustle of the building for that of the street, intending to make for the El. If he hadn't automatically scanned his surroundings for any hint of danger, he would never have seen them.

They came up from behind, one on either side, their hands outstretched. Men, grabbing for him, just as he'd been grabbed to be taken to Noah. Just as Martin had pushed him down the stairs.

Isaac froze in place, terror coursing through his veins.

A musty smell permeated the interior of the house, accompanied by a hint of sour milk. The once-fine home had been divided into a number of smaller apartments, and the lack of windows in the hall turned the interior gloomy. The carpet runner was threadbare, and the furniture of the parlor Da led him into bore old stains never properly cleaned. No pictures hung there, not even of the family Da had chosen over Bill and his mother. The curtains dangled limp over the open window, lacking even a hot breeze to alleviate the close air.

Da seated himself in a wing-backed chair whose velvet upholstery had been worn smooth long ago, without so much as the offer of a drink for the son he hadn't seen in over fifteen years. "Close the door behind you," he ordered. "Mr. Colombo leaves his apartment door open so he can hear everyone else's business."

Bill did as asked, then seated himself in a chair across from his father. He meant to keep things professional, but instead found himself asking, "How are you, Da?"

Da let out a snort. "How does it look?" Bitterness filled the words like poison.

"What happened?"

"It's none of your business, but why not?" He shrugged. "When Marlene—that was my wife—died, her family cut our allowance in half. Their money was the reason we could afford to live here, back when the neighborhood was decent." He scowled at the memories. "I invested most of what we'd put aside to try and make up for it, but most of the deals went sour for one reason or another. I had to let go of more and more servants. Then the Poles and Italians started moving in, and everyone who could afford to left for uptown. The neighborhood went to hell, but I couldn't leave, especially once Martin was gone and Marlene's parents cut off their support altogether." He eyed Bill's shiny shoes. "Are you really here on police business, or did you just come to gloat?"

Bill didn't know how to reconcile the vigorous man of his memories with the one in front of him. He'd once thought Donald Granger was the strongest man in the world, better than any of his playmate's fathers, even if he wasn't around as much as Bill would have wished. He dimly recalled being lifted up and tossed, only to be caught in powerful arms and tossed again, his childish voice shrieking "Do it again, Da; do it again!"

He'd lived half his life with the knowledge that man had judged him unworthy. But maybe the strong, brave father had only been a child's fantasy. Maybe he'd never really existed at all.

"I need to know where Martin is." Bill was surprised his voice didn't shake. "Does he live here?"

Da's expression darkened. "No, he doesn't live here, the miserable fairy. I threw him out when I found out about him. He came back, told me he'd 'tried to take care of the problem,' but I knew better."

A chill like ice water ran down Bill's spine. "What are you talking about?"

"Martin joined the MWP. He was going to put his witch blood to good use. Help support me in my old age. He was a good hand at hexes, always practicing them on the kitchen table, night after night. Things were going well, and then he came to me. He overheard a couple of familiars talking, and one of them—a Jew fairy—said Martin was his witch." Da's features twisted. "Everyone knows a witch's familiar reveals his true character."

"That ain't true," Bill protested. "It just means their magic is compatible."

"Don't lecture me in my own parlor, boy," Da snapped. "At any rate, I told Martin I wasn't going to have a Jew-loving pervert in *my* house."

Bill's fingers slowly clenched, and his heart thumped against his ribs. Whatever he'd expected when he came here, it wasn't this. "What did you do?"

"I threw him out, of course. Told him I wouldn't have anything to do with him. But that boy always did have a stubborn streak." Da shook his head. "He showed back up the next day. Said he'd tried to do in the little cocksucker, and gotten fired for his trouble. Wanted me to take him back in, at least until he got another job. Spend my hard-earned money on him, even though he was some kind of deviant. I said I'd call the police on him if I ever saw his face around here again. It must have stuck that time, because I haven't seen hide nor hair of him since."

Bill couldn't seem to get enough of the stifling air into his lungs. *This* was the man whose approval he'd wasted years longing for? This hateful, greedy, selfish creature?

"So you're useless," he said. "This whole interview was a waste of my time."

"Don't you judge me," Da said, riled. "I told you not to come back here. Not my fault if you can't listen worth a damn."

"I'll judge you as I please." Bitterness coated Bill's throat as he rose to his feet. "Martin's familiar is the best man I know, and I won't hear the likes of you say otherwise."

A sneer crossed Da's face. "So you're a Jew-loving fairy too."

"Aye. I suppose I am. And thank goodness for it." Bill put his shoulders back. "You're a hateful, twisted, wreck of a man, and I realize now I was well rid of you."

He turned toward the door, opened it, then paused as something occurred to him. "All those years ago, you said you left because I didn't do well enough on the witch tests. But that was just an excuse, wasn't it? You left because of Marlene's money."

Da snorted again. "Do you really think I'd give up a house with servants and my own carriage, to live in squalor with some Irish whore? I deserved better than that."

"No," Bill shot back. "We deserved better than you."

He left his father's house behind him. Unlike the last time, the sound of the door slamming filled him with peace rather than shame.

Isaac's muscles locked into place. He was back in Sloane's office at the Rooster. On the stairs at the Coven.

Seized from behind, overpowered no matter how hard he fought.

Two men had a hold on him, one to either side. They lifted him off his feet, cursing as they hauled him toward an enclosed wagon. One of them slapped a paper hex against Isaac's arm. "Be bound to your human form!"

At his words, rage poured through Isaac's veins, sluicing away terror. He might not take on mastiff form, but it was his *choice*. He was the one who got to decide his shape, not anyone else.

Now these bastards thought they'd take that from him, the same way Noah had kept him in dog form for so long?

No.

Isaac snapped his head back, felt the crunch of a nose against his skull. The man yelped and loosened his hold. Isaac yanked one arm free. The moment his feet hit the ground, he kicked behind him, aiming for the second attacker. The heel of his boot scraped across a shin, drawing forth a snarl of pain.

"Hold him!" one of the ruffians shouted.

"I'm trying! Martin said he wouldn't fight back."

Martin had sent them. He'd spotted Isaac on the dock yesterday, and had sent these men to take him and…what? Kill him somewhere away from witnesses? Bring him to Martin?

Isaac fought back in a frenzy. Biting, kicking, scratching, an enraged growl rumbling out of his throat. He'd kill them both before he let them drag him off.

"Here now!" a man exclaimed. "What are you doing? Police!"

One of Isaac's attackers backed away. "Fuck it—leave him—we get hauled in, it's the labyrinth for us!"

They both let go of him and ran for the wagon. The waiting driver snapped a whip at the horse, and it took off with a jolt. As it disappeared, a police whistle sounded behind Isaac.

"Are you all right?" asked the man who had raised the alarm. He was a heavyset man, dressed like a clerk, who regarded Isaac with kindly eyes. "Robbers assaulting people in the middle of the day! I just don't know what this city is coming to."

Isaac didn't bother to correct him. "Thank you for helping."

"Of course, of course." The man checked his pocket watch. "I really do have to get back to the bank, though."

As he scurried off, Isaac answered the questions of the beat copper who had come running, but his mind was only half on his words.

Martin had tried to kill him once before. It seemed he meant to finish the job.

Bill returned to the Coven to find Isaac sitting shirtless in Owen's lab, with Owen applying healing hexes to his head and bruised arms.

"Martin sent men to grab me," Isaac explained, his mouth a flat line.

Bill's stomach fell, guilt and relief and anger all mixing together inside. "The devil! Are you all right? What happened?" Without waiting for an answer, he hastened to Isaac's side. The marks of fingers showed on Isaac's arms, and he winced when Owen probed the back of his head.

"I'm fine, Bill." Isaac took his hand. "They ran when they realized a crowd was gathering. Apparently, Martin had told them I wouldn't fight back." Isaac's lip curled into a snarl. "He was wrong."

"The more fool him," Malachi said from his perch on the edge of a table.

Hell. If only Bill had been with Isaac. Martin had recognized one or both of them last night, and yet Bill had been too caught up in his own pain to consider his half brother might threaten them directly.

"They must have followed you," Bill said aloud. "Unless Valentine is in on it with them."

Isaac shook his head. "Valentine didn't know I was coming today. If Martin—or whoever he's answering to—has an informant in the police department, he might have gotten your name in connection with the case. It wouldn't be hard to find out where you lived. If familiars are involved, willingly or not, a witch could have followed me onto the El and communicated my destination to the wagon driver through the bond. Or the horse pulling it could have been a familiar, even, in contact with his witch."

"Da said Martin claimed to be a fair hand at hexes, when he was with the MWP," Bill said. He didn't want to upset Isaac further by bringing up those days, but didn't see any other way around it. "Are we certain he's answering to someone else?"

"Any hex that could affect the serpent familiar the way it did is far too sophisticated for someone who was only 'a fair hand' at hexes to invent," Owen said, stepping away from Isaac. "Knowing how to draw a hex doesn't equate to understanding why it works as it does."

"Not to mention, the men who tried to grab me used the same hex as the Dangerous Familiars Squad." Isaac pulled his shirt back on. "The one to bind a familiar to human form." His eyes went flinty with silent anger.

"I'm sorry?" Bill said uncertainly.

Isaac shook his head. "It doesn't matter. The newspaper was a dead end, by the way, so I hope your father was willing to give you Martin's address."

"Nay. He and Da—" Bill caught himself. "No. To hell with the man. He gave up the right to be called that a long time ago. *Donald* had a falling out with Martin a few years ago. Tossed him out on his ear and told him not to come back."

Isaac put a sympathetic hand to Bill's arm. "I take it your visit didn't go well."

"Donald's a vindictive old bastard whose funeral will be attended by no one but the priest and the gravediggers." Bill paused, then shrugged. "But I got a few things straight in my head."

The fingers on Bill's arm tightened gently. "Are you all right?"

"You know what? I am." Bill nodded, half to himself. "I truly am."

"I almost forgot." Isaac glanced at Owen. "The men who tried to grab me said if they were hauled away by the coppers, they'd end up in the labyrinth. Did Tom come by earlier and tell you about what happened yesterday?"

Mal and Owen exchanged a silent look. "Yes," Owen said, his voice pitched low. "I don't know exactly what Granger referred to when he threatened his underlings with the labyrinth, but...well. I have some ideas. Ones I don't want to speak aloud here."

Bill frowned. "You think this has to do with…?"

Senator Pemberton, he meant, and everyone there knew it. The MWP had problems with traitors before. No one felt safe talking about such matters openly here, not anymore.

Owen went to a desk and scribbled an address. "Come here tonight at nine o'clock," he said, handing the slip of paper to Isaac. "Mal, if you'd let the others know?"

"Aye," Mal said, hopping off the table. "I'll see you gents tonight."

CHAPTER 16

BILL KEPT A close watch on the crowds around them that evening, as he and Isaac rode the trolley up Broadway. After the attack on Isaac this morning, he'd stayed close to his love's side, not even bothering to go back to his own precinct and report to Donohue. The captain wouldn't be happy about it, but Bill had survived being yelled at by the man before, and likely would again.

They left the trolley behind at West 78th and made for the address Owen had given them. A row of townhouses looked out over the street, their stoops shaded by trees.

"Nice neighborhood," Isaac remarked.

Bill knocked on the door. A moment later, it swung open to reveal an amazon of a woman. She stood at least six feet tall and was built like a blacksmith. White-blonde hair hung in plaits to her waist. "Who are you?" she demanded.

Had they come to the right house? "Bill Quigley, ma'am," Bill said, taking off his hat. "This is Isaac."

Owen peered around her. "Bill, Isaac, I'm glad you made it. You're the last to arrive." He patted the woman on one muscular arm. "This is my sister-in-law, Ingrid. Don't worry, Ingrid, they're friends."

Bill wasn't at all sure that was how he'd describe their relationship, but it caused the woman to unbend. "Forgive me. I have a protective nature. Please, follow me."

When she turned her back to lead the way deeper into the house,

Owen mouthed "Swan familiar." Bill made a mental note not to get on her bad side.

They passed by displays of the house owner's wealth: gilded mirrors, marble floors inlaid with hexes to keep the inhabitants in good health, and ceilings painted with pastoral scenes. The only time Bill had ever been in such a fancy house had been when he'd caught Malachi fleeing a Fifth Avenue mansion.

Ingrid led the way into a library. "We dismissed the servants for the evening so we could speak freely," she explained. "There is tea and cake, if you wish it."

The library felt more lived in than the rest of the house: its chairs worn, books scattered atop tables, a basket of knitting near the hearth. Cicero was busy talking to a young man Bill didn't recognize, whose fashion sense rivaled the cat's. Dominic examined the books on the shelves alongside Nick, while Rook, Jamie, and Tom ate cake on a cushioned bench in front of an open window. Mal had taken on fox form and curled up in one of the chairs.

Another man Bill didn't know sat in a wheelchair. On the table beside him was a contraption resembling a typewriter with overlarge keys.

Ingrid and Owen both went to him. "This is my brother Peter," Owen said, beaming. "He was gracious enough to lend us his house tonight."

Silvery eyes the same color as Owen's met Bill's gaze. Peter's face spasmed into what might have been a smile, and one withered hand twitched in his lap.

"Pleased to meet you," Bill said, bobbing his head.

"Thank you for your help," Isaac added. "This is much more comfortable than squashing into Rook and Dominic's apartment."

"That's our other brother, Nathan, making friends with Cicero," Owen added. "I'll probably regret bringing them together." He clasped his hands in front of him. "I assure you, my brothers—and Ingrid, of course—are completely trustworthy."

Peter's hand twitched again. Perhaps it was a signal, because Ingrid said, "Shall we get down to business, then?"

"Indeed."

She bent and kissed Peter's head. Then, in a flash of light, she transformed into a mute swan. The appearance of a giant bird caught everyone's attention, and silence fell. Ingrid hopped onto the table with the strange contraption, paused—then began to peck at the keys.

"Shall I?" Owen offered. Peter's head jerked, presumably in

approval, and Owen began to read from the paper in the machine. "Thank you all for coming tonight. It's good to meet so many friends of my brother's. Honestly, I think Nathan and I are a bit shocked to discover Owen actually has friends." Owen broke off and shot his brother a look.

It took Bill a moment to understand what was happening. Ingrid wasn't just Peter's wife—she was his familiar. Peter communicated his words through the bond to her, and she typed them out. She had to be in animal form for the communication to work, which explained the strangeness of the typewriter.

"Thanks for having us," Jamie said, raising his plate of cake as though making a toast. Everyone else murmured assent.

The swan continued to type, and Owen read, "Owen has told us the truth behind the massacre at his wedding, and the blood hexes, and the Wraith murders. Ingrid and I will do whatever is within our power to put a stop to Pemberton and his allies."

"Hear, hear," Nathan called.

"The floor is yours, Owen."

The clacking keys fell silent. Owen straightened and glanced around the room. Mal lifted his head, amber eyes gleaming, and Bill suspected they shared their own silent communication.

"I believe I know what the connection is between the missing children, the altered familiar, and the labyrinth," Owen said. The gaslight gleamed from the golden rims of his spectacles. "The details, the location, Granger's role in it all, I can't speak to. Not to mention, I could be wrong," he added hastily.

"Get on with it," Nick said. "There are children's lives on the line here."

"Yes, of course." Owen tucked his hands behind his back and began to pace. "Has anyone else followed the reports of the excavations at Knossos?"

It sounded familiar, though Bill couldn't place it. He glanced around and was somewhat reassured by the other blank looks. But Nick said, "The palace they dug up on Crete. The one the papers say belonged to King Minos."

"So it's an archaeological dig?" Nathan asked.

Owen nodded. "Yes. It's significant because it revealed details of a civilization known to us only through the tales of the Greeks, tales recorded long after the Minoans—the ancient inhabitants of Crete, that is —vanished. There are many interesting points irrelevant to tonight's discussion, but one of the things claimed by the legends—and supported by the excavations—is that the royal family were all familiars."

Isaac leaned forward, intent on listening. "So anyone who wasn't a familiar, who only carried the blood, couldn't inherit?"

"No." Owen said, "I mean they were all familiars. *All* of them."

A look of unease passed over Nick's face. "Did they only marry each other, then? Because even having two familiar parents doesn't always guarantee the children will shift. It's more likely if it's first cousins marrying, though still not a given."

Bill's pulse quickened. The missing children were potential familiars to the last. Was there some way of making sure that potential became reality? Of creating more familiars?

Owen met Nick's gaze. "If I told you all of the men were bull familiars, and all the women serpents?"

Nick shook his head, like a horse tossing its mane. "Not possible. The form we take isn't carried in the blood. I'm a horse, and Rook's a crow. Our mother was a hawk, and our grandfather a sea turtle."

"And Alfonso was a rat snake," Bill said through a dry throat.

"Indeed. I'll speak more to his fate in a moment." Owen turned back to the rest of them. "The truth is, no one knows what determines the animal form of a familiar. Environment seems to play a factor—we don't find polar bear familiars in the tropics, for example."

Cicero shrugged sinuously. "It's magic."

Owen looked annoyed. "Further study is required. The point is, such a uniformity of familiar forms, even within a family, is unheard of. One might dismiss it as some strange case, except evidence suggests some of them were persons one might suppose were…er…" He trailed off and looked helplessly at Nathan.

Nathan arched a brow. "Assumed to be the wrong gender at birth?"

"Exactly. Yet, they took the familiar form associated with their proper gender. Nathan, you would have been a bull, not a snake. Which to me suggests human intervention."

Even though the library was warm from the day's heat, Bill felt as though he'd been plunged into a snowbank. "What if the hexes work differently on kids than adults?"

Nick let loose an impressive string of curses. Owen winced, but nodded. "Indeed." He held up his hand. "Bill, you mentioned Alfonso. I want to talk now about the best known legend of ancient Crete and King Minos."

"The minotaur," Isaac said. He'd gone pale, as if at some horrible realization.

Bill put a comforting hand to his shoulder. Then, remembering the company they were in, slid his arm around Isaac and pulled him in close. Cicero smiled at them, and Bill felt a blush creep over his cheeks, but he didn't let go.

"What's a minotaur?" he asked. "I didn't have as much schooling as some."

"Same here," Tom said.

Owen took off his spectacles and drew out his handkerchief to polish them. "I would like to make it clear the legend long post-dates the disappearance of Minoan civilization. None of the people depicted in it may have existed at all."

"Please do get to the point," Nathan said. "If I wished to listen to a long, drawn out lecture, I would have gone to university."

Owen replaced his spectacles to glare at his brother. "My *point* is that the legend involved a maze called the labyrinth. For reasons we don't need to discuss here, Minos's wife, Queen Pasiphaë, supposedly gave birth to a son who was half-bull when he emerged from the womb. He was referred to as the minotaur, and imprisoned within the labyrinth, where he survived on the flesh of those thrown in with him."

"How unpleasant," Cicero said, putting a hand to the base of his throat.

"Needless to say," Owen went on, "it is beyond unlikely such a creature would have survived to be born, let alone thrived on a diet of human flesh afterward. But what if there is a scrap of truth behind the legend?"

"You're referring to what happened to Alfonso," Isaac said. His body was tense against Bill's, waves of unhappiness radiating from him. "How he was part snake, even in human form."

"I am." Owen bowed his head briefly. "Let us imagine a son of the royal family failed to take on bull form when he reached puberty, perhaps because he didn't get the proper hexes at the right time. Or perhaps there was a royal adoption of a child from another family, one old enough to have shifted already into his natural familiar form, which wasn't that of the bull. To correct it, the hexes normally used to ensure royal offspring were the proper type of familiar were applied."

"But he'd already shifted into something else, so the hex didn't work the way it was supposed to," Bill guessed.

"Perhaps?" Owen spread his hands. "This is wild speculation on my part."

"But they've been digging up this King Minos's palace?"

"*A* palace, at any rate."

"You've got good copper's instincts," Bill said. Owen looked rather pleased at the compliment. "We've seen old hexes over and over again from Pemberton's people. Forgotten things we don't recognize and so don't know how to fight. Whoever knew about the blood hexes, the mechanical hex maker, the conquistador's poison, and all the rest of it, would surely be keeping a close eye on this excavation."

Tom nodded. "They bribed someone on the dig, or smuggled something out themselves, maybe. Now we've got missing kids, and an adult who turned into a different type of animal, then couldn't turn all the way back."

Isaac shuddered. "But why?"

"It'll be about controlling familiars and making a profit off of them." Nick stamped his foot angrily. "One way or another." Rook gave him an exasperated look, which he ignored.

"I've a question." Tom folded his muscular arms over his chest. "Owen's told us what the labyrinth is in the myth, but what did Martin and the others mean by it?"

Jamie looked uncertain. "You don't think some maniac has built a giant maze somewhere, do you?"

"That would be hard to hide in the city." Dominic sat in one of the comfortable chairs, hands clasped over his belly. "They could be transporting the children to the countryside, I suppose."

"The farther you take someone, the more chance there is to get caught," Nick said. The corner of his mouth curled up. "Or so I hear."

Bill suspected there was a story behind the comment, especially given the fondly exasperated glance Jamie gave Nick. "Let's concentrate on Greater New York to start with," Bill said. "Pemberton has rich friends who might have almost anything in the basement of their Fifth Avenue mansion."

"I can attest to that," Owen said dryly. "Bowling alley, swimming pool, second ballroom, inescapable maze…"

Mal let out a yip that sounded like a laugh.

"Ask your fancy friends, if you can do it without drawing suspicion," Nick said. "Jamie and I will keep an ear out among the ferals. I'll start knocking on doors personally first thing tomorrow. If we hear anything, no matter how far-fetched, we'll let you know."

Bill rubbed at his eyes with his free hand. "Martin is wanted for Jake's murder now, so that will give me some leverage with my captain.

Especially since Martin shot at me, too. Most coppers don't look kindly on suspects who take potshots at officers of the law. I'll make sure the river police know to keep an eye out for the tug he was on, and have an artist draw up a likeness to send around. If we can find Martin, we might convince him to give us the name of whoever he's taking orders from."

"What about the MWP?" Isaac asked. "By rights it is an MWP case. Tom, Cicero, I know you have the court case soon, and Owen is more useful in the laboratory—no offense—"

"None taken."

"—but what about you Rook, Dominic?"

"The Police Board is still keeping a close eye on the MWP." Dominic ran an ink-stained hand distractedly back through his hair. "Remember, they're the ones who replaced Ferguson with Pemberton's man, Lund. Temporarily, as it turned out, but clearly someone on the board has ties to Pemberton."

The typewriter clacked, and Owen read Peter's message. "I can hire a private investigator."

"Do we dare involve anyone else?" Isaac wondered.

"Hold off and let's see if I get anywhere," Bill said to Peter. "It ain't a bad idea, and if I can't find anything to lead us to Martin in the next two days, we'll look into it."

"In the meantime, neither you nor Isaac should go anywhere alone," Dominic said. "Bill, you haven't been specifically targeted yet, but we shouldn't assume things will stay that way."

Bill shook his head. "Donohue ain't going to let me keep working the case if I walk in there with a familiar."

"Then have someone who isn't Isaac escort you tomorrow." Dominic glanced at one of them, then the other. "That person can wait outside while you're in the precinct station."

"Does Martin know about you?" Isaac asked. "That you're his brother, I mean. Do you think your father would have told him?"

The question gave Bill pause. "I assumed he'd recognized me, or at least my name, but I can't say for sure. He was watching out the window, the day Donald threw me off his doorstep and told me not to come back. But Donald wouldn't have wanted to make a fuss if he could avoid it, not while he was depending on his wife's family to supply him with money. Martin might not have any idea the copper investigating him is his half brother."

Would it have made a difference if he did? Would he have been as quick to fire on Bill yesterday?

"It won't hurt to be cautious," Dominic said. "Come to the MWP tomorrow before you go to the precinct, at least."

"Aye."

Isaac pressed his side against Bill's. "I'll look through our old records at the Coven. It sounds as though Martin was living with your father when he was hired, but there might be some clue in his file to point us in the right direction."

"I can help," Rook said.

Isaac nodded. No one spoke immediately, and after a moment, Owen looked around. "I think that's it? Very well."

The typewriter clattered. "Thank you all for coming. Good night, and good luck." A pause. "I have the feeling we're going to need it."

CHAPTER 17

ISAAC ACCOMPANIED BILL back to his apartment in unspoken agreement. Almost as soon as he'd locked the door behind them, Isaac wound his arms around Bill's waist from behind. "Bed?"

Bill pressed back against him, felt Isaac's prick hardening through the barrier of their trousers. "Aye, if those bruises ain't troubling you."

"Thanks to Owen's hexes, they're practically gone." Isaac nipped at Bill's ear. "Come with me."

Bill's cock hardened as Isaac drew him into the bedroom. They kissed hungrily as they peeled off their clothes, as if they couldn't get enough of each other's skin. Isaac's eyes almost glowed with desire, and once they were naked, he caught Bill's face between his hands. "I love you, mi corazón."

"You're amazing," Bill whispered. His heart seemed to have swelled against his ribs, constricting his lungs. "I never met anyone like you."

"Probably just as well," Isaac said with a self-deprecating grin. Then he pressed his body against Bill's, distracting him. "Say you want me."

As it was fairly obvious, given that Bill's prick was rubbing against Isaac's belly, Bill figured he must need to hear it out loud. "I want you, Isaac. Whatever you'll give me, I want."

Isaac's expression softened, and he kissed Bill again. "Lie down on the bed."

Bill went without hesitation. Isaac crawled in on top of him, prick trailing over Bill's skin as he bit and nipped at Bill's neck with his teeth.

Bill squirmed with pleasure and let his hands roam. Over Isaac's shoulders, down his back, to his arse. The hamsa amulet swung and flashed in the moonlight streaming through the window when Isaac sat back. Bill took the opportunity to pinch first one nipple, then the other, and now it was Isaac's turn to groan and squirm.

"Will you fuck me?" Bill asked.

Isaac bit his lip, a flash of white teeth against the kiss-swollen flesh. "I was thinking I'd denied myself the pleasure of sucking you off for too long. But there's no reason I can't do both."

He slid out of bed to fetch the oil from its box. When he returned, he held the oil in one hand, and the dildo in the other. The grin he gave Bill was pure wickedness.

Bill's mouth went dry, and his cock leaked clear fluid in anticipation. "Saint Mary, you're going to be the death of me," he said, but he drew up his legs to give Isaac access to anything he wanted.

"Now that would be a waste," Isaac said, and unstoppered the oil.

Bill bit back a groan when Isaac began to work the dildo in. It was nice and thick, sleek wood polished to a high sheen. It had cost him a fair bit of coin, but if he'd thought it worth every penny before, he was doubly sure now.

"You love it, don't you?" Isaac murmured. His pupils nearly swallowed the brown irises. His breath became ragged with lust. "Taking a big cock."

Bill let out a low moan when he felt its entire length stretching him. "Aye, please," he babbled, "fuck me."

Isaac did, shifting the dildo's angle until he found just the right one to make Bill nearly come off the bed. Bill gripped the sheets in his hands, his prick aching with need. Isaac leaned forward, his hair brushing Bill's thighs and balls, and wrapped his lips around Bill's cock.

And stopped moving the dildo. Bill made a sound torn between pleasure and protest as Isaac slid down, taking him to the root, then drawing slowly off. Isaac licked his lips and grinned. "Mmm. You taste so good."

Bill squirmed on the dildo. "Don't stop."

"Oh, but I want to draw this out." That wicked look was back, and it sent heat racing through Bill.

He bent his head and began to work Bill's cock again. Isaac's wet mouth engulfed Bill's prick, while the dildo spread him open, maddening in its stillness. Isaac drew Bill almost to the edge, then stopped sucking and thrust with the dildo instead. He switched back and forth, until Bill was nearly begging for release. It all felt so damn good, better than he'd ever imagined.

"Tell me you're enjoying this," he panted.

"That's too mild a word." Isaac's voice sounded strained. "I'm going to finish you now, and then fuck your mouth."

"Yes," Bill said, before words deserted him. Isaac sucked and fucked him at the same time, and all he could do was clench his fingers in the bedsheets and feel pleasure cresting like a slow wave, until it finally broke and crashed down on him. He came with a shout, and Isaac moaned around his cock and swallowed everything Bill had to give.

The mattress shifted as Isaac climbed up to straddle his chest. Bill grabbed Isaac's cock by the base with one hand and wrapped his lips around the head. He wasn't as accomplished at the act as Isaac, but he desperately wanted to become so. He must have been doing something right, though, because within moments Isaac let out a gasp of warning and spilled in Bill's mouth. He tried to swallow, but some of it ended up leaking out the side of his mouth and onto his chin.

Isaac clung to the headboard for a long moment, as though his legs didn't want to move. Then he slid off of Bill. Bill reached around and pulled out the dildo. His arse felt sore, but he couldn't bring himself to care.

Isaac collapsed beside him, head on Bill's shoulder. Bill bent his head and kissed him on the nose. It brought a laugh from Isaac, followed by a more proper kiss on the mouth. "That was incredible," Isaac said, at the same moment Bill murmured, "Amazing."

They both laughed and snuggled in closer. Isaac ran his fingers through the hair on Bill's chest. "I'd like for you to meet my family."

Bill glanced down in surprise, but Isaac's attention was on his chest. "I'd like that. Do you think they'll approve of me?"

Isaac chuckled. "I won't say we didn't have our disagreements when I was younger, but they love me no matter what. And that means they'll love you, too."

"Are either of them familiars?"

"No. But my uncle was. Their family were Orthodox and looked down on familiars. My father was very close to his brother, so after my uncle shifted, they left home and chose a poor life on the East Side among the immigrants. It was hard at times, but Father says he never regretted it, especially after meeting my mother and having me." Isaac was silent for a moment. "Did you know, we don't give up our names? Jewish familiars, I mean. Goyim might call me Isaac and nothing else, but

I came to the Torah Yitzhak ben Avram, and that's how I'll be buried."

"I didn't know that." Bill nuzzled Isaac's hair. "I want to learn everything about you. Whatever you want to share. I can't say as I'm a fair hand at speaking English, and my Gaelic is even worse, but I'll try to learn that language you speak if you want me to. If it's important to you."

Isaac lifted his head. His eyes shone with love, and Bill felt as though his heart had leapt straight out of his chest and into Isaac's. "You're really something, aren't you, Bill Quigley?"

Bill snorted. "I'm something all right, and I'm sure my captain will be happy to tell me exactly what when I report in tomorrow."

Isaac laughed and put his head back down. "It's called Ladino," he said. "I'll teach you a few words to impress my parents, and we'll go from there."

Though it would have been faster for Bill to go to the precinct directly from his apartment, he was mindful of the potential dangers, and instead escorted Isaac to the Coven. "Are you going to be all right with looking up Martin's information?" he asked as they climbed the stairs. "You can wait until I get back, if you need to."

Isaac cast him a fond look but shook his head. "No. I'm certain it won't be easy, but nothing about this is. I'll be all right, though."

"If you're sure." Once they were through the door and out of the public eye, he caught Isaac's hand and gave it a squeeze. "I figure I'll ask Sionn if he wants to go to the precinct with me."

"Oh. Um, Sionn." Isaac played with the silver chain around his neck. "We had a…bit of a falling out."

Bill came to a halt. "About what?"

"You, actually." Isaac's cheeks darkened. "Sionn accused me of toying with him. I had told him I didn't care if the two of you had a relationship, or if you bonded with him. Then I ended up snatching you out from under him. I'm not blaming him for being angry," Isaac added hastily. "I didn't do it deliberately, but I lied when he asked me."

Bill winced. He hadn't spared Sionn much thought in the last few days, which had been damned selfish of him. He'd done poorly by the man, then not had the balls to face him. "I'll definitely ask him to come with me, then. It'll give us time to talk."

"He might not want to talk."

"I'll find someone else to play bodyguard if he refuses." Bill shrugged. "But I at least owe it to the man to hear him out."

"He changed offices, but I'm sure you'll find him." Isaac brought

Bill's hand to his lips, then let go. "I'm going to the detectives' area to wait for Rook, then the two of us will go to records."

"I'll see you when I get back, then."

He watched Isaac walk away. It still astonished him that this brave, beautiful man actually wanted him. When Isaac vanished from sight, he turned reluctantly toward the offices shared by the unbonded familiars.

It didn't take long to find Sionn. Predictably, the owl didn't look pleased to see him. "Detective Quigley," he said coldly. "If you're looking for Isaac, I don't know where he is."

"I was looking for you, actually." Bill took off his hat and held it awkwardly. "I have to report in to my captain, and I could use someone to watch my back on the way. I figured it would give us a chance to talk. Or for you to curse my name, if you'd prefer."

Sionn eyed him thoughtfully. He really was a handsome fellow, and if Bill had never met Isaac, he wouldn't have minded seeing where things went between them. "Why do you need someone to watch your back?"

He'd hoped to at least get out of the building without bringing Isaac up, but it wasn't to be. "Isaac and I have kept looking into Sister Brigid's murder and the missing kids. Someone isn't too happy about that. You're an owl; if we're set upon, you can fly straight to the nearest beat copper in a few seconds."

"I ain't bad in a fight," Sionn protested. Then he grinned ruefully. "Well, if the other fellow doesn't see me coming."

Bill grinned back. "I'll try to keep them distracted, if it comes to it."

Sionn rose to his feet. "All right. Let's go."

Feeling relieved, Bill led the way back outside. They fell in beside each other as they made for the El. The day was young enough for the heat to still be bearable, though the stands selling lemonade and cold drinks were already doing a brisk business.

"I'm still annoyed with Isaac," Sionn said after a few minutes. "Things were going so well between you and me."

Bill tried to think how to respond. "I ain't used to this sort of thing," he said at last. "Relationships. But I wasn't fair to you, and I'm sorry."

Sionn shrugged. "It happens. I won't pretend not to be disappointed, though. I think we would have gotten along well as witch and familiar."

"You deserve better than I could have given you," Bill said firmly. "You're a good fellow. You ought to have someone who can love you with his whole heart, not half of it."

"That's kind of you to say." Sionn's smile was thin, though, as if he didn't believe it.

Despite the uncomfortable beginning, they chatted the rest of the way about inconsequential things: baseball scores, favorite saloons, the neighborhoods they'd grown up in. The tension eased, and by the time they reached the precinct, Sionn's presence at his side no longer felt awkward. With any luck, maybe they'd eventually be friends again.

"My captain ain't going to be keen on anyone from the MWP," Bill said when they stopped outside the precinct station. Not to mention it would be harder to keep up the lie that hexes weren't involved, but Bill didn't say that part aloud. "Do you mind waiting on me out here? I'll be as quick as I can. I'll buy lunch to make it up to you."

Sionn pretended to consider. "All right, but I pick the restaurant."

"Deal."

Bill ran his edited story through his head as he climbed the steps and went inside. He'd give Donohue the truth about everything except their suspicions about the hexes. That would satisfy Donohue for a bit, and maybe convince him to give Bill a bit of help tracking Martin down.

Conversation fell silent when he entered. Bill glanced around uncertainly, but none of the coppers seemed willing to meet his eye.

"Morning," he said uncertainly. He was used to some hostility, but this was more. Different.

Liotta shuffled some papers nervously. "Captain said he wanted to see you as soon as you bothered to show up."

Not a good sign. Bill had earned Donohue's displeasure before, after arresting Malachi only to have the thief slip away on him. It hadn't been fun, but he'd survived. Steeling himself for a dressing down, he made his way to the captain's office.

Donohue sat at his desk, cigar filling the room with smoke, despite the early hour. When he saw Bill, he yanked it out of his mouth and stubbed it out angrily. "Quigley. About time you sashayed your way back here."

Bill hovered in the doorway, in case Donohue decided to start throwing things. "Sorry, captain, but this case is running me ragged. I'm going to get right on my report—"

"You mean your pack of lies?" Donohue challenged.

Silence fell between them. Bill's pulse beat fast in his throat. Donohue knew. Somehow. "Sir?"

"Don't play dumb with me." Donohue leaned forward, as though he might spring over the desk at any moment and throttle Bill. "You falsified your earlier report to make it sound as though there weren't any hexes involved."

"Let me explain." Bill's mind grasped for any excuse Donohue might believe. "The suspect we're after—he's my half brother. The MWP have it out for him. He used to be one of theirs, who they fired. If you'll just let me—"

"Shut it." Donohue held up a hand, and Bill's jaws snapped closed. "I don't give a damn about your brother, or your excuses, or you. You lied on a report and made me look like a fool." Donohue sank back in his seat again. "You're off the force."

The words didn't register for a moment. "Sir?"

"You're fired, Quigley. Your career as a copper is over. Done with." Donohue thrust out his hand. "Give me your badge and get the hell out of my sight."

The MWP records were stored in the basement of the Coven, below the huge room where hexmen and hexwomen labored to create the hexes used by both of New York's police forces. Most of the basement storage was given over to dusty cabinets stuffed with evidence from the fifty-five years' worth of cases since the MWP's founding. It was strange to think about the fragments of life—and death—held within the cabinets, so dreadfully important at the time, now dusty and forgotten.

Just like Isaac's commendation.

The old personnel files were stuffed into a dim corner; clearly no one expected them to be of later interest once they were stored, at least judging by the level of disorganization.

"I should have gone with Bill and let Sionn help you," Rook said. "An owl might actually be able to read in this light."

"I'm not Sionn's favorite person at the moment," Isaac replied. "Ask Cicero if you really want to know why."

"Let me guess, it involves Cicero sticking his whiskers into things that don't involve him."

"A bit." Isaac shrugged.

"How am I not surprised." Rook peered at one of the labels on the cabinets then shook his head. "I'll run and get a hexlight. Don't have fun while I'm gone."

"No chance of that," Isaac muttered.

Rook's footsteps receded. Despite the busy headquarters overhead, very little noise penetrated the underground room. The shadows seemed thicker than when Rook had been with him. Isaac rubbed at his arms.

It wasn't *that* dark. Certainly not as dark as the tunnels he'd been held captive in. But the dim light and silence, the sense of being close to the living world yet unable to reach it, reminded him of them. His nerves drew tight, every sense on alert.

To calm himself, he pressed his hands to his mouth, as a reminder he was in human form and not animal. Not in a cage. In just a few minutes, Rook would be back with the hexlight.

Still, every creak of settling building, every distant rattle of pipe, stoked his nerves to new heights. Was that a mouse chewing up the records, or a stealthy footstep?

He stared in the direction the noise had come from. The rows of cabinets blocked his vision.

He'd just go and look. Telling himself he was being a fool, he took a step forward.

Something—a piece of rope?—struck the ground with unexpected force, right where he'd been standing.

Startled, he took an instinctive step back. Then the rope began to move, and he realized it wasn't rope at all, but the brown length of a serpent.

Chapter 18

BILL STOOD ON the steps in front of the precinct, blinking in the sunlight. His mind spun in circles, like a machine with a slipped gear, and he couldn't quite work out what to do next.

Fired. Off the force.

He'd spent his adult life as a copper. If he'd learned other skills along the way…but he hadn't, because he'd never pictured himself as anything else.

He'd have to find a job. He had a little money set aside, but he'd used most of his salary to afford the luxury of his own apartment, and rent would be coming due in a week.

What was he going to do? To hell with that—how was he going to keep helping with the investigation? He was just a member of the public now, not the MWP liaison. Sure, Owen had broken the rules by sharing information with his brothers, but they weren't playing an active role chasing down suspects. He couldn't just abandon the missing kids to their fate.

"Bill?" Sionn said, in a tone that suggested he'd called Bill's name unnoticed several times already. "Something wrong?"

"Aye." Bill heaved a sigh. "Somehow, Donohue found out I wasn't entirely honest concerning the details of the case in my earlier report. I've been fired."

"Oh no." Sionn's freckled face drew into an unhappy frown. "I'm sorry. Why didn't you tell him the truth?"

"I wanted to stay on the case." Bill rubbed at his face. "So much for that."

"How do you think he found out?"

"Hard to say." Bill started to walk back in the direction of the El. "It could be as simple as he looked over the coroner's report on Alfonso and saw it didn't agree with what I'd told him."

Sionn's eyes narrowed uneasily. "Does the captain usually look over coroner's reports, or does he leave that to his detectives?"

"Nay." Bill sidestepped a pushcart selling oysters. Could someone have tipped Donohue to the fact his least favorite detective was lying to him? But who? Someone from the coroner's office, an ally of Martin's with the MWP, or Martin himself? "But to be fair, Donohue and I ain't been getting along anyway. He could have taken a closer look at the case in hopes of finding an excuse to get rid of me."

Not everything was part of a plot, and Bill had known the risk. Still, it sat uneasily with him.

"What the devil?" Sionn murmured. "Bill, look at that."

A figure dressed in gloves and a heavy cape, the hood drawn up to obscure its face, stood across the busy street, unseen face turned toward them.

In the winter, the figure wouldn't have been remarkable. But no one would go out in the full blaze of summer dressed like that, unless they wanted to hide their face for some reason.

Having inhuman aspects to their features, for example.

The moment the figure realized they'd spotted it, it turned and fled. Bill bolted after, dodging in front of a wagon filled with beer kegs and knocking a woman's hat off. Sionn let out a startled shout and followed.

Bill reached the other side of the street without being run over. He caught sight of a flap of cape as the figure ducked away into a less-crowded thoroughfare. "Stop! Police!" he shouted—Sionn still had a badge, at least, so it wasn't quite a lie.

The figure made for the waterfront. Thin children stared as they ran past, and rag-pickers paused in their work, watching curiously. "Get the beat copper!" Bill yelled, and hoped someone would be inclined to obey.

The figure ducked into a sort of courtyard walled in on three sides by crumbling tenements. Bill slowed. "This could be an ambush."

"I'll take a look from above," Sionn said, and shifted into owl form. The tiny red owl flapped hard, climbing steadily toward the roofline—

A falcon smashed into him, like an arrow thrown by an angry god.

Bill cried out. There was an explosion of feathers from the impact, and Sionn dropped like a stone, vanishing somewhere amidst the tangle of roofs and wash lines. The peregrine pulled out of its dive just before striking the ground, and landed on the shoulder of the caped figure.

Shock coursed through Bill's veins, filling his mouth with a metallic flavor. Could Sionn have survived a hit like that? Even if the peregrine hadn't used talons or beak, it had been diving at stunning speed when it crashed into Sionn's much-smaller form.

He drew out his gun and aimed it at the two, for once glad that coppers were required to provide their own weapons. At least Donohue hadn't been able to take his gun along with his badge.

"You're under arrest," he said, though he had no authority to do so. "You've assaulted an officer of the law, and you'd best hope he's still breathing, or it's the electric chair for you."

The figure let out a wet, racking laugh. "Do you think I'm afraid of the electric chair after this?" it asked, lifting its hood.

It was far less human than Alfonso, its skull so distorted into a wolfish snout that Bill couldn't tell if it was a man or a woman. The falcon let out a small whistle, as of distress, and rubbed its head against the fur-covered face.

Bill's heart slammed against his ribs, but he forced himself not to react. "We have a hexbreaker," he said. "Surrender, come with me, and he'll help you in return for information."

A look of startled hope flickered in the wolf's golden eyes. "The hexbreaker…could undo this?"

"Don't be stupid," said a voice from behind Bill. "He's lying to you."

Bill spun, but a hand seized his wrist before he could bring up his gun. He found himself staring into the face of his half brother.

"Hexed shoes, to keep you from hearing me," Martin said with a grin. Then he slapped a paper hex against Bill's forehead. "Now sleep."

For a moment, Isaac was nearly light-headed with the realization the serpent would have struck him if he hadn't moved at exactly the right instant. Then the snake let out a thwarted hiss, revealing a set of fangs dripping with venom.

It wasn't the same sort of snake as had been sent to kill Sister Brigid, but Isaac didn't doubt its poison would prove fatal, even if not as quickly. Brigid had to die fast enough so as not to arouse an outcry among the sleeping sisters whose cells lay beside her own. But Isaac had stupidly let Rook leave him alone in a basement away from the busy parts of the

Coven. If something delayed Rook, no one would find him until it was far too late for an antivenin hex to do any good.

It lunged a second time. Isaac leapt back, but it was coming fast now, slithering over the floor between him and the only way out. He ran to one of the cabinets and threw it blindly open. A heavy volume of bound reports tumbled out, and he caught it instinctively before it could hit the floor.

The serpent struck again, but Isaac used the book like a shield, blocking the bite. He had to get past, back into the company of other people, before his luck ran out.

The flutter of wings heralded Rook's return. The crow swooped down and snatched the serpent by the tail, lifting it into the air with him. It twisted wildly, trying to climb back up its own body to bite.

Rook dropped it before it could sink its fangs into his leg. Isaac hurled the book in his hands at the snake, hoping to injure it enough to make it give up. Instead, there was a crunch audible even over the loud thwack of the book hitting the floor.

The serpent's tail coiled and thrashed madly, but the movements were its death throes. Its head lay beneath the heavy tome, crushed by the weight.

Rook landed and took back human form. "I leave you for ten minutes, and you get into a fight for your life!"

"It isn't my fault!" Isaac cautiously lifted the volume in hopes he was mistaken, but there was only pulp left where the snake's head should have been. "I didn't mean to kill it."

Rook put a hand to Isaac's arm. "It certainly meant to kill you."

"But it—he or she—was a person." Isaac sagged. "Someone who might have been able to tell us where Martin is. Maybe even a victim."

Footsteps clattered loudly on the stairs. "Are you all right?" Dominic shouted. "Rook?"

Of course—Rook would have alerted Dominic through the bond. "I'm fine," Rook said. "A snake familiar just tried to kill Isaac, though."

Dominic spent most of his time behind the desk, and between that and Rook's excellent cooking, the run had left him out of breath. Even so, he jogged to them and flung his arms around Rook.

Rook hugged him back. "I'm fine, Dominic," he repeated. "Not a scratch on me. Isaac?"

"No injuries. I got lucky." If he hadn't stepped away at the right moment, or if Rook had gotten distracted by something shiny…

Rook must have seen him shiver, because he pulled away from

Dominic and held out his hand to Isaac. "Come on. Let's get upstairs, have a drink from the bottle I know Cicero has hidden in his desk, and let someone else look over the scene." He shook his head. "Ferguson is going to have an apoplectic fit when he finds out there was an attempted murder in the MWP."

As they started back toward the stairs, there came yet another series of footfalls running down them. Cicero met them at the bottom, his hair in disarray. "There you are!" His yellow-green eyes fixed on Isaac, and Isaac felt a sinking sensation in the pit of his stomach.

"What's happened now?" he asked, dreading the answer.

"Word just came from Bellevue. Sionn's there—he was attacked and badly injured."

No. The shadows seemed to creep closer, threatening to obscure Isaac's vision. "Where's Bill?"

"I don't know." Cicero's mouth flattened in distress. "But he wouldn't have left Sionn lying in the street for a beat copper to find. I'm afraid…I'm afraid something terrible must have happened."

They arrived at Bellevue to find Tom there ahead of them. For an instant, Isaac was surprised to see him—but of course, Bill was Tom's best friend. Tom and Cicero had dropped everything else when they heard something might have happened to him. Isaac had been in such a daze on the way over he hadn't even considered why Cicero was with him but Tom wasn't, just leaned on his own friend in miserable, worried silence as they rode the El.

Rook had come with them, to act as messenger if need be. Tom waited just outside the ward, against the wall so as not to impede the flow of nurses through the doors. "Have you spoken to Sionn?" Isaac asked as soon as they were within earshot.

Tom shook his head. "The doctors put him out with a sleeping hex while they set his bones. He ought to be coming out of it anytime now. I asked them to hold off on the stronger pain hexes until we can talk to him."

Tom led the way into the ward, past beds of ailing patients. Even with the windows open to catch any breeze, the place stank of incontinence, vomit, and old blood. Isaac suppressed a shudder—he'd spent time here as a patient himself, first when Martin attacked him, then after being rescued from Noah.

Sionn lay near one of the windows, his freckles dark against skin gone the color of milk. His red hair clung to his forehead, damp with sweat, and even with the covers drawn up Isaac could see the bandages swaddling his right arm and much of his chest.

A doctor spotted them and came over. "He should wake up soon," the doctor told Tom. "He'll be in a great deal of pain, so I'd like to hex him as soon as possible after you ask your questions."

Isaac had managed to submerge most of his fear for Bill on the way over, but seeing the extent of Sionn's injuries brought it roaring back. "Will he be all right?" he asked, as though Sionn's chances at life would somehow insure Bill's as well.

The doctor grimaced. "I'm not certain about *all right*. But he will live."

"What happened to him?" Cicero asked.

"That, we don't know yet. But his injuries appear to have been caused by an impact of some sort. The bones of his right arm were shattered in multiple places, as was his collar bone."

Rook drew in a harsh breath, his skin going gray. "That's not good news for a bird familiar."

"I'm certain it isn't," the doctor said gravely. "Some of the ribs on that side were fractured as well, though at least they're in place and the lung sounds whole. If you find out what happened, please let me know, in case it changes his course of treatment."

Sionn stirred and let out a low moan. "We will," Isaac said, and hurried to the bedside.

Sionn's eyelids fluttered, revealing golden irises. As consciousness reasserted itself, he went motionless, the instinct of a small owl hiding from predators.

Isaac crouched by the bed. He wanted to grab Sionn by the uninjured shoulder and demand to know where Bill was. Instead, he took a deep breath and said, "Sionn, it's us. You're safe in the hospital. What happened to you?"

"Water," Sionn whispered. Cicero hastened to pour a glass from a nearby pitcher and hold it to his lips. Sionn's throat worked as he swallowed; then he sank back against the bed. "Everything hurts."

"I'm sure it does. We'll make sure you get the best pain hexes, but first, we need to know what happened."

"Peregrine falcon." Sionn's face contorted in pain. "We were being followed. Chased him down—it was a trap. I took to the sky, thought I'd spot an ambush on the ground. But the ambush was in the air." His mouth went white with remembered pain. "The falcon hit me out of nowhere. I fell."

Not good. "Where is Bill? Do you know?"

"They took him. I saw it. One of them hit him with a sleeping hex, and he went down. They dragged him off." Sionn closed his eyes, then opened them again. "I was in and out of consciousness for a while after that. Finally managed to shift into human form and try to move. I couldn't get far, but the beat copper was nearby. I guess someone listened to Bill and went for the police." He swallowed. "Bill was fired. Off the force for falsifying reports."

Isaac couldn't possibly have cared less about that at the moment. "Did they say where they were taking him?"

"No. I'm sorry, Isaac."

Tom put a comforting hand to Sionn's uninjured shoulder. "It's all right, Sionn. You didn't do anything wrong. Is there anything else you can tell us?"

"I don't think so."

"Then I'll call the doctor and get you something for the pain. You rest up and get better, hear?"

"Aye." Sionn managed the ghost of a smile. "It could be worse. If it had been a wild falcon and not a familiar, it would have eaten me."

Tom went to fetch the doctor, and the rest of them started away from the bed. "Isaac?" Sionn called. "Find Bill, will you? He's a good man."

Isaac met yellow eyes clouded with pain and nodded. "I will."

No one said anything until they were back in the free air outside the hospital. "What now?" Tom asked. "We have to find Bill, but where the blazes is he?"

Isaac shook his head slowly. Bill was gone. Probably in Martin's clutches by now.

If Isaac closed his eyes, he'd see Martin's face as it had been the day he'd tried to kill Isaac. Twisted with rage, filled with hate. Isaac's body tensed, half expecting the blows of fists and feet.

Martin had tried to destroy Isaac for no more reason than Isaac told him he was his witch. Now that maniac had Bill at his mercy. Isaac's heart quailed to imagine what Martin might be doing to Bill at this very moment.

Somewhere in the vast city, the man Isaac loved was being held captive. Despite what he'd told Sionn, Isaac didn't have any idea of how to find him.

CHAPTER 19

ISAAC SAT AT his desk in the Coven, staring at the tiny pile of evidence he and Bill had collected in the hope inspiration might strike.

There wasn't much to see. A copy of the coroner's reports on Brigid and Alfonso. A list of the missing orphans. The address to the boarding house. Young's arrest records. Notes taken in Bill's messy hand, and Isaac's neater one. The coded messages sent in the newspaper, directing Alfonso to kill. The newspaper with the final message, which Alfonso had never gotten the chance to cut out and add to his collection.

None of it told him anything more than he already knew.

There came a knock on the door, and Cicero poked his head in. He and Rook had volunteered to go back to the basement and look for Martin's file, as they'd never gotten around to retrieving it earlier. Isaac's heart lifted momentarily. "Did you find something?"

Cicero shook his head. "No. I'm sorry, Isaac."

Isaac's throat tightened and his eyes burned. "We're not going to find Bill in time. Martin is going to kill him, and if we're lucky we'll find his body in the river."

For once, even Cicero didn't have any reply. Isaac stared at the scraps of paper, the reports, and anger welled up to mingle with despair. Why hadn't he told Bill how he felt earlier? Why had he wasted years, wallowing in his own misery, too afraid of grief to reach for happiness? Now Bill needed him, as he'd never needed Isaac before, and he couldn't do anything but sit here helplessly.

"Useless," Isaac snarled, and swept the papers off the desk and onto the floor in a single, violent motion. "Useless, useless, useless!"

Cicero hurried to him. "Don't," he murmured, wrapping his arms around Isaac's shoulders. "You can't blame yourself."

"Bill *needs* me, and I can't...I can't..." Isaac's words trailed off. He shut his eyes, let Cicero hold him. Longing for it to be Bill's arms around him, Bill's scent in his nose.

"Let's just...look at the clues again," Cicero suggested. "Maybe a pair of fresh eyes is just what the case needs."

Isaac nodded mutely. Cicero let go of him, and they both bent to pick up the files and cuttings. The newspaper had scattered everywhere, and Isaac gathered the pages and put it back to rights. As he sorted through the pages, a headline caught his eye. It was the article Valentine had complained about writing, the day Isaac had encountered him at Freida's apartment.

THE MONSTER OF BLACKWELL'S ISLAND
FISHERMAN SWEARS ABANDONED LUNATIC ASYLUM HAUNTED

Claims to be Teetotaler

Mr. Y. Kowalski is in the habit of night-fishing in the East River, in particular along the banks of the islands. On Saturday last, he chose the northern end of Blackwell's Island as his casting spot, where he has dropped his line undisturbed many times before. This evening, however, he saw something extraordinary.

According to Mr. Kowalski, shortly before midnight he was startled to see a strange figure running across the lawn in front of the former New York City Lunatic Asylum. As our readers know, the Lunatic Asylum was closed some six years ago, and is rumored to have been sold to a private concern who intend to open a hospital within the old building.

When he saw this unexpected activity, Mr. Kowalski believed the figure to be a prisoner attempting escape from the Penitentiary which also occupies the island. The moon was full and the sky clear, so he drew closer in hopes of later identifying the individual to the police, should the escape succeed.

What a shock he received, then, when he beheld the figure was not human at all—perhaps not even among the living. In his own words, Mr. Kowalski reports: "It was a monster. There's no other word for it. The thing was eight, nine feet high and went on two legs like a man, but it was no man. It had a head like a bull, with great big horns, and a tail, and was shaggy all over. It bellowed and waved its arms at me, clear as day. I wasn't staying anywhere near something like that! I threw my rod overboard and rowed like the devil himself was after me."

When asked what he believed the creature to have been, Mr. Kowalski volunteered the opinion that the monster was in fact the ghost of some unfortunate familiar who had died during confinement at the asylum, and now wandered the earth in a tormented state between human and animal form.

Isaac felt the world slow around him, acutely aware of the heartbeat in his chest. He read the article again, then a third time, to be certain.

"Isaac?" Cicero asked, hovering beside him. He looked as though he wanted to touch Isaac, but wasn't certain if he should.

"I know where they are." Isaac thrust the paper at Cicero. "The labyrinth Martin mentioned, the story of the minotaur Owen told us…"

Cicero frowned at the headline and started to speak, but Isaac rushed over him, "They've been coming and going by boat, every time we've seen them. We know they needed somewhere to take the missing children. Somewhere to try their hexes on people like Alfonso. Somewhere to take prisoners like Bill." He stabbed a finger at the paper. "That's where they are. That's where *Bill* is. The abandoned insane asylum on Blackwell's Island."

Bill regained consciousness slowly. His impressions of his physical state swam slowly through the haze fogging his head, reaching him one at a time.

His mouth tasted foul. He was seated upright.

He couldn't move.

His eyes flew open in alarm. Something pressed against either side of his skull, holding his head firmly in place. By rolling his eyes as far down as possible, he could just make out the thick leather strap around his chest and upper arms, as well as two leather cuffs anchoring his wrists to the heavy wooden chair. A jerk of his legs discovered a similar restraint around both ankles.

A surge of fear cleared away the last lingering effects of the sleeping hex. The room around him looked to have been abandoned for some time, from the peeling paint on the wall to the cobwebs festooning the corners. A strange sort of wooden cage, almost like a low bed, sat on the floor directly across from him.

Where the devil was he?

Footsteps approached, and a door creaked open, though Bill couldn't turn his head to see it. A moment later, Martin Granger stepped into view. In one hand he held a small glass of whiskey. "Well, well," he said. "If it isn't Dad's dirty little secret."

A mix of shame and fury burned through Bill, and he jerked uselessly on the straps around his wrist. Martin tutted.

"Don't bother trying to escape." He sat down on the strange cage-like contraption. "You're strapped into a tranquilizing chair, the sort they put violent lunatics in. It's meant to hold men fueled by the strength of madness. So you aren't getting out." He sipped his whiskey and leaned forward, peering at Bill. "I'll admit, I'm curious about you. It's your fault my mother died."

"I don't know what the hell you mean." Bill wasn't certain how he might escape, but keeping his brother talking would give him the chance to think. "I never met the woman, never even laid eyes on her."

Martin's lip curled. "You came to our house and made a scene. Dad threw you off the stoop, but it was too late—I'd already seen you. I asked him who you were. He cuffed me and told me it was none of my business." Martin took a larger swallow of the whiskey. "So I made it my business. I snuck into his room and went through his things. He wasn't nearly as careful as he should have been. But then, neither was I."

He turned away and stared at something out of Bill's line of sight. "Mother came to find me, and discovered me with the evidence in my hands. Receipts for rent for an apartment. A half written letter addressed to a woman who clearly wasn't his wife. More receipts for shops in New York, dated during times he was meant to be away from the city. A photograph of another woman and a baby, with 'To Donald, with love from your adoring Mary and Billy' written on the back. It destroyed whatever happiness she had in her marriage, and turned her into a shadow of herself. After that, she simply…wasted away."

"That ain't my fault," Bill said. "Nor yours. Seems to me the one responsible is the man who said vows to her and then broke them."

Martin surged to his feet. "If you hadn't come there, none of it would have happened! I wouldn't have thought to go through Dad's things. No one would have ever known. What did you think—that we'd open our door to gutter-trash like you?"

"To hell with you." Bill's heart raced, and he tested the restraints around his wrists again. They didn't give an inch. "You can look down on me and Ma all you want, but at least I ain't murdering nuns and kidnapping helpless kids."

An ugly expression crossed Martin's face. "Sister Brigid was a fool. She didn't have the courage of her convictions—in either direction. She took our money, knowing she wasn't doing the Lord's work, but then got cold feet and threatened to expose us. What did she expect—that we'd let her sell us out without lifting a hand to stop her, just because she wore a habit?"

"Sister Brigid's gone to her final judgment, one way or another," Bill replied. "But you can't justify the kids."

"They aren't children—they're familiars."

"Potential familiars."

A nasty smile crawled across Martin's lips. "Not when we're done with them."

Oh Christ. Saint Mary, Holy Familiar, have mercy. Owen had been right. "You're using hexes from that place in the papers. Crete."

A startled look crossed Martin's face—then he scowled. "How the hell do you know that?"

"Why should I tell you?"

Martin buried a fist in Bill's gut. It knocked the wind from his lungs, and he tried to curl instinctively to protect himself. The tranquilizing chair held him motionless.

"The boss won't like that," Martin said, half to himself. "Maybe he doesn't have to find out though." He turned back to Bill. "It was the dog who figured it out, wasn't it? The Jew fairy who ruined my life. Good thing I meant to kill him anyway."

Bill managed to draw in a breath, though it hurt. "Isaac didn't do anything wrong. It ain't his fault you're a—"

"Shut up!" Martin threw the whiskey glass. It struck the wooden clamp holding Bill's head in position and bounced away. "You don't know anything. You never had any future, any prospects, but I did! I'm a witch. I'm owed a familiar worthy of me. Instead, I got some limp-wristed, cocksucking piece of filth."

Bill spat at him. It was the only thing he could do, imprisoned as he was, and the spittle landed right on Martin's cheek.

Martin hit him again, and then again. Bill gritted his teeth, trying to hold in a bellow of pain. "I'll bet you fucked him, didn't you?" Martin demanded. He left off punching and grabbed Bill by the jaw, fingers digging in. "You're both working against me, of course you are. You're jealous of everything I have, but you aren't taking it away from me again, you hear? In a few weeks or months, I'll finally have the familiar I deserve."

Bill's stomach and chest hurt so bad he could barely draw breath to speak. "What do you mean, the familiar you deserve?"

Smugness replaced much of the anger on Martin's face. He let go of Bill's chin and stepped back. "I'm working with powerful men. Men of vision. The Dangerous Familiars Squad overstepped the bounds of what the public would tolerate. But the threat of dangerous familiars still exists. Thanks to the Minoan hexes, that threat is about to just…go away."

The hairs on the back of Bill's neck stood up. "What do you mean?"

"We can choose the form a familiar will turn into." Martin picked up the whiskey glass from the floor and examined it for cracks. "No more rounding up lions and bears in the public eye, no more locking them away for the common good. We simply make sure every familiar from now on will be of an acceptable type. Nothing vicious or frightening." He tipped his head back. "No more ugly surprises, when a witch can have a familiar made to order."

Bile coated the back of Bill's throat, and he swallowed hard to keep it down. "It won't work. You can't kidnap every potential familiar in the city."

Martin looked at Bill as if he were stupid. "Kidnap? Don't be foolish. This is only the beginning. A test of concept, if you will. Once we have all the problems worked out, a series of new sanitariums will open. Places where potential familiars can come and be taken care of, have a few hexes cast on them, and go on with their lives without having to worry they'll turn into anything dangerous. Naturally a law will be passed to make certain they undergo treatment, just as the law says anyone who has smallpox must go to the smallpox hospital, for the public good. Anyone who breaks the law and turns into an unacceptable form will be sent to the Menagerie for the rest of their lives." Martin shrugged. "The public will love it. It'll all be very advanced, very modern. Very…humane."

Bill's stomach twisted. *Sanitarium* was a pretty name mean to disguise something horrible. Martin knew it—after all, hadn't he mockingly referred to Alfonso as "patient" in the coded messages, and himself as "Dr." G?

The worst part of it was, the scheme would work. After the massacre at Owen's wedding, people had been scared. Happy to see laws passed, so long as those laws didn't affect *them*. Who could object to the idea of keeping tigers off the street, without sounding like he didn't care about public safety? If a so-called humane alternative was offered, anyone who protested it could easily be portrayed as some kind of radical seeking to destroy the very fabric of society.

"Let me guess," Bill said. "Senator Pemberton—or some company connected with him—will be the one building and profiting off these sanitariums."

Martin grinned. "I told you I know powerful men." The grin faded. "I was curious about you, but now that we've had this little chat, I can put you behind me and get on with my life. The dog should be dead by now."

Horror swamped Bill. "What have you done to Isaac?"

"A shame we silenced Alfonso—I could have used him again. But there are so many familiars in the jails and the Menagerie." Martin paused. "Of course, I would have preferred to do it myself. Wrap up my own loose ends. But those incompetents I sent after him failed, and I decided I'd rather meet my dear, dear brother than see the dog again."

So Isaac might not be dead. Martin had sent an assassin, but if Isaac stayed inside the Coven, surely he'd be safe. Bill clung to that hope, even as despair closed in around him.

"I'll finally be rid of the past and have the future I deserve," Martin went on. "I'm going to have the first pick of new familiars. There's one girl I think will be perfect for me. She's going to be beautiful, I can tell already. I asked that she be made into a dove—appropriate for a female familiar, don't you think? I can't wait until I bond with her."

"I hope she guts you like a pig," Bill said.

Martin hit him again. "There's something to remember me by," he said, when Bill could breathe again. "Not that you'll have long to remember anything." Lifting his voice, he called, "Boys, I'm ready. It's time to take him to the labyrinth."

Chapter 20

Isaac stood in the prow of a yacht as it cut across the East River, making for Blackwell's Island.

They had no real plan and no time to make one, other than get to the island as quickly as possible. Owen had immediately offered the Yates family yacht, on the grounds they didn't know who to trust among the river police.

"Father hardly uses it now that he lives in Newport year-round," Owen had explained. "Nathan and I can sail it, and it's spacious enough for us and anyone we rescue."

Rook flew to Caballus to alert Nick and Jamie, and they'd all convened at the docks where Owen, Malachi, and Nathan waited. Those three would stay with the boat, while Isaac, Cicero, Tom, Nick, Jamie, Rook and Dominic went ashore. If a police boat happened along, Owen would rely on the Yates family name and play the part of wealthy eccentric to allay suspicion.

Tom joined Isaac at the prow, peering into the darkness ahead, broken only by the lighthouse at the northernmost end of Blackwell's. Though an electric plant had been proposed, installation never occurred, and the institutions of the island remained lit only by kerosene lanterns.

"Miserable place," Tom said. "I had to go to the Penitentiary once, back when I was an ordinary copper. This is where New York sends everyone it don't want to think about. The sick to the Charity Hospital, the criminal to the Penitentiary, the old to the Alms House, the poor to the Work House, and the mad to the Lunatic Hospital. They're kept out of sight here, where nobody else has to think about them, or worry if they're treated well. When they die, they're buried in anonymous graves on Hart Island. Forgotten while they live, forgotten when they die." He shook his head. "Sometimes, people on my beat would end up here. Neighbors, men and women I talked to most every day. But they got too old, or too poor, or too inconvenient."

"I'm sorry," Isaac said.

Tom sighed. "So am I."

Isaac glanced up at him. Tom was tall and broad, nearly the size of Nick. His fair hair stirred in the wind, his eyes fixed on the island ahead. "Thank you. For helping. This might get dangerous—it probably will—so just…thanks."

"Bill is my best friend," Tom said. "He stood by me when nobody else on this earth did, not even Cicero. I ain't going to let him down."

The yacht avoided the ferry landing and continued along the western side of the island. The light house slid past, followed by a line of trees, then a thicker grove which might have been intended to give the asylum's inmates a pleasant place to stroll on their supervised outings. This must have been where the fisherman spotted the minotaur.

It had bellowed at him, waving its arms. To drive him away…or because it sought his help?

In the legends, the labyrinth had been a prison. Was it the same today? Had the minotaur escaped wherever it was being held, seen possible salvation in the form of a boat, run toward it…only to see the fisherman react in horror and flee?

If so, what had happened next? If it had entered the river, it had probably drowned, the currents around the island forming as much a barrier as the walls of its institutions. Perhaps it had stood there on the grass, watching its only chance of rescue vanish into the night. Staring at the electric lights of the city that seemed so close, just on the other side of the water.

The yacht slowed and dropped anchor. Owen came to join them. "The asylum is just ahead."

"They'll be somewhere no one will notice light coming from a supposedly empty building," Isaac murmured. "Interior rooms. Basements."

"The labyrinth is often assumed to have been underground," Owen said.

"Could there be tunnels beneath the asylum?" Isaac asked

uncertainly.

Owen and Tom both shrugged. "I've never heard of such a thing," Tom said. "But that don't mean they ain't there."

"The Blackwell House still stands on the eastern side of the island, I believe." Owen's spectacle lenses flashed briefly in the moonlight as he turned his head. "There were other dwellings, long ago torn down to make way for the various institutions. Perhaps some of them had need of underground construction. New York City was quite the haven for pirates in the seventeenth century. Captain Kidd himself was a prominent citizen."

"Maybe we'll get lucky and find some pirate loot down there," Cicero said, draping himself against Tom's shoulder. "I'd look just amazing in gold and jewels."

"Is everyone prepared?" Dominic asked. "Equipped with charged hexes? Hexlights?"

Isaac touched the pouch tucked into his pocket. As they didn't know what they'd be facing, Owen and Dominic had distributed a wide variety of charged hexes, including ones for unlocking, causing sleep, preventing pain, and casting light.

"Then let's go," Dominic said. "Rook, if you'd be so kind as to scout ahead—but for God's sake, watch out for that falcon."

"I wish we had an owl," Rook muttered. "Crows can't see well in the dark, you know."

"Neither can falcons, so at least there's that," Owen said.

Cicero peeled himself from Tom's shoulder. "I'll scout ahead on the ground."

Rook took on crow form and glided toward the trees, vanishing almost instantly into the inky shadows. The rest of them disembarked; the moment he was on land, Cicero changed shape as well. His black fur blended into the night as he raced ahead.

"Cicero reports the smells of multiple familiars and humans," Tom whispered. "None fresh, but they've been here recently."

"Are any of them Bill?"

Tom listened for a moment, then shook his head. "He's not sure. They're mixed together and not fresh enough."

It didn't matter. If Bill still lived, Martin would have brought him here. This had to be where they were hiding the children.

One way or another, it all ended here.

"All right," Isaac said. "Let's see if we can't find the true monster of Blackwell's Island."

* * *

Bill fought the men who came to release him from the chair, but there were too many of them. They struck him with fists and feet, until his left eye was swollen and the taste of blood filled his mouth. One held a thick leather belt with wrist cuffs attached to either side. Like the chair and the wooden cage, it looked like the sort of thing used to restrain the mad. They strapped Bill into it and hauled him out of the room.

They passed into what might have been an office at one time, now empty except for a lone desk and chair, and from there into a long hallway. Benches lined the hall on each side below the windows, and Bill was shocked to see night had fallen while he'd been unconscious.

From there, they exited onto a landing, then down several flights of stairs, until they descended into what appeared to be some sort of basement. The air stank of mildew and damp. Bars divided off one end of the room, and to his horror Bill saw children huddled behind them.

The missing kids. They were packed into the makeshift prison, filthy and scared—but alive. If he could just get away, he could lead a rescue party back here.

He flung his weight back, digging in his heels. But the guards seemed to have expected a renewed struggle, and dragged him bodily across the floor. Away from the children, and toward another door on the other side of the room. It opened onto a narrow corridor lined with damp brick, which in turn lead to a second, smaller room. What the room had been used for, Bill couldn't guess—storage, he hoped, as it would have been a lightless, airless place to put the inmates. In the center of the floor was a metal grate set into the brick.

Martin stopped beside the grate. "Escort my brother a little way in," he ordered. "Not far—I wouldn't want any of you to get lost. Just deep enough in so he can't find his way back in the dark."

Whatever waited for Bill down there, it couldn't be good. "I'm ashamed to be related to you," Bill snarled. "You murdering son of a bitch. I'm coming back for you, do you hear me?"

Martin tsked. "Don't you papists know the story of Cain and Abel? Killing your brother is the worst possible crime. Why do you think I'm letting you take your chances in the labyrinth, instead of throwing your body in the river?"

He bent to unlock the grate, then swung it open. Taking out his gun, he fired it casually into the opening. "There. That should keep them back for a bit."

Bill's heart hammered. "Keep who back?"

Martin's grin showed all his teeth. "You'll see."

The grate opened on a brick-lined shaft leading down. One of the guards swung onto the rusted iron ladder bolted into one wall. While Martin trained his gun on Bill, another guard unlocked his restraints.

"Despite what I said about Cain and Abel, I will shoot you if you run," Martin said conversationally. "As will any of my men."

For a moment, Bill considered trying anyway. If nothing else, maybe he could wrest the gun away from Martin and use it on his brother, before the guard killed him.

But as badly as he wanted Martin to bleed, dying here wouldn't save the kids. Maybe this labyrinth had another way out. Some opportunity for Bill to escape, or signal for help.

"Oh, and one more thing." Martin took the stub of a tiny candle from his pocket, along with two matchsticks. Still smiling, he tucked them into Bill's vest pocket. "Don't say I didn't give you a chance."

Bill knew cruelty when he saw it. Being left in the dark underground would be bad enough. But having two precious matches and a bare stub of candle, knowing he had to conserve them, making the agonizing choice of when to use them, praying the candle didn't go out, would add another dimension of suffering. How much more hopeless would he feel when the tiny flame guttered away for the last time?

"Didn't your whore mother teach you any manners?" Martin asked. "Thank me."

Bill gritted his teeth. He wanted to spit in his brother's face again, but then Martin would surely take the candle and matches back. If Bill was to have any chance of finding a way to escape, he'd need them. "Thank you."

"Very good." Martin stepped back and gestured grandly to the ladder.

Bill climbed down, the rust rough against the palms of his hands. The first guard waited at the bottom, gun drawn and his face pale with nervous fear. The shaft let out into a brick-lined tunnel, similar to the one where they'd found Isaac that fateful New Year's Eve.

The thought of Isaac, of what might have happened to him, spilled fresh fear through Bill. He struggled to concentrate on his surroundings, so as not to betray himself in front of his guards. The brick here was older, and much rougher. Wooden trusses shored up the walls at regular intervals, hexes carved deep into their surfaces. Whatever magic had been used to keep the tunnels from flooding or collapsing, it had been strong indeed to have survived for so long.

The second guard dropped from the ladder. "Walk," he said, giving Bill a shove.

Bill walked. Damp clung to every surface. Mildew crawled across the walls. Water pooled on the uneven floor at intervals, splashing underfoot. The tunnel didn't run straight for long, instead branching and intersecting with other tunnels at irregular intervals. Bill did his best to count steps and memorize turns.

"Far enough," one of the guards said. "Sit down while we leave."

Bill sank to the floor obediently. Shooting nervous glances around, the two ruffians hurried away, taking the lantern with them.

Darkness descended. Bill held his hand up in front of him. Nothing—he might as well have had his eyes closed.

Fear scrabbled at the back of his mind, but he did his best to shove it away. Giving into panic wouldn't help anyone.

Was Isaac all right?

He had to believe Isaac wouldn't be taken unawares by Martin's assassin. Otherwise he'd lie down and never get up again. No, Bill would escape, get help, save the kids, and find Isaac waiting safely for him back at the Coven.

Then he'd fall to his knees and beg Isaac to never, ever leave him. He might not be a copper anymore, but they'd find some way to make it work. They'd have good lives, perfect lives, because they'd spend all of their days together.

Unless Bill died down here. Or Isaac was already dead.

"No," Bill whispered, and the sound of his own voice startled him in the silence.

There had to be some way out of here, other than the basement entrance. No one built a system of tunnels like this and didn't have them lead anywhere. He just had to clear his head and *think*.

No way to tell direction, even if he'd had a light. No food, but at least the puddles on the floor would offer water. Maybe he could think of a clever way to mark the intersecting tunnels so he'd know where he'd been, even in the dark. Could he pry loose some bricks and place them at intervals to mark his path? Or only ever make right-hand turns? Or—

A soft splash echoed through the tunnels.

Bill held his breath, listening intently. Since the footsteps of the guards had faded, he hadn't heard anything save for the occasional drip of water. But the splash had been too loud to have been made by a water droplet. A piece of brick falling from the ceiling, maybe?

Another splash, then another. Then the scratch of what must be

nailed boots against brick, accompanied by an odd dragging sound.
Something else was in the dark with him.

Chapter 21

From the outside, the asylum had an almost castle-like appearance, thanks to the crenellated patterns atop the walls. Several outer structures were scattered about, in various states of disrepair: kitchens, housing for patients once the main building became so overcrowded no more could fit inside, something that might have been a workshop for the groundskeepers. Someone had scrawled "while I live, I hope" on one of the outer walls. A former inmate? One of the familiars Martin had kidnapped? Perhaps even the minotaur, during its escape attempt?

No light showed within the vast bulk of the asylum itself. The building consisted of two wings, set at right angles and joined together by a fifty-foot high octagonal tower, which only enhanced its fortress-like appearance.

"How do we get in?" Jamie whispered. His face was set in a line of grim determination, and he held his gun ready, barrel pointed at the ground. Even without a uniform, he looked every inch the soldier he'd once been.

"I imagine there are alarm hexes everywhere." Dominic peered at the building as though he might discern them through the darkness. "Tom?"

"I'll take care of them," Tom agreed. "I would say we go in a window instead of a door, but Cicero says they're all barred. Does Rook see anything useful from above?"

"No. As he made clear, his vision is no better than ours in the dark.

What about Cicero?"

"He's still looking." Tom fell silent, his own eyes closed, concentrating on watching through Cicero's instead. "There's a guard patrolling outside—he has a shuttered lantern."

Nick pulled out a length of black ribbon and knotted his long hair into a messy bun. "Where?"

"Not far from the end of the building nearest the woods. He—"

Before Tom could finish, Nick was gone, moving with surprising silence for such a large man. "Always charging off," Jamie muttered. "Come on, before he gets his fool self in trouble."

As they rounded the small knot of trees, there came a faint clatter from ahead, nearly lost beneath their own soft footfalls. A moment later, Isaac glimpsed Nick hauling a man into the shadow of the trees.

The clatter had come from the guard's dropped lantern. A tiny glow, shielded by the canopy and branches, showed Cicero had taken on human form and picked it up. He adjusted the shutter until it was barely cracked, emitting just enough illumination to reveal Nick holding the guard pinned against a tree, his hand clapped over the man's mouth.

"Good work." Jamie patted Nick on one broad shoulder.

The guard's eyes bulged above Nick's hand. He was pale and smelled faintly of fish; another worker from Fulton's Market, perhaps, or one of the boats plying the river. Had Martin found employment there after being fired from the MWP and thrown out of his father's house?

Nick leaned in, his face just a few inches from his captive's, one arm braced threateningly across his neck. "I'm going to take my hand from your mouth," he told the man. "Try to yell for help, and it'll be the last thing you do. Answer my questions, and you'll live to see another sunrise. Understand?"

The man nodded as best he was able. Nick let out a long breath and removed his hand from the man's face. Instantly, he began to gasp in air. "Please…"

"Where are the children?" Nick demanded over his plea.

"Th-the basement of the asylum. The boiler room."

"How do we get inside?"

The guard swallowed. "Through the door in the octagon. It leads right into the basement."

"Hexed and guarded no doubt," Tom said. "How many of you lot are there?"

"Six or seven, I never bothered to count."

Isaac pushed in impatiently. "Bill Quigley—is he here? Where is he!"

"I-I don't know who that is."

Isaac *growled*, leaning in closer. The man's eyes widened in terror.

"Th-they brought someone in earlier," he babbled. "I don't know who he was, but Martin wanted to talk to him personally, once the sleeping hex wore off. Once Martin was done they put him in the labyrinth."

Isaac's blood turned cold and sluggish in his veins.

"What happens in the labyrinth?" The dim light reflected in Tom's eyes, his mouth set in an angry line.

The guard tried to shake his head, but Nick shoved him harder against the tree, lifting him off his feet. "Answer the man."

"It's a bunch of old pirate tunnels that don't lead anywhere, at least not these days," the prisoner gasped. "That's where they put the familiars who aren't useful, who can't be threatened or bribed into helping. The ones who lose their minds after the hex takes hold, and aren't all the way human anymore. Or who can't change back and forth at all." He squeezed his eyes shut. "They're wild. Mad. They'll tear anyone apart. It's a death sentence down there."

Isaac wanted to fling himself on the man. To hit him, bite him, scream into his face. But none of that would help Bill. "How long as he been in the labyrinth?"

"Long enough to have been ripped limb from limb."

"To hell with that," Tom snarled. "How do we get down there?"

"There's a grate in the basement floor. But it's locked and hexed, and even if it wasn't, you *don't* want to go down there with them."

Nick glanced over his shoulder. "Are we done?"

"Aye," Tom said in disgust.

"You promised you wouldn't kill me—" the man started. Nick punched him before he could finish, and he crumpled into an unconscious heap.

"We could have used a sleeping hex," Dominic said mildly.

"He wasn't worth wasting magic on," Nick replied. "How are we doing this?"

"I have to get to Bill." Isaac's hands had gone cold in the warm summer air. If what the guard said was true, if Bill had been torn apart by maddened familiars…

No. He couldn't let himself believe it.

"We have to get the kids out and away as fast as possible." Nick glanced at Jamie, who nodded. "We can't risk them getting caught in a crossfire or being used as hostages."

Tom rubbed at his face. "All right. We'll go in fast and hard."

"Just the way I like it," Cicero said.

"This ain't the time, cat. We'll have the element of surprise on our side, but not for long. Dominic, Jamie and I are armed. We'll concentrate on whatever guards they've got in there. Nick, you shield the kids and get them to safety. Cicero, you and Rook do whatever you can to provide any needed distractions."

Dominic stiffened. "There's an owl on the roof."

A sentry. "Did it see Rook?" Isaac asked urgently. If the owl sounded the alarm, their chances of getting inside were nil. Instead, they'd be fighting men entrenched in the building, while Bill was trapped in the labyrinth, maybe hurt, maybe dying…

Dominic communed silently, his expression growing stormier by the minute. "Rook, what were you thinking? I suppose, but…fine." He sighed and focused on his surroundings again. "While we were distracted by the guard, he decided to land near the owl. She was tied down, and her wing feathers plucked out. He took human form, then freed her so she could do the same. She's not…very human even now, apparently, but she can speak. She says she was supposed to raise the alarm at any intruders, or else her captors will never undo the hex that's made her this way. But a falcon told her the MWP hexbreaker can help, at least according to the policeman the falcon helped capture. The owl is taking the risk that's true."

It must be the same falcon who had hurt Sionn. Isaac's gut tightened in anger, but he kept his silence.

"Tell her I'll do my damnedest," Tom said.

Jamie checked his gun. "Then let's move, before something else goes wrong."

Bill's heart slammed against his ribs, his pulse roaring so he could hardly hear anything else. He took a deep breath, trying to stay as quiet as possible.

So he wasn't alone. Martin had indicated as much when he fired the warning shot earlier. He'd meant to put Young in the labyrinth, so chances were it was him Bill had heard.

Please let it have been him Bill had heard.

Young had tried to kill him, but that was before the man had been dumped in an underground maze of tunnels. Likely he'd be desperate for any alliance at this point. God knew Bill was.

And if it wasn't Young whom Bill had heard?

Then it was some other poor soul trapped here by Martin. If nothing else, they might know which tunnels *didn't* lead to an exit, which would save Bill wasted searches. Two people working together to escape would surely have a better chance than one.

His decision made, Bill called, "Lucius Young, is that you?"

He'd pitched his voice more softly than he would have normally. The utter darkness made him oddly reluctant to shout, as though he feared attracting the attention of something terrible.

There came no answer, but whoever it was must have heard him, because the noises stopped. Then they resumed, this time distinctly drawing closer.

The lack of a response unnerved him, so he tried again. "Who is it? What's your name? I'm not going to hurt you, even if it is Young. I figure we can work together to get out of here. Do you have any candle or matches left?"

The only reply was the scratching steps, coming closer.

The hairs on Bill's arms stood up. The scratching didn't sound as much like nailed boots as he'd first thought. And what was that awful dragging? Had whoever it was found something down here, something useful enough to lug around with them?

"I'd feel better if you'd say something, friend."

Whoever it was had come close enough for Bill to hear their rasping breath. Yet still they didn't speak.

Moving very slowly, Bill reached into his pocket and took out the candle stub and one of the matches. He hadn't meant to use a match so soon, but the situation was too unnerving. Maybe his assumption of an alliance had been wrong. Maybe being stuck in the dark had driven Young mad, and he was even now preparing to stave in Bill's head with a chunk of brick.

The match flared, its tiny light blinding after utter blackness. The face hovering only inches from Bill's didn't belong to Young.

It didn't belong to anything human at all.

A twisted mishmash of man and alligator stared at him, nightmare teeth filling the long jaws. Scales covered its entire body. A long tail dragged behind human legs, feet tipped in claws.

It opened its mouth and roared.

The rescue party raced across the lawn to the door leading into the octagonal tower, choosing speed over stealth. Nick charged in the lead in horse form, Jamie on his back. Cicero clung to Tom's shoulders in cat form, and Dominic puffed and panted in the rear. A guard stepped around the side of the building; Jamie fired a single shot, and either luck or skill were with him, because the man dropped before he could cry out.

The gunshot would draw attention, of course. But they were about to do that anyway.

Jamie slipped off Nick's back when they reached the door. He landed badly on his wooden leg, but Tom was there to catch him by the arm before he fell. Tom put his hand against the door, then stepped back. "Hexes are broken."

Nick spun around and kicked behind him, powerful hindquarters smashing into the door. It flew back off its hinges and down a short stair leading into the basement.

Tom was through the opening first. "Police! Drop your weapons and put your hands up!"

Isaac raced after him, followed by the rest, Rook swooping in over their heads. Two men sat at a table at the bottom of the stairs, a stack of playing cards and a bottle of whiskey between them. To the left was the brick bulk of the furnace, now cold. That part of the room had been walled off by bars, new enough to gleam in the lantern light. Behind the bars huddled a group of filthy children, perhaps thirteen in number.

The missing orphans.

One of the men went for a gun, only to have Rook dive into his face. He yelled and fell back, and Tom barreled into him at full speed. The other backed away, eyes wide and hands up.

"Where's the entrance to the labyrinth?" Isaac demanded.

The guard pointed at a door set in the wall opposite the children. "Through there and down the hall—but for God's sake, don't let the monsters out! They'll kill us all!"

Isaac flung open the door, which didn't seem to have a lock, and started down the hall. Dominic hurried after him. "If the imprisoned familiars are beyond reason, we can't release them while the children are still here. It would be too dangerous."

The hall ended in a small room whose door was long gone. A rusty grate was set in the floor, held shut by a heavy padlock. Alarm hexes were likely set on it, though at this point it hardly mattered whether he set them off or not.

"Then lock it after me," Isaac said. "I have an unlocking hex."

Dominic's face had paled. "And if they have enough of their minds left to take it off your body?"

Isaac waited to feel the weight of decision fall across him. Of choice.

He waited to feel afraid, or trapped, or uncertain.

He didn't. He realized then, he'd already made his decision.

He wasn't certain exactly when, whether it had been when he suggested Bill meet his family, or when he'd realized Bill was missing, or in some other, quieter moment. Perhaps it was when Martin's men used the hex on him, and he'd felt anger rather than fear, because it was his right to decide his life for himself.

Either way, the knowledge had settled into bones that had begun to ache again with the longing for the mastiff form haunting his dreams. So he simply said, "Then give me an uncharged one. Bill's a witch. We'll come back together, or not at all."

Dominic shook his head. "No! I'm not locking you in to die, and I'm not making you pay that sort of price to escape. You go back and help the others—I'll find Bill."

"You'll never find him in time." Isaac met the other man's eyes. "It's all right, Dominic."

Shouts and cries echoed down the hall—reinforcements must have arrived. Dominic swore and pulled out a scrap of paper and his inks. His fingers flew as he sketched out an unlocking hex and pressed it into Isaac's hand.

Isaac took all the charged unlocking hexes save one from his pockets and gave them to Dominic, so no one—or nothing—could loot them from his body if things went terribly wrong. The final one he pressed against the padlock. "Unlock."

It clicked open. He swung the grate back on a ladder leading down a narrow chimney into darkness. A cold breeze streamed up from below, chilling his skin.

"I'll see you soon," Isaac said, and hoped it was true. Taking out a hexlight, he swung onto the ladder. The grate clanged into place above, the click of the padlock echoing down the chimney.

Holding the hexlight between his teeth, Isaac descended into darkness.

CHAPTER 22

BY THE TIME Isaac reached the foot of the rusty iron ladder, his palms were sweating and his pulse beat fast and thready. The brick-lined tunnel, the clustering shadows, all forcibly brought back memories of his captivity by Noah and the theriarchists. He knew—had known from the moment the captured guard said Bill was in this underground maze—that there would be only one way to find him. Just as in his dreams, he would have to track Bill by scent.

Which meant taking on mastiff form. Alone.

Bad enough to view these tunnels from a human perspective. But in his other shape, the shape that had experienced his long imprisonment, the memories would be even more overwhelming.

Assuming, of course, the shock of taking on his other shape wasn't too much after all this time. What if he couldn't track anymore? What if he failed yet again?

His magic, his familiar nature, could do nothing but fail. It made him vulnerable, not strong. Vulnerable to Martin, to Noah. It would betray him now, just as it always had.

No. He took the hexlight from between his teeth and curled his hand around it, the edges cutting into his fingers. Bill would argue with all of that. Tell Isaac he was wrong, that he was taking too much of the blame on himself, not putting it where it belonged.

Bill needed him. Isaac couldn't find his way through the maze, couldn't find Bill, by wandering randomly.

He needed to do this. For Bill.

"And for me," he said aloud. "I'm doing this *for me.*"

Because Cicero had been right—Isaac deserved more than the half life he'd been living. Deserved to be his whole self, human and dog, a familiar. Deserved the happiness Bill offered so generously.

He'd never lose the memories of his captivity, of Martin and Noah and the darkness of the tunnels. But he'd keep the rest. All the moments of joy, of pride, he'd experienced in mastiff form.

Most importantly, he'd keep himself. Martin, Noah…he'd almost let what they'd done take his very essence from him.

No more. He was done carving parts of himself away.

Isaac put the hexlight on a clean bit of brick. Then, taking a deep breath, he reached for the magic he'd denied for so long.

It hurt from neglect; it was slow, and halting, but the magic was *there.*

It felt like moving a muscle gone stiff from disuse. A sort of body-wide ache, billowing out from his bones, threading through his muscles. Something cramped, and he cried out, but the sound was a dog's whimper. A sense of disorientation crashed down over him, the angles and proportions of the world incomprehensible. His legs were the wrong length; he forgot to account for his tail and struck the wall behind him. Colors faded, leaving behind muddy shades of yellow and blue. His sense of smell blossomed however, so many scents he couldn't sort through everything for a moment.

Except Bill's was among them.

Isaac shut his eyes and breathed deep, letting it center him. Then he took a step, and another. Going on all fours didn't feel entirely natural yet, but he could only hope it grew easier as he moved. He put his nose to the ground, snuffling until he found Bill's trail.

Isaac took up the hexlight in his teeth, since he no longer had hands. Then, head down to follow the scent, he began to run.

Bill flung himself back from the alligator-man, its teeth barely missing his skin. He rolled, came to his feet—and ran.

The match went out almost instantly. He threw his arms in front of him as a shield, moving as quickly as he could, his hands striking walls as the tunnels intersected and split. His own flight made far too much noise to tell whether the creature was in pursuit, but his imagination populated the dark with monsters of every kind. This was where Martin kept the true horrors, the adult familiars whose bodies were too twisted by the hexes to leave the asylum without instantly attracting attention. Had

Alfonso and the wolf-creature who had led him into Martin's ambush been the only ones still human enough to let out?

Owen had said the labyrinth was a prison for monsters. Only none of them had thought to take it literally.

Bill's foot collided with something in the dark.

He sprawled full-length on the ground, the rough brick tearing skin from his hands. Curling in on himself, he waited for claws or teeth to descend and rip him to shreds.

Nothing happened.

The roar of his pulse slowed. Silence had once again descended upon the tunnels, broken only by the drip of water. Either he'd outrun the alligator, hampered by its human gait coupled with a dragging tail, or it had never tried to chase him to begin with. As for what he'd tripped over, it didn't seem to be moving.

Holding his breath, he stretched out his hand.

His searching fingers encountered the cold, waxen flesh of a corpse.

Bill snatched his hand away, barely choking back a cry. Then, steeling himself, he reached out again. It was a face he'd touched; he felt the jut of nose, jerked away from the rubbery lips. Did the body belong to Lucius Young? Some poor familiar?

Had Martin seen fit to equip them with matches and candle stub as well?

Searching the pockets of a dead man in the dark was as unpleasant as Bill would have imagined it to be. When he felt the stub of candle and a remaining match, he nearly wept with relief.

He ought to conserve the matches. But how had the man, whoever he was, died? If a familiar, had some internal malformation like the ones the coroner had found in Alfonso's body killed him? Or had he come to a violent end at the claws of the creatures trapped here?

Bill struck the match and set it to the candle wick. The tiny flame flickered, then caught. After the darkness, it seemed to blaze brighter than the sun. He could clearly make out Young's face, jaw slack in death. The tangle of limbs, as though he'd been tossed here like so much trash.

Blood soaked his clothing in multiple spots: right thigh, left shoulder, and stomach. Bill reluctantly tugged the cloth aside to reveal enormous puncture wounds, larger and rounder than any knife would make.

Something had murdered him down here. With his candle in his pocket, had he even seen it coming?

A faint series of cries echoed through the tunnel, though none sounded made by human throats. Bill pressed himself against the wall, heart tripping in his chest. His hand shook, causing the candle to flicker, so he dripped a bit of wax on a dry spot, then secured the stub to it.

How long would it burn? He had two candles now, at least, but neither was more than a nub. An hour's worth of light between them both, at most.

He tried to think past the fear. He needed to put out the remnant of the candle, risk the darkness, and try to find some way out of here before the maddened familiars killed him.

Footsteps sounded in the tunnel ahead of him. Not the sort of steps made by human feet, though. This was the clomp of massive hooves.

Bill braced himself, casting about for any weapon, even a loose brick to throw, but finding nothing. Closer it drew, and closer, and God now he could *smell* it: earthy and musky, like a livestock yard in the sun.

It stepped to the edge of the light cast by the candle, and Bill felt as though his heart stopped. He was indeed in the labyrinth.

The minotaur was huge, too large for the low tunnels. It stood painfully, awkwardly, on two legs, but those legs were more bovine than human. No clothing would have fit it; only thick, woolly hair clad its arms and legs, the bare chest rippling with muscle. Its head was that of a bull, with no human features at all. Yellow foam flecked its nostrils, and matted the fur around its mouth. It let out a snort, the blast of fetid breath causing the candle flame to gutter madly.

Two enormous horns jutted from its skull, curving menacingly forward. Even in the dim light, Bill could see they were stained dark from blood.

Its tiny eyes met his, and even though it had no human features, he could read the hate in its gaze. It had killed Young, and now it was going to kill him too.

"Don't," Bill whispered. But there was no air left in his lungs, and the sound was as feeble as the flickering candle flame.

The minotaur let out a furious roar and pawed the ground in preparation to charge.

There was nothing to be done. He couldn't outrun the monster, and certainly he couldn't outfight it. Bill closed his eyes against the sight of those terrible horns and conjured up the memory of Isaac's smile. Of how he'd laughed in delight when they made love. If Martin's assassin had succeeded, if Isaac was dead, they'd be together again soon. If not, Bill would wait for his love on the other side, just as he'd waited on this one.

There came the clatter of claws on brick, and a pure, clean light showed even through Bill's eyelids.

Startled, he opened them. A mastiff stood between him and the minotaur, all his hackles raised, a deep growl issuing from his throat. He'd dropped a hexlight, and the clear illumination showed the minotaur in all its terrible glory.

Then Isaac shifted into human form, never taking his eyes off the monster in front of them. "Back away from my witch," he said, the mastiff's growl still in his voice. "I've come to save us all."

Isaac crouched in front of Bill, staring defiantly at the minotaur towering over them. There were others hiding in the dark—he'd smelled them as he tracked Bill. Alligator and lion, boar and bear. He sensed them gathering, well behind the minotaur. Watching.

That was the key. They watched with *intent*. They weren't mindless things bent on killing, no matter what Martin's lackeys claimed. They were familiars, abused and locked away in dark tunnels, just as he had once been locked away.

Which made them no different than Freida, or any of the others Isaac had tried to help. Odd, that it had taken Bill to make him realize the only one Isaac hadn't tried to help was himself.

The minotaur snorted, the blast of breath hitting Isaac in the face. It smelled rancid, hungry, as though its mismatched parts couldn't be nourished by whatever food was thrown down here by its captors.

"Isaac, be careful," Bill said. Isaac reached blindly behind him with one hand, felt Bill's fingers grip his own. But he didn't look away from the minotaur.

When he refused to move, the minotaur snorted again, then let out a deep bellow. The sound was terrifying, but Isaac locked his knees and refused to yield.

A rasping voice spoke from somewhere in the darkness behind the minotaur, from a throat so changed from human it could barely form the words. "You are allied with the ones who did this to us?"

"No." Isaac kept his gaze focused on the minotaur, even though he answered the other. He had the feeling the minotaur was, if not their leader, then their protector. "Neither is Bill. We've been trying to stop Martin Granger. I've come to save you."

"They killed Young," Bill said.

"One of the ones who hurt us." The voice turned into a snarl. "You have no idea what he did."

Bill cleared his throat. "Martin's been using you to dispose of the men who've failed him. Though I don't blame you for wanting a bit of revenge, we ain't with them. I'm Bill Quigley, and this is Isaac with the Metropolitan Witch Police. Martin captured me—and I guess Isaac, too."

He sounded strangely relieved at that, but Isaac didn't have time to question. "No. I came with some other MWP officers. As I said, we're here to save you."

A moment of silence followed his pronouncement. The minotaur turned to the other familiars behind it. Someone whispered, and then other voices joined in.

"There's no time for a debate," Isaac said impatiently. "I'm sorry, but our friends are even now holding off Martin's men. I can get us out of here, but you need to come with me now."

The minotaur turned back to Isaac. Its large, dark eyes regarded him. How long had it been in such a state, neither human nor animal, desperate to survive in the lightless tunnels?

"I know you're slow to trust," he said. "What you've been through is terrible, and it won't be easy to move past. But I swear, I will help you all get off this island. Whether or not the hexbreaker with us can change you back, I won't abandon you."

The minotaur thrust out its hand. The back was covered in shaggy fur, and its fingers had fused into two larger digits, each tipped with a malformed hoof.

Isaac clasped it without hesitation. "Do you want me to lead us out of here, or do you know the way?"

The minotaur let out a softer snort and released Isaac's hand. Without waiting, it turned and began to walk away. "Hurry," urged another of the familiars.

Isaac helped Bill to his feet. Bill's clothes were torn and filthy, his palms raw with scrapes, his skin smeared with mud and dust.

He'd never looked so wonderful.

They embraced the moment Bill was back on his feet. Isaac shut his eyes and breathed in Bill's scent.

"I was so worried about you," Isaac said, at the same time Bill said, "Saint Mary, it's good to see you in one piece."

"Hurry!" the familiar rasped again.

They broke apart, but Isaac caught Bill's hand in his own. He held up the hexlight in the other, revealing the assorted familiars ahead of them. All were as much animal as human, and he desperately hoped Tom could free them from their unnatural state.

"You took on mastiff form," Bill said quietly, as they followed the minotaur.

Isaac nodded. "Scent was the only way I could find you in this maze."

Bill was silent for a moment. Then: "Are you…are you all right?"

"Better than I have been for a long time." Which should have been a ridiculous thing to say, considering their surroundings and circumstances, but it was true.

Bill grinned. "I'm glad. Saint Mary, for a moment I thought Cú Chulainn himself had come to my rescue."

"Who?"

"One of the great heroes of Ireland." Bill squeezed his fingers. "The Hound of Ulster, they called him. He was a dog familiar like yourself, who guarded his people against anyone who would hurt them."

"I'm no hero," Isaac protested.

"I beg to differ. You took on dog form to find me." His eyes shone in the hexlight as he looked down at Isaac. "I know that wasn't easy. I'm so proud of you, love."

Isaac felt as though his chest couldn't contain his heart. He wanted to kiss Bill, to hold him, to sit and talk about everything they'd been through.

But there wasn't time. Their friends were upstairs, possibly fighting for their lives.

The minotaur knew a much quicker route back to the ladder. The familiars gathered around the exit, some of them hissing and muttering to themselves in excitement, others silent.

"There's one thing," Isaac said. "The grate above is padlocked. We didn't know…I'm sorry, but there was some question of everyone's… mental state."

The alligator familiar growled. "You mean you thought us unreasoning monsters, ready to tear you apart."

"Dominic argued we couldn't risk the children, and I agreed," Isaac said. "He locked the grate behind us, but I have an unlocking hex. It just needs to be charged."

Bill's face fell. "Oh." Then he visibly rallied. "Minotaur, you look strong. Maybe you can break the lock open, now that the guards are otherwise occupied?"

It was probably how the minotaur had escaped before. "There's an easier way, Bill," Isaac said.

Bill shook his head. "No. I ain't forcing that on you. We'll try something else."

"You aren't forcing anything on me." Isaac grabbed his hand. "I already made my decision."

Understanding filled Bill's expression. "Back there, when you saved me, you said...you called me your witch. But that's Martin, not me, as much as I wish to God it was."

Isaac stepped closer. His pulse thudded at the base of his throat, but he realized he didn't feel nervous at all. "Blind instinct, blind magic, wants Martin to be my witch," he said, gazing up at Bill. "But I'm *choosing* you."

Bill's hazel eyes widened slightly, and he seemed at a loss. "But there are other witches, stronger—"

"You're the one I've chosen. You, Bill. Not anyone else."

A look of wonder crossed Bill's face, followed by an uncertain smile. "All right, then." He hesitated. "But if you change your mind, we don't have to go through with it. Or we can have Tom break the bond. Or—"

"I know." Isaac put a finger to his lips. "I know, mi corazón."

"Hurry!" snarled the alligator. "Less talking, more doing!"

Bill shot him an unfriendly look, then turned back to Isaac. "What now?"

"Close your eyes." Isaac stretched up on his tiptoes. His heart rate sped, and for an instant he felt a trickle of reflexive fear, an echo of ugly memories. Tunnels and darkness, thirst and aching hunger, and the bond, and pain.

He breathed in Bill's scent, and his pulse calmed. Bill's eyelids felt delicate against his lips as he kissed first one, then the other. "Let me in, Bill," he whispered.

Bill's mouth curved in a smile. "Always."

"Keep your eyes closed and look through mine." Sliding into mastiff form still hurt, and probably would for a while, like a muscle needing exercise. But the pain quickly vanished, and he was suddenly aware of Bill, there, behind his eyes.

It didn't feel like a violation as it had with Noah, because he wanted Bill there, more than he could have imagined.

"Incredible," Bill whispered aloud.

"It is," Isaac agreed, felt Bill's shock when he heard the words. *"You know how this works, don't you?"*

"Aye, but it's one thing to know, and one to experience."

Isaac shifted to human form, took out the hex, and pressed it into Bill's hand. "Now, witch," he said with a smile, "make some magic."

CHAPTER 23

BILL'S ARMS TREMBLED as he hauled himself up the ladder, though not because of the physical strain. His hands hurt like the devil, and he was exhausted, but none of that could compare to the knowledge that sent his mind reeling.

Isaac had *chosen* him, when he could have had anyone—or even no one.

Bill had spent half his life knowing Donald had picked Martin over him. That he wasn't worthy enough, wasn't special enough, for his own father to want him.

Isaac wanted him, and not because of some instinct, or because his magic thought Bill's meager witch talent would work in harmony with it. He wanted Bill for Bill's own self, and no other reason than that.

At the moment, it stunned him. Later, if—when—they got out of here, Bill would let himself feel the full joy of it. For now, they had to save the hexed familiars and stop Martin once and for all.

Bill reached the top of the ladder. Taking a deep breath, he focused on the hex in his hand.

It felt different than before. Less like a flat drawing, and more like a cup. A container, wanting to be filled.

So he did his best to fill it.

Magic flowed, from Isaac through him, and into the hex. Maybe it was less a raging river of power and more of a trickle through a straw, but it got the job done.

The magic left behind a sort of warm place, tucked up against his heart. "Isaac?"

Isaac was just below him on the ladder. "That's the bond."

"Are you all right?" If it reminded Isaac too much of what Noah had done to him, Bill would have Tom break it the first second he could.

"I am." Isaac's voice was warm. "I really am."

Bill reached over his head, threaded his fingers through the bars of the grate, and pressed the hex to the padlock. "Unlock!"

With a strong hex, the hasp would spring open and the lock fall off, sometimes even through the barrier of a door. With the one fueled by Bill's small talent, the lock clicked open but nothing more.

He bit back a curse and tugged on the padlock, manipulating the shank free. Once the lock was out of the way, he gave the grate a hard shove, and it swung open.

They were free from the labyrinth.

The sound of gunfire echoed down the hall toward them.

The minotaur let out a bellow. Bill scrambled out of the way, as did Isaac, and the prisoners poured up and out of the labyrinth. Without hesitation, the minotaur charged toward the gun shots, and the rest of them followed.

They emerged into chaos. A quick glance showed the barred door open, and the children gone from their cell. Near the door, a table turned on its side suggested Tom, Dominic, and Jamie had attempted some sort of holding action. But Martin had too many men, and the makeshift position had been overwhelmed.

Now Tom exchanged blows with a ruffian nearly as tall as himself. Dominic hid behind one of the basement's support columns, gun in hand, his face pale. Jamie wrestled with another attacker, both of them fighting for control of his weapon. Martin stood on the interior stairs, sighting down his gun at Jamie, while three more men charged down past him and into the fray. Cicero darted out in front of the leader in cat form, tripping him just as he reached the foot of the stairs. He tumbled to the ground with a curse, but the other two leapt over him.

"Jamie, look out!" Bill shouted. If only he had a gun, or any weapon at all.

The minotaur bellowed again, the sound so loud it seemed to shake the very foundations of the asylum. Martin's hand jerked, and his shot went wild, smacking into the floor well away from Jamie.

Then the minotaur lowered its horns and charged.

The man wrestling with Jamie let go of him and tried to run, but he was too slow. The minotaur's horns caught him in the small of the back, and he was thrown into the air as though he were a bale of hay.

The rest of the familiars rushed after the minotaur, snarling and snapping. Within seconds, the desperate struggle turned into a rout, Martin's lackeys fleeing the wrath of the familiars they'd abused. The minotaur wreaked havoc among them, goring the fleeing men with its horns, then crushing their bodies beneath its hooves when they fell.

Martin's face went white at the sight. He looked around frantically, then seemed to realize how fast the battle had turned against him.

"Martin!" Bill yelled. "I told you I was coming back for you, you son of a bitch!"

Martin sprinted up the stairs, making for the asylum proper. No doubt he meant to escape before Bill had the chance to catch up with him.

To hell with that. Bill paused only long enough to scoop up a gun dropped by one of fallen guards, before giving chase.

By the time Bill made it through the fight to the stairs, Martin had vanished from sight. Swearing silently, he took the steps two at a time to the next level. They let out into a plain hall, probably meant for nurses and other low-ranking staff. Martin's footsteps rang off the peeling walls as he fled toward the end.

"Stop!" Bill yelled. He aimed and fired, but missed. Cursing, he lowered his gun and broke back into a run.

The hall ended abruptly in the open core of some kind of octagonal tower. Stairs curved around to the right, leading up to a balcony encircling the second floor. The stairs resumed on the opposite side, again leading to a balcony on the third floor, the pattern repeating until the uppermost story was reached.

There didn't seem to be a door to the outside on this level. Martin reached the stairs and ran up them—some room or hall on an upper floor must lead to another part of the building, and then to an exit.

Bill's legs ached as he hit the stairs not far behind Martin. His brother glanced over his shoulder, lips twisted into a snarl of hate and fury. "You can't win!" Martin yelled. "Not against what's coming."

Bill didn't bother to respond, saving his breath for the chase. Ordinarily he might have kept up with Martin, but after running blindly through the dark tunnels below, crashing into walls and falling on hard bricks, his battered legs could only do so much. Martin made it to the balcony first, then to the next set of stairs and up to the third floor. Bill followed, but by the time he reached the third-floor balcony there was no sign of his quarry.

Bill froze, listening as he had in the labyrinth. He was dimly aware Isaac had reached the octagon, but all his concentration was focused on finding Martin. His brother must have dodged through one of the doors leading off the balcony—but which one?

Gun at the ready, he paced forward as silently as possible. He checked the first room he passed, but it was empty, nothing left to even show what purpose it had once served. The next looked to have been an office of some sort, now filled with cobwebs. The third was a sewing room, with five dress forms draped in heavy cloth to keep the dust off.

Damn it. Martin couldn't have gone far. He had to be up here somewhere. He—

The floor creaked just behind Bill.

He turned, just in time to see Martin step out of the sewing room, still trailing a length of cloth behind him. Then Martin's fist cracked into the side of his head.

Stars flashed in his vision, and the world spun around him. Martin kicked his leg; Bill went down heavily. The gun fell from his hand. Martin punted it over the side of the balcony.

Bill rolled onto his back, then froze. Martin stood over him, the black bore of his pistol pointed at Bill's forehead.

"This is why Father chose me," Martin said. "Because no matter what happens, I'll always be better than you."

Isaac charged in mastiff form up the octagon's stairs, muscles stinging, lungs gasping for air. The bond burned like a beacon in his chest, behind his heart.

Bill cried out just above and ahead, and fear propelled Isaac up and onto the landing. Bill lay near the edge of the balcony, gripping the railing with one hand, as though he'd meant to use it to stand. And over him, gun pointed at Bill's head, stood Martin.

The world seemed to slow around Isaac. He could feel the bond with Bill, warm and alive, nestled against his heart. When he looked at Martin...

He felt only rage. The mindless yearning of his unbonded magic was gone.

He was free.

A growl tore his throat, and his haunches gathered to spring. Some glimpse of movement out of the corner of his eye must have warned

Martin, because he started to turn. But he was too slow.

Isaac's jaws closed on the wrist of the hand holding the gun, his full weight slamming into Martin's body. They went down in a heap, and Bill shouted Isaac's name.

Isaac let go of Martin's wrist to avoid swallowing any blood. Martin yanked his arm back, but Bill latched onto it, struggling for the gun. One of Martin's boots slammed into Isaac's head, momentarily stunning him.

Bill pried the gun from Martin's hand. It fell to the ground. One of their feet caught it, sending it spinning off, though Isaac didn't see where it went.

Martin punched Bill in the gut with his free hand. Bill bent over, grip loosening on Martin's wrist. Martin wrenched free and staggered to his feet.

Isaac sank his teeth in Martin's trouser leg, yanking him off balance. Martin fell heavily against the balcony railing, which groaned beneath his weight. His eyes widened with terror at the sight of the floor three stories below, and he shouted: "Stop! I surrender!"

Isaac let go of the trouser leg and bared his teeth. Bill scooped up the dropped gun. "I ain't a copper anymore. Isaac, do you want to put him under arrest?"

Isaac shifted. "Gladly," he said. "Martin Granger, you're under arrest for kidnapping, assault, murder, and anything else we can throw at you."

Martin held up his hands. "My lawyer will have me out in an hour."

"You shot a man in cold blood in front of two police officers." Bill stepped closer and lowered his voice. "While you're rotting in a prison cell, waiting your turn at the electric chair, Isaac and I are going to be free and happy. Living our lives without sparing you a thought, because you ain't better than me. And Isaac deserved a hell of a lot better than you."

Rage flickered in Martin's eyes, and he bent swiftly over, hand going to his boot. Isaac grabbed his arm, but he was too slow. Martin drew the hidden knife from his boot, bringing the blade up in a wide strike—

The gunshot was painfully loud against Isaac's sensitive hearing. He let go of Martin's arm, jumping back as blood poured down from the hole in Martin's chest.

Even as Martin crumpled to the ground, Isaac turned toward Bill. Bill dropped the gun, and caught Isaac in his arms. Both of them shook like leaves and stank of fear, but that didn't matter. The only thing that counted was that they were both alive and together.

With a flutter of wings, Rook landed beside them, before shifting into human form. "Are you two all right?"

They broke apart. "I am," Isaac said. "Bill?"

Bill avoiding looked at Martin's corpse. "I think so. I've got a lump forming on my head, but a hex for the swelling and I'll be fine."

"I'll have Dominic draw something up." Rook nudged Martin's body with his toe. "You got him."

Isaac nodded. Though Bill glanced at him with concern, at the moment he couldn't feel anything but relief. "We should get back downstairs. They might need our help."

"I think a giant bull-man was all the help we needed," Rook said dryly. "Not to mention a half alligator and a boar. All of Martin's men are either dead or probably wish they were."

"What about our side?"

"Jamie got grazed by a bullet, and I don't think Dominic will ever leave our desk again, but otherwise unharmed. Nick got the kids to the yacht, though he did have to trample a guard to do it. Tom's going to try his hexbreaking on all of the prisoners, children and adult alike, but he wants to wait until there's a doctor on hand."

Isaac nodded. Hopefully the children who hadn't yet shifted would be easily freed to take whatever form nature would have dictated. As for the mutated adults, the shift back to their normal state—assuming it happened—could be a shock to the system. Tom was probably right to wait.

Bill let out a long sigh. "It's over, then."

Isaac glanced at Martin's slack face, then turned away. "Some things are." He touched Bill's cheek tenderly with his fingers. "But you and me…we're just beginning."

CHAPTER 24

"LET'S TOAST," CICERO called above the cacophony of the crowded saloon. He raised his glass high. "To another triumph for Thomas Halloran, hero of the hour!"

Tom blushed. "Keep it down, cat. I ain't no hero."

"Really Thomas, don't be so modest. First you broke the hexes on all those children, then restored a group of monsters to human, and *then* carried the day in court against the gang kidnapping and force bonding familiars."

Bill exchanged a glance with Isaac. Bill had worried all day about the verdict, pacing in circles in front of the courthouse. He could probably have flashed his shiny new MWP badge and gotten in, but he hadn't wanted his presence to distract Isaac from his work. But when the verdict was read, he'd felt Isaac's burst of happiness through the bond.

"It wasn't just me who did any of that," Tom protested to Cicero. "I mean the hexbreaking, aye, but nothing leading up to it."

"True, I *was* indispensable," Cicero agreed. "Really, if you think about it, I'm the one who made it all happen. To me, then!"

Bill laughed and clinked his tankard with Cicero's glass of wine. "Aye, cat, I don't know what we would've done without you."

Isaac snorted. "I'd like to toast Freida. Without her testimony, the gang would have gotten away with it. She was so brave."

"You helped her be brave," Bill said.

It had been two weeks since the night on Blackwell's island. Isaac took mastiff form far more often now, and had discovered an unexpected benefit. Some of the victims he was trying to help, even though they were familiars, found his dog form a better comfort. Especially in places like court, where they couldn't talk freely anyway.

Isaac had sat at Freida's feet every day of the trial, and been her silent protector during recesses. Or not so silent; Isaac confessed he'd growled at a few men who'd insisted on pressing Freida too close.

True to his word, Eli Valentine ran a series of articles highlighting the plight of familiars. When news broke about what had happened on Blackwell's Island, the timing had worked in Valentine's favor. Newspapers as far away as California reprinted some of his pieces.

Isaac surprised both Bill and Valentine by offering to do the interview Valentine wanted. When Bill asked why later, Isaac only shrugged and said he was ready to talk about it now.

"It happened," he said. "It's something that will always be a part of my life. A part of me. But it isn't who I am, if that makes sense."

The memories Isaac lost hadn't returned, even though he took dog form on a regular basis. Likely they never would. When Bill hesitantly asked Isaac if that bothered him, Isaac answered with a sad smile. "I won't lie. If I could forget the tunnels, I would. But not at the cost of myself."

They drank a few more rounds with Tom and Cicero, then said their goodnights. They'd found an apartment more convenient to the MWP than Bill's old one, and turned their steps toward it now. The heat had broken, and the breeze whistling between buildings cooled Bill's skin after the warmth of the saloon.

They made a quick stop at the apartment to grab a blanket, Isaac pausing to touch the Mezuzah mounted on the door frame. Then they climbed to the building roof. With the nights cooler, no one felt the need to sleep up here, so at the moment they had the space to themselves. Bill spread the blanket, and they settled onto it to look out over the city.

"It was a good day," Isaac said, leaning against Bill.

Bill slipped his arm around Isaac's shoulders and pressed a kiss into his hair. "Aye. It was."

"Don't forget, tomorrow is Friday. We'll go straight to my parents' apartment after work."

"I ain't forgotten," Bill said wryly. "Far too nervous to forget."

"Don't be." Isaac fell silent for a while. Then he said, "Do you think you'll ever see your father again?"

"Nay." Bill wished his answer could be different. "If he came to me with an apology, or…I don't know, an open heart? Then maybe I would. But he ain't the type to do either."

Isaac glanced up at him. "Do you think he knows about Martin?"

"Couldn't help but know if he reads the papers," Bill said sourly. Thank goodness no reporters had made the connection between him and Martin, and Bill certainly hadn't told them.

The company slated to take over the old asylum and turn it into a sanitarium for familiars had expressed horror when the story came to light, and denied all knowledge of Martin's wrongdoing. Unfortunately, none of the underlings who had survived the night had known enough to point a convincing finger at anyone higher up than Martin.

Pemberton and his cronies had slipped away yet again. "We'll get them someday," Owen had said, when they gathered at Peter's house in the aftermath. But Bill couldn't help wonder how many other innocents would suffer before that day came.

"I heard some of the children are staying with Nick and Jamie," Isaac said, breaking into Bill's gloomy thoughts. "Three of them, I think? One had a younger sister who was still in the orphanage, so I guess they've got her now, too."

All thirteen missing children had been rescued. Elwood's reunion with his son had brought a tear to Bill's eye. The newspaper coverage of their ordeal had led to the remainder being adopted by other familiars, so at least none of them had to return to the orphanage.

"Nick does seem to have a way with kids," Bill admitted. Certainly he'd been the one to keep them calm on the race to the yacht, and later on the ride back to Manhattan. "Jamie, too."

"Rook claims Jamie is the strict father, and Nick the one they've got wrapped around their little fingers." Isaac grinned. "I'd pay money to see that."

Bill laughed. "So would I. Well, if it makes them happy, so be it." He paused. "What about you, love? Are you happy?"

Isaac remained silent for a long moment. The city around them still bustled, despite the hour. The distant laughs and shouts of men and women drifted up from the streets below, mingling with the clatter of the El as it made its way past a block over. The wind had dispersed the smog of coal smoke that usually draped the city, and the stars twinkled above in their multitudes. Over the East River, the moon shone like a beacon.

"I am." Isaac tipped back his head and looked up at Bill. "For a long time, I thought I'd never really be happy again. I thought I didn't deserve to be. I imagined I'd spend the rest of my life alone, watching everyone I cared about slowly drift away. Watching *myself* drift away, or at least half of me." He smiled. "But I was wrong about all of that. Thank you for helping me see it."

"I think you helped me just as much," Bill leaned in and kissed Isaac gently. "I love you."

"I love you too, Bill Quigley," Isaac murmured.

Their lips met again. They kissed and held one another, while the moon rose into the sky.

Share Your Experience

IF YOU ENJOYED this book, please consider leaving a review on the site where you purchased it, or on Goodreads.

Thank you for your support of independent authors!

End Notes

First, thank you so much to my sensitivity readers: Neta B., Einat K., Rebecca A., and Udi. Thanks also to my wonderful patrons on Patreon, including Robin H., Scott M., Dusk T., and Alaska B.

The New York City Lunatic Asylum on Blackwell's Island closed in 1894. In our world, the building was repurposed as the Metropolitan Hospital, but the setting of an abandoned asylum was too good for me to pass up. For anyone interested in what conditions were like while the asylum was in operation, start with *Ten Days in a Mad-House* by Nellie Bly, an investigative journalist who went undercover as a patient there.

Though NYC was a pirate haven at one time, the pirate tunnels beneath Blackwell's (now Roosevelt) Island are of my own invention.

I also played fast and loose with the timeline for excavations at Knossos. Arthur Evans began excavations in March 1900 in our world, which doesn't leave much time between then and July 1900, when *Hexhunter* takes place. We'll assume he got started in 1899 in Hexworld.

Floating baths began to be used in the early 1800s, as an alternative to the public bath houses which couldn't keep up with demand. The floating baths were maintained by the city, and free to the public. Their use continued until the 1920s, when the rivers became too polluted for swimming.

About the Author

JORDAN L. HAWK is a trans author from North Carolina. Childhood tales of mountain ghosts and mysterious creatures gave him a life-long love of things that go bump in the night. When he isn't writing, he brews his own beer and tries to keep the cats from destroying the house. His best-selling Whyborne & Griffin series (beginning with Widdershins) can be found in print, ebook, and audiobook.

If you're interested in receiving Jordan's newsletter and being the first to know when new books are released, please sign up at his website: http://www.jordanlhawk.com. Or join his Facebook reader group, Widdershins Knows Its Own.

Printed in Great Britain
by Amazon

59870803R00109